Bluestone
Michael Peron

Dedicated to Ella (of course).

1. Incident

Teetering back and forth on the balls of his feet, he read the sign above the door. His eyes registered a few letters, combined their general order into words, and his mind connected these words to memories and knowledge. But the connection was weak. Though he saw the words, his mind was elsewhere.

Two days ago, he was absolutely sure of himself. Yesterday, he double checked the market reports—everything was favorable. Today, Stewart was hesitant.

As he entered the store, the door playing a jingle to announce his presence, he knew he had to stop this deliberation at some point. A decision had to be made. The Fenix corporation seemed to be on the verge of a revolutionary breakthrough, and a large investment could set him up for thousands of credits in profit. Of course, if it was all a bunch of gas, if the rumors weren't true, then he'd be in the hole a pretty penny. What, then, was he to do?

Stewart shuffled toward the back of the small shop, passing various electronic novelties: semi-holographic walkie-talkies… bulky, expensive proto-fusion generators… and surveillance cameras that became essentially invisible with some clever bending of light. Once he reached the back end of the store, he stopped to look at the selection of robotic brains spread out in even shelves along the wall.

So, what were the motives? Well, for one thing, Fenix had a concept that seemed to work. Their cerebral units—the equivalent of robot CPUs —contained the safest, most reliable software to date. And safe software usually meant one thing: being one step closer to robotic altruism.

Stewart was no expert in the matter, but robot history was relatively new. For years, strong AI—artificial intelligence that matches or exceeds human intelligence—had been labeled the final frontier of the science. After the complicated mess of the earlier 21st century, cerebral units were showing signs of learning. But there was a difference between following a series of simplified, programmable rules, and being able to show true reasoning skills, or even self-awareness. To make matters worse, there was the constant fear the robots would revolt or even exterminate mankind. This meant that any endeavor to bring strong AI had to be coupled with a programmed desire to help humankind. The complexity of the task was monumental, but the motivation was clear. And so roboticists set about trying to integrate a sense of altruism into the cerebral units. That was where Fenix came in, and that was where Stewart had to make his bet.

He scanned the shelves left to right as if he were reading a book, noting variations in size and structure. He had come to this antique store to do his own bit of field research. Normally, the sale of cerebral units was under the tight control of the government, and you couldn't buy robotic brains without the corresponding body. Upgrades or replacements were growing rarer by the day, and when they did occur, the process consisted of contacting the original company and sending the robot back for several weeks. At an antique shop, however, one could browse dozens of scrapped cerebral units. In fact, as a result of the strict policies regarding robotic brains, a flourishing collector's market had risen. But Stewart wasn't here because of a hobby; he was here to interpret his deal.

"Need any help?" Stewart glanced to the left and saw a clerk eyeing him politely from above his bifocals.

"Thanks, no," came the unenthusiastic answer. For a moment, as the clerk turned back to what he was doing, Stewart almost felt sorry for his apathetic response, but he had his monetary future on his mind and needed to focus.

He turned back to the display, and concentrated his attention on the third brain in the second row, about an arm's length above him. The descriptive tab under it read FENIX CORPORATION in large, bold letters. Underneath the title was a long number followed by a short paragraph. Ignoring the description, he reached upwards, bringing the grapefruit sized device down into his hands for examination.

Its shape was almost perfectly spherical, and despite being less than half the size, it was heavier than most bowling balls. Its surface was smooth steel, interrupted only by three evenly spaced, ovular holes along one line of longitude, and an etched version of the serial number on what could only be referred to as the front. Stewart handled it carefully, almost caressing it with his fingers. The holes were for wires and circuitry, and there was no conceivable way of opening the casing without completely ruining the inner workings. The serial number, S9-821-21522205, indicated that the brain had belonged to an S9 class. Cerebral units were engineered specifically for their future body, in order to maximize efficiency and minimize customization. In fact, just as there was no way to open the brain's casing, there was no way to remove the brains from their robotic bodies without actually destroying them in the process. This complete integration represented another precautionary measure by the government, but it was mostly the public's idea. People have a constant fear of mismatched robots displaying erratic behavior, mostly due to the incredible strength of the machines. Thanks to the integration process, the public slept sounder, and Stewart knew the details of the robot, including its production number and date of creation.

"2152?" he thought out loud. "This does belong in an antique shop."

He realized he could have made that distinction simply by the model number. The S9 class had been infamously phased out in the last decade after a good sixty-odd years of service. There were probably quite a few of the S9 brains floating around antique shops, due to the special nature of their elimination. The news had labeled them "renegade robots," although the moniker was simply a typical exaggeration by the media towards the already nervous masses.

Generally, models filtered through the classes—first as novelty items of the rich, then as indispensable luxuries of the middle class, and finally as providers for the poor. Once they became extremely outdated, the government recalled each individual robot electronically and recycled the expended metal and parts. The S9s, however, failed to respond to the recall order. After extensive investigation, the Bureau of Robotic Affairs located a flaw within the receiver software of the robots, preventing them from knowing of the recall without manual explanation. The event was covered extensively, and thanks in part to the public's growing aversion to robots in general, the BRA was able to round up the vast majority of the existing S9s.

He glanced up at the tab again and realized there was no price. He turned toward the clerk and lifted the brain to indicate it, "How much for S9-821?"

The clerk gave him an inquisitive look. Then, as he pressed a button Stewart couldn't see, he said, "Price, cerebral unit, ID S9821." Immediately, the number 2370 appeared on the monitor behind the clerk.

Stewart's raised his eyebrows in slight disbelief. He had expected the brains to be expensive, but he did not expect a price above 2000 credits, or even 1800. A price tag of that magnitude made the ball in his hands quite a luxury. Thankfully, he hadn't planned on actually purchasing it.

With added care after finding out the price, Stewart replaced the brain above its tab. He placed his arms on his sides, and, with a feeling of reassurance, smiled. Although the astronomical price tag had more to do with cerebral unit scarcity than general quality, it made him feel better. Truthfully, the shop could give him little empirical support for his decision, but as he made his way to the exit, Stewart made up his mind. Fenix claimed it was on the verge of integrating the fabled robotic altruism and damn it all, he believed them.

Once out the door, the bustle of the shopcenter interrupted his thoughts. He was no longer in the comforting arms of the antique shop's silence. In fact, he realized, the only other person he had noticed in the shop was the clerk. Now he was faced with an unsightly example of the chaos that is crowds. He glanced left and right, establishing his position, and noticed a distant exit sign with an arrow. Weaving between clusters of people and the occasional robot, he made his way to freedom.

- - -

"Stolen!?" Lauren couldn't believe what she had heard. How on Earth...? Noticing the look of terror cross Gregory's face, she realized how harsh her exclamation must have been. She tried her best to compose herself, and went on in the calmest voice possible.

"Are you absolutely certain?" She wasn't very convincing... even to herself.

"There are no signs of it, ma'am, whatsoever. All seven prototypes are gone, and every last file has been compromised and deleted."

There would be no end to this, she thought. "Is the technical staff probing into recent links?"

"Yes ma'am, but apparently the possibilities of location are low. The hackers swept the links, and they swept them thoroughly. Technical says this was a massive effort, ma'am."

For a moment, Lauren was speechless. She looked around helplessly, as if a solution were hidden among the decorations of the office. Of course it was a massive effort, she thought. Anyone that had the ability to access their files was bound to be an expert.

"What about backups? Recovery disks? Saved versions?" She was almost begging him.

With a sigh, Gregory shook his head. "All gone, ma'am. The backups were deleted, as were all previously saved versions. As for recovery disks, they were taken along with the prototypes."

Slowly, absent-mindedly, she let herself fall into her chair. Someone had managed to wipe Project Bluestone clean. No files and no prototypes meant no production.

Feebly, without looking up, she whispered, "Call the board. Announce an emergency meeting. Have everyone there in ten minutes."

With visible relief at being able to leave, Gregory nodded and hurried to the phone.

Lauren watched him while her mind wandered. Here she was, barely a decade out of university, freshly promoted to lead the most powerful robotics corporation on Earth, and they were under some sort of attack. Of course, their recent advertising extravaganza probably had something to do with it. As soon as rival companies heard whispers of robotic altruism and strong AI, they would do almost anything, legal or otherwise, to get their hands on the technology. That's why they had done everything within their power to protect Project Bluestone. Obviously, it wasn't enough.

"Ma'am, they're ready." Lauren looked up and nodded at Gregory. Well, she thought, here goes nothing. Out she went, into the hallway, passing the sign next to her door which read "Lauren Care, President, Fenix Corporation." Time to face the board.

- - -

Freedom was not what Stewart found once he made his way out of the shopcenter. To be sure, walls no longer enclosed him, but outside it was equally congested. Roads in the city were filled with manual automobiles, and traffic in Houston was almost constant. Considering the slow but sure decline of manually-driven cars and their transportation infrastructure, he was at a loss as to how they were clogging the streets. High above, beyond the thousand meter mark known as the Canopy, the sight of an occasional aero-vehicle hinted at things to come. For the time being, however, you were more likely to see a bird; and this was in the middle of a city.

With a glance to the left, he discerned the faint glow of a Diama sign, and without the slightest hesitation, moved in the direction of the station. As he ascended the two flights of stairs, he felt a small sense of pride in his race. That humans could create such a complex transportation system as Diama was remarkable. On reaching the top, he gazed with admiration at the superconductor track, which guided small, magnetically levitated pods across vast expanses of land at incredibly high speed with astonishing accuracy. And all of it planned with mathematical precision! Come to think of it, the only interaction humans had with the system was during emergencies. The countless calculations required to stabilize pods, let alone allow them to weave between each other without collision, were entirely left to supercomputers. Human interference would create problems in a system so complex. Even the supercomputers were monitored mostly by robots. Therein lay the paradox, thought Stewart. The public was content to let robots control from behind walls, but as soon as they became visible, they were a threat.

He shook his head in an effort to clear it. It was just past noon, and his wife had expected him an hour ago. With clarity of purpose, he approached the sliding glass doors and waited for the scanners to locate his Personal. A red light turned green, the glass slid away, and he proceeded through the opening. Two robots watched from opposite corners of the station, ready to help at a moment's notice. He made his way to the section for single occupancy, entered the idle, one-person Diamapod at the front, and sat in the (always surprisingly) comfortable seat.

Sensing the weight, the pod's speakers proclaimed, "Identifying..." while a sign lit up under the windshield in case Stewart was deaf. Accustomed to the process, Stewart let his mind drift for a few moments. Seconds later, the words disappeared, and the door to his right closed gently.

"Destination?" Again, subtitles. This time, however, a standardized keyboard appeared at perfectly comfortable height in front of his chest. Or, at least, the lit outline of a keyboard appeared – created by a sophisticated array of lights. But Stewart had no use for it.

"Terminal A663," he said, clearly pronouncing each letter and number. The keyboard vanished, and his desired destination appeared in the subtitle slot with a question mark for verification: "Terminal USTXHOA663?"

"Yes."

There was a pause, maybe half a second of computation, and the pod slowly accelerated. In that small bit of time, the pod had, with the help of computers at the station, decided a route and deduced at what exact velocity and acceleration it would navigate the course in order to avoid others already in motion.

"Warning: Prepare for acceleration." As the pod was giving the heads up, a cushioned brace fell into place, securing him in case of an accident.

And then it happened. Stewart's Personal had informed the pod of his health, age, and any special circumstances. Using this information (which indicated a man in his thirties with no sickness or disabilities), it propelled him to an astonishing speed. And for all the grumbling that he engaged in after each and every launch, he had to admit something: it was fun.

After the initial shock, he gazed through the windshield at the quickly shifting surroundings. Jacqueline wouldn't be happy, and he knew it. She would think it foolish of him to waste his time in a shopcenter, let alone in an antique shop. But he needed some sort of reassurance, and it was the best he could come up with. He glanced at the panel reserved for subtitles. The timer read six minutes and change. Enough time to close the deal, he thought. With noticeable strain, thanks to the brace, he maneuvered his arm into his right bottom pocket and removed his Personal. He touched the rectangular screen in his hand with his right thumb and it lit up in immediate recognition of his fingerprint. After the scan, the imprint was erased in a very complicated, molecular-level process that Stewart was unfamiliar with. The device itself, however, was quite familiar. Personals were a basic necessity in that time period. They acted as a phone, a wallet, ID... and most importantly, granted access to the Cloud, the collective communication protocol that had evolved from the Internet.

Presently, Stewart logged into his Market account and proceeded to confirm his investment in Fenix Corporation. Over four months worth of credits flowed from his account to the robot business. Each one of those 4288 credits was now actively promoting the development of robotic altruism.

Three and a half minutes. He clicked a lock button on the left side of the Personal and placed it back in his pocket. At that precise moment, he realized how hungry he was. He hadn't eaten lunch, and it was nearly half past noon. Maybe Jacqueline had decided to roast some turkey? It was Friday, after all, and good days usually meant great food. Or tomato soup? He loved her tomato soup.

Lost in these thoughts for some time, Stewart felt the familiar deceleration that signaled arrival. The pod announced, "Terminal USTXHOA663" as it advanced along a downward ramp. With a gentle halt, he finished the journey. The brace was lifted, and the door slid open. Stewart hopped out onto the paved station, looked about as if to be completely certain of his arrival, and made for home.

- - -

Lauren frowned. Seven aggravated board members, and no excuse to be heard of. She had explained the theft in a calm and precise manner, and the growing look of disgust on each of their faces added to her troubles. Why her? Why now?

"What is your plan?" One asked with noticeable agitation.

"We contacted the DCI and the BRA. The DCI sent three analysts who should be here shortly."

Another interjected, "The Department of Criminal Investigation? Are their analysts planning to uncover something Technical hasn't already?"

"We're the experts in robots, but they're the experts in computers, and, more importantly, links. Other than the analysts, we'll need DCI help in physically tracking the prototypes."

"Despite the fact that whoever did this was clever enough to manage deactivating our own built-in trackers?"

Lauren felt the irritation creep into her voice as each member shared his or her equally negative views. "Yes, despite all that."

"And what of information? Are we planning on revealing this to the public? Surely not."

There was a general murmur of approval.

"No, at least not until we have more details. The DCI and the BRA have agreed to keep the information under wraps until legally possible."

"Can the government be trusted in matters of robotics? They've been trying to end us since the beginning of the industry."

What ignorance! Lauren was almost left speechless. At least the rest of the board had asked relatively sensible questions! "Yes, they can be trusted," she replied with impolite emphasis. "They are acutely aware of the benefits of robotic altruism, not to mention strong AI—entire industries, which now run only partially on robots, could be left to themselves, if only we had the altruism engrained in their cerebral units. They know as well as we do that these two technologies need to emerge hand in hand."

The youngest man among them, who had remained silent during the preceding cross-examination, spoke up from the opposite end of the table in a surprisingly respectful voice. "Madam President, that the government understands the necessity of secrecy is indeed undeniable fact. However, was it wise to contact the BRA? Many roboticists of many different companies find work in the Bureau. If word gets out of our failure… well…" He let the thought float above the oval desk of the meeting room.

Lauren let a moment or two pass before quietly responding. "We have realized this, Mr. Rubger, and I assure each one of you that the BRA knows only that an incident has occurred, nothing more, nothing less. By law, we are required to report any such incidents to them, and we are in fact stretching our legal rights by not supplying any more information."

Mr. Rubger nodded in gentle approval. Lauren was exceptionally thankful to him for quieting the other six, but her Personal was vibrating.

"Excuse me, ladies and gentlemen, but my Personal is indicating the analysts have arrived. I will inform you all of any developments. Meeting adjourned."

With one last glance at Mr. Rubger, whose eyes she could not catch, she left the room and made for the stairs. Just by the feel of the hallway, she knew rumors were spreading. She encountered several pairs of averted eyes, and whispers were brought to an abrupt stop at her passage. Could this be any worse? At least the robots were non-judgmental. She watched a few of them pass, and found their static disposition oddly comforting. They could care less, she thought, and this development had a lot more to do with them than any of the whispering employees around her.

She was so concentrated on the hallway's scenery that she nearly collided with three tall men dressed in matching suits. Their faces bore no hint of emotion, filled instead with immeasurable seriousness. Even their outfits, worn with precision and virtually immaculate, expressed solemnity. At that very moment, Lauren foresaw the exact image of future humanoid robots. She was so surprised by their impression that she found no words with which to speak. Finally, after considerable hesitation, she asked, "Are you the DCI analysts?" What answer did she expect?

The middle one gave a curt but polite "Yes."

"Then follow me to the database port, please."

As she motioned them down the stairs to the main level, she noticed a suitcase in each of their right hands. Everything about them gave an impression of meticulousness. It was not until a few steps down that she realized this was the first time she had encountered DCI operatives. The organization was incredibly secretive, and, supposedly, incredibly effective. There was quite an interesting history, albeit a short one, behind the formation of the DCI. As Earth proceeded to unify under one global initiative, (driven, for the most part, by the Robotic Revolution) organizations, departments, and bureaus molded into worldwide entities. Slowly but surely, the boundaries on maps began to fade. Currently, countries still existed, but not in the archaic sense. There was an Earth Legislature, along with Earth Presidents and Earth Court, all working to unify the globe, step by step. It was through that very Earth Legislature that the DCI came to be. With war becoming increasingly impossible (again, thanks to robots), there was a general desire to form an exceedingly efficient police/detective force from the remnants of former intelligence and defense agencies. The Legislature, on a vote of 9843-1788 (106 abstaining), established the DCI in 2201. In the eighteen years since its inception, it had gained an infamous reputation. Now she knew why.

And these were only analysts, she thought. What of the actual police? She had heard stories, of course. Everyone had. But she had always dismissed them as exaggerated. By the looks of the three men behind her, she was probably wrong in doing so.

After crossing the main lobby towards the edge of the building, they made their way down a wide set of stairs to a large, white wall. "Right through here," she announced at the armored door. A small panel to the right emitted a low hum. She pressed her hand against it and felt the warm tingle as it analyzed her handprint. The entire panel turned green, and a touch keypad appeared. She entered a seven-digit code, and in a clear voice, pronounced, "Lauren Care." The panel became green a second time, and there was an audible click, as if something quite massive had just unlocked. Slowly, the foot-wide armored door swung inwards.

Such a grand creation, she admitted. And yet it was useless.

Once the entry was clear, she led the men into the domain of supercomputers, robots, and labs known as R&D. The labs were dominated by a pristine white, with occasional brushes of black. Coupled with the staff in their white coats and the audible hum of a vast array of electronics, the area gave quite an impression. Dozens of humanoid robots marched about, carrying out orders or operating semi-autonomously. With a glance back, Lauren saw just a hint of awe on each of their faces. She couldn't help but smile in pride. This sector was the very heart of the corporation. While the portal behind them began to shut, she led them to a port of the supercomputer, where her technical staff was investigating any anomalies they could discern.

"Gentlemen?" She leaned over to where the six company men were busily inspecting several computer terminals teeming with wires, each one of them with a Personal in one hand and a Portable in the other. The larger, more powerful Portables were each busy calculating, adjusting, searching…

They looked up inquisitively, noticed three of the most formidable figures they had ever seen, and began packing their gear. Lauren turned to the analysts.

"It's your game now."

The middle one nodded and they set to work at once. Lauren watched them and frowned. What now? Was she supposed to wait?

"If you find anything, please contact me by Personal."

"Yes ma'am." They didn't so much as look up.

She turned back toward the door. All she could do now was be patient.

- - -

There was never as beautiful a delicacy, he felt, as a plate of his wife's roast turkey. Especially when that plate sat next to a bowl of her tomato soup. Why, then, did he refrain from indulging himself in the pleasantries of the table?

It's in her face, he thought.

There he sat, acting oblivious to the delicious meal, looking directly at his wife. He couldn't bear the tension she had crafted against him. She knew how to say things in just the wrong way. The words were innocent, of course. But the voice was not trying to say, "Welcome home, dear." It said, "Where were you? Why have you let me worry about you? I messaged your Personal, why didn't you reply?"

He was ashamed of not noticing the message until he was on the doorstep, but he was offended at the manner in which he was being treated. If he had gotten the message, he would have replied. But that argument was of no use. "Why didn't you send your own?" He could hear her say it. Up to this point, neither had said anything argumentative, but the air tingled with impatience. He knew he was in for it, but he had to speak up.

"Sweetie... I'm sorry I didn't reply to the message." If there were any way he could convey the honesty of his statement, he would've done so in a heartbeat.

Jacqueline stopped her own eating, lowering the fork and knife. She looked up at him and knew from more than a decade of experience that her husband was being honest. Still, she was bitter.

"Why didn't you send me a message to tell me you'd be late?" It was a plea, not a scowl.

Stewart let out a gentle sigh. He knew her well. "I was caught up in my own little world... I didn't even know what time it was until I left the shopcenter."

"Was it really necessary to go there? How did some ancient lump help make the decision?" She hated herself for arguing with him.

There was another sigh in response. "I'm sorry sweetheart. Next time I won't let myself get distracted like that..."

How could she resist his helplessness? "Oh Stewart..." She lifted herself from the chair and embraced her husband before he could even react. "I'm sorry. It's just I get so worried... Especially with the shopcenters – you know how those crowds can be..."

He kissed her on the cheek. "Look, I really should have messaged you. Next time, I promise I won't forget." He hoped, with every fiber of his being, that he would hold to that promise. His forgetfulness could become his undoing—it had happened many times before.

For a moment, she wrapped him even tighter and kissed his forehead. Then, gently, she let him go.

He looked up into her eyes. And, letting a smile spread across his face as he tried to be sarcastic, he said, "Now will you let me eat this food? Goodness." His laughter distorted the last word.

As was her usual response to his sarcasm during emotional moments, her face gave the impression of shock but her eyes could not hide their laughter. She waved her arm as if to shoo him away and returned to her seat. He grinned, watching her. He knew what was coming.

She sat, beaming, and proclaimed, "Go on! Eat the damn food!"

His grin widened, and he delighted himself with the feast set out before him.

- - -

It had been less than ten minutes when Lauren's Personal acted up. She glanced at the screen, and seeing no message, only a source, she knew they wanted her to return to R&D. Surely they hadn't given up already? Technical had been at it for maybe half an hour, and yes, they had admitted the search was futile, but DCI was supposed to be the best of the best. What was this, then?

Absent-mindedly, she placed her hand on the print-scanner. They couldn't have possibly found anything, could they? They weren't *that* good…

"Lauren Care."

The door opened again. This time, she scarcely had to enter – the analysts were waiting for her by the entry, cases in hand, not a wrinkle in their suits.

"Yes?" She wondered, for a second, if she should cross her fingers.

As usual, the middle one spoke for all three. "After careful examination of your entire linkage history, we located sixteen critical points of possible entry. Judging by the nature of the crime, however, the hack has occurred in light of your company's Project Bluestone, correct?"

She nodded.

"Based on the assumption that the criminals must have, therefore, exploited the system sometime after the initiation of Project Bluestone, we eliminated twelve critical points. Your data indicates that Project Bluestone began on June the 30th of 2215, and in the four years, two months, and twenty-three days since then, your terminals have been open to attack four times. That's three openings in the recent past, and the exploited one today. We swept each of these links, starting with today's, and have gathered quite a bit of information."

Lauren respectfully interrupted, "How was it that my technical staff missed these details?"

The analyst replied, "Your staff cannot legally sweep the links. They can merely analyze the first and second layer of data. The remaining eight Tiers are heavily encrypted, and the DCI is the only organization authorized to explore them. I beg your pardon, but I will assume you have little knowledge of links, the Cloud, and how data transmits between locations?"

Without showing too much of her embarrassment, she nodded.

"In that case, the best analogy I can give you is of layers, called Tiers. We are the only ones capable of peeling into the final eight."

"Please continue – you said you gathered information?"

"Yes. Today's link was quite sabotaged, and the hackers managed to reach Tier Four data." There was a momentary pause as he remembered something. So they're human after all, Lauren thought. "I have to add one detail to my explanation of the links – the layers count down to Tier One. In other words, the criminals responsible for this were able to infiltrate five Tiers of data illegally."

"Is that easy to do?"

There was the faintest hint of surprise on his face. "No. In fact, it should be impossible, and we've never encountered any criminal threat past Tier Seven. We are dealing with very masterful computerists, ma'am, and I must not understate how crucial it was that you let us take a look at this."

For the third time, she nodded, and with a bit of impatient emphasis, asked, "What information did you gather?"

He responded, "The five infiltrated Tiers were distorted almost beyond recognition. However, we did manage to extrapolate the source of the link from shards of data left in Tier Nine and Seven. Based on our analysis, the hack originated somewhere in the southern United States, maybe northern Mexico. No other coherent data could be obtained from today's link."

She gaped awkwardly. Sure, they had found something… but it was useless.

"Was there nothing else?"

"Not in today's opening."

"Is that it then? We have an incredibly large source region?"

"Pardon me ma'am, but I said not in today's opening. We did, however, gather data from the other three links, along with an extra, unrelated link."

"Wait," she paused, doing some calculations in her head. "I thought you said there were only four total, including today's?"

"You are confusing normal links with links that could be hacked. Since the inception of Project Bluestone, or in fact since the inception of Fenix Corporation, your R&D supercomputers have had a constant flow of normal, secure links. In the four years and change that Bluestone has been active, only four of those millions and millions of links were insecure. What we're trying to let you know is that four vulnerable links, along with one specific secure link, have given us pertinent information regarding today's hack."

"Ah, I see. Well then what did you gather from the three previous vulnerable links?"

"As I have mentioned, we are dealing with expert computerists, and our analysis shows that the earlier three links were also hacked. Being that the culprits were so well versed in the art, your supercomputers and your technical staff noticed nothing. The distortions mapped by our Portables matched certain patterns in today's hack, meaning we can attribute all four hacks to the same criminals. The purpose of the three earlier infiltrations seemed to be the gathering of sensitive data. They used complex software to fool your terminal's automatic security into believing the links were secure. Then, once the connection was established, they spread hook protocols over Tiers Six, Seven, and Eight, which combined at your mainframe into fully automated inspection programs. These programs searched for data in your supercomputer that was related to Bluestone and sent it back, scrambled again over Tiers Six through Eight. Their methods were quite effective, but your computers are quite advanced, and it took them three links to obtain all the necessary data. Then, at the next critical point that occurred, they entered the system full force, and that's what happened today. One conclusion we can draw is that of their constant observation. Whoever did this had to have quite a few computers, constantly at work, waiting for the one vulnerability in the system that would allow an attack. Once your terminals misplaced a 1 or a 0, their computers took advantage of the insecure link and hooked in. In summary, this was a well-planned and lengthy operation."

Lauren nodded. That made matters a bit more complicated. "When did the first hack occur?"

"A year, two months, and thirteen days after the beginning of Bluestone. You cannot gauge that as the starting point, however. They could have been waiting for that opening since day one."

"Yes I understand." No use arguing there. They were right, no matter how desperately she wanted them to be wrong. Why her, for Earth's sake? "So you've explained to me the method of the attack. Was there any more information on location in the first three hacks? Anything of use in the investigation?"

"Yes, there was. Because they didn't want to trigger an alarm in your computers, the culprits were unable to distort the data as much as in today's hack. This, in turn, enabled us to pinpoint their location with a much higher accuracy."

"Excellent! Where?"

"Well, ma'am..." He hesitated. "There is one problem..."

She looked at him, wondering if there would ever be an easy solution to the predicament she found herself in. "Well?"

"I must remind you that we are dealing with professionals here. They knew the risks of low-scale hacks, and each of the three infiltrations originated in a different location. The first came from somewhere in the

Orlando, Florida area, the second from an area slightly north of the Arizona-Mexico border, and the third from a barren patch of Texas southeast of El Paso."

Lauren tried her very best to hold back her outward surprise, but she felt somewhat dizzy and took a step backwards. The men betrayed no response, and waited for her to compose herself.

"So all-in-all, we have absolutely no leads?"

The front man shook his head. "There's still the safe link that we mentioned. Based on our analysis, it has significant meaning to the case."

All her despair washed away and was immediately replaced by an unnerving anxiety. "How?"

"We traced a routine credit investment link that occurred approximately seventeen minutes after the attack. You see, despite the hack, business continued, and your mainframe received approximately four hundred such investment links in the first half hour after the incident. The one we singled out, however, had an unusual quality."

"What sort of unusual quality?"

"Well, typically, investment information channels through Tier Four, with some other informational attachments in Tiers Seven and Nine. This link, however, had additional information traveling through Tier Six."

"So there was an error?"

The analyst nodded. "The crucial detail regarding this supposed error is its Tier. Tier Six was the chief Tier used by the hackers for data disruption. We believe that this investment link is not an error, but a deliberate attempt to erase some extra data they accidentally left behind."

"I see… and what are the chances of it being just an error?"

"Infinitesimally small. As I have just explained, your computers have experienced only four insecure links in the last four years, and they compute thousands every minute."

"So you think this error was actually the criminals, and not only that, but you were able to pinpoint an exact location this time?"

"Yes. In fact, we were able to pinpoint the Personal of origin."

Lauren was absolutely and completely attentive. "Who?"

"A certain Stewart Anders."

2. Flight

Stewart looked up from his desk. He had just finished eating maybe thirty seconds earlier and was about to start his work when an audible knock came from the front door.

Hm, he thought to himself. That's what I get for trying to do work on a Friday.

"Is it for you?" Jacqueline's voice wandered from the living room.

"I don't know," he said as he passed her and made for the door. Glancing at the video feed, he saw a dark-haired young man in a suit. Even through the lens of the camera, Stewart could sense the man's impatience. Who in Earth's name...

He tapped the button next to the feed and the door slid away gently.

"Can I help you?"

"Stewart Anders?"

"Yes, who's asking?"

"I think you need to let me in."

Without even waiting to finish the sentence, the man edged past Stewart and into the house. He was relatively fit, to a point where he could have overtaken him, yet when he turned to face the owner of the household, his face betrayed a hint of fright.

Stewart, reacting only to the rude entrance and not noticing the man's expression, exclaimed, "What exactly do you think you are doing?"

With a wince, the other replied. "I'm sorry to intrude, Mr. Anders, I... I should explain..."

Almost immediately, Stewart saw the man's fear, and a wave of sympathy flooded over him. There was a quick reversal, and he was calm —kind, even—in his words. "Let's start with the basics, shall we? Who are you and how do you know who I am?"

The young man seemed very relieved at the change of tone. "I apologize again, Mr. Anders. My name is Lucas—Lucas Roberts—and I'm very sorry to have to ignore your other question but we're going to have to skip the formalities—your life is in grave danger, sir."

Coupled with the man's sudden arrival, the announcement caught Stewart completely off guard, but before he could compose an answer, Jacqueline emerged from the living room.

"Excuse me but who exactly are you and what exactly is going on?"

The young man, upon seeing her, almost recoiled in surprise. "A wife!" And then, as if to himself, "This makes things much more complicated..."

Stewart, finally able to comprehend what had been said, asked, "And how is it that my life is in danger?"

"Danger!?" Jacqueline turned her head to Stewart in alarm.

Lucas answered for him. "Yes ma'am, danger. This is going to seem bizarre, but your husband is about to be apprehended by the DCI."

"The DCI!" exclaimed Stewart. "Why?" And then, as an afterthought, "And how do you know this?"

The man's next words were cautious. He seemed distracted and Stewart thought he noticed a hint of guilt. "There has been a misunderstanding... the details are far too complex to explain at the moment. I beg you to believe me and I tell you again, your life is in grave danger. We must leave immediately!"

"Leave?" Stuart was incredulous. "What in the hell do you mean?"

Before Lucas could answer, the buzzer on the door went off three times in rapid succession. His face went pale as he whispered, "They're here!"

- - -

She let the aroma flood her nostrils before taking a sip, and her headache subsided ever so slightly. Slouched in her chair behind her desk, Lauren let the hot cup of tea consume her thoughts for a few soothing seconds.

Tidbits of information flashed across the table, which acted as a large touch monitor. In front of her lay a concise but comprehensive report on the attack, sent to her office moments after the departure of the DCI analysts. The efficiency of their organization was amazing, if not a bit frightening. She had also been provided with an informational folder on the suspect Stewart Anders, and was told she would be notified by Personal of any developments. The rest of the office (and by now presumably the whole building, she realized) was positively buzzing with gossip. She hadn't made an official announcement yet, but she would be hard-pressed to find just one employee who hadn't gotten wind of some sort of emergency.

And that was quite a dilemma. If a rival corporation perceived any sort of weakness at the heart of Fenix, their attack would be relentless. She had to act quickly, and she was acutely aware that the future of her career, as well as the future of the company, was on her shoulders. There was just one problem—she hadn't the slightest idea how to alleviate the situation.

Another sip. Oh, ignorance is bliss, she thought to herself. A knock on the door snapped her into consciousness, and she saw Gregory leaning through the open entrance to her office. He hesitated.

"Ma'am, Mr. Ross is still waiting for your official announcement…"

Sighing, she put down the cup of tea and got out of her chair. The Chairman of the Board was a particularly influential man, and she could not afford to gamble with his patience.

"Thank you, Gregory."

Thank you indeed. As she made her way toward the Chairman's office, Lauren found herself at a complete loss. She was familiar with the typical emergency protocol, but this was beyond anything her training could have prepared her for. When she finally reached the announcement chamber, what would she say? Should she lie, explaining that the company had effectively neutralized the threat, in order to prevent annihilation by their competitors? If she told the truth—that their most valued project, more than four years in the making, had been wiped clean—stocks would plummet, the company would falter, and with pressure from the competition, Fenix would fall.

Her irritation from the board meeting returned. Why her? Why now? And, she then realized, why like this? The theft of their project data would have been a manageable crisis. She would announce the burglary and they would hunt down the perpetrators. Meanwhile, Fenix would continue to work on Bluestone to its completion. But the theft of their data and all forms of backup? That was unheard of! She had been assured, countless times, that their recovery disks and prototypes were safe to every degree possible. Immediately after her debriefing with the DCI analysts, three new DCI agents arrived to investigate the hardware robbery. Instead of Portables, they carried all sorts of forensic analysis materials and detective gadgetry. Where the analysts had searched for the computerized breach, these men were meant to probe the security breach. Someone had managed to infiltrate the most heavily guarded sector of the building and nab all the backups, as well as the prototypes. This, of course, was no small feat. Prototype robots are human size and made of an assortment of metals that could not just be carried around—some sort of transport would be necessary for such weight. All told, quite a hefty amount of cargo had to make its way out of the facility undetected. It was up to the new agents to find out how.

The thought occurred to Lauren that she had never seen a female DCI operative. To be sure, she had only encountered six in her lifetime, but even their dramatized, televised counterparts were all men.

Must be a social convention, she thought. There had to be *some* women in the organization. It's not like men are the only good detectives...

In an instant, she realized just how right she was. Blessing her wandering mind, she strode with a new sense of confidence. Men were not the only good detectives... She had a plan, and a good one too.

- - -

Stewart frantically tried to calm his thoughts. DCI agents? Here? Now? For him? Impossible… he hadn't done anything… a misunderstanding? Who was this man? Lucas Roberts? That name was completely unfamiliar. Why was he in their house?

It was Jacqueline who retained composure and tried to verify their fears. She flicked on the intercom and asked, "Who is it?" The answer came, calm but forceful, "This is the DCI. You have thirty seconds to open the door or we will break in. Is Stewart Anders there?"

During this exchange and Stewart's bout of shock, Lucas had quietly walked to the back door and inspected the area visible out the back window. As Jacqueline prepared to answer the agents, Lucas returned and cut off the intercom.

"We need to go, now."

"Go? Are you insane?" Jacqueline looked at him in horror. "You can't escape the DCI! And my husband's innocent, don't you understand?"

Lucas looked at her helplessly. "Ma'am… your husband is innocent, but that won't help him. There is more going on here than you can understand, and if we don't leave now you may never see him again!"

Jacqueline was furious that this stranger even dared utter such words. "Why should we trust you!? Maybe you're the one they're really after!"

But Lucas was done arguing. He grabbed Stewart by the arm and pulled him out of his confusion and into reality. "Stewart Anders you are coming with me one way or another." He looked to Jacqueline. "You have about four seconds to make up your mind."

And with that, Lucas took Stewart forcefully out of the house. Jacqueline didn't hesitate a moment—she was out the backdoor with three seconds to spare. But as the midday sun warmed her face, she knew no matter how fast they ran, even three years wouldn't be enough to escape the DCI.

- - -

Mr. Ross drummed his fingers impatiently on the mahogany desk laid out before him. The situation was still sinking in. Everything gone? And with a green CEO in charge, no less. Where was she, anyways? How many more times would she test his patience? As he reached for the intercom to find out what could be taking her so long, the doors opened and in walked Ms. Care, surprisingly confident given the circumstances. Ross studied her for a moment with slight confusion.

"Why in the world are you so peppy?"

Lauren took the comment in stride, and began to pace back and forth in front of his desk. "Mr. Ross, I have an idea for the official announcement." She paused, turning her head to look at him.

He did little to hide his lack of confidence. "By all means, share it."

Lauren returned to her pacing. "We are not going to straight out lie to the public. For one thing, it's unethical, and now that we've explained everything to them, the BRA would be so far up our ass about it that we would be forced to tell the truth within a week's time." Again, she paused. Ross gave her a quick nod, and she continued, "We also agreed at the emergency meeting not to divulge the loss of Project Bluestone because, frankly, our company will die—also within a week's time." She stopped her pacing but did not look at Ross. He waited as she determined the best way to put forth her plan.

"Mr. Ross, I suggest a compromise." She turned to face him. "I will announce that there has been a terrible attack on our company, and that we have lost both software and hardware critical to an ongoing, high-priority research effort. However, with the board's permission, I would like to add a bit of a lie—small enough for the BRA to ignore and large enough for our company to stay afloat."

At this, Ross sat up at full attention. "I'm listening."

Lauren smiled. It was at this most critical moment, while the future of her company was uncertain—grim, even—that the new CEO would finally gain the trust of the chairman of the board.

"After announcing the loss, I will explain that we had one last, top secret backup, located in my own office, which the plot failed to get a hold of and that will soon bring us right back on track." As she spoke, she could see Ross's eyes light with hope. "In addition to keeping us safe from our predatory competition, this false information will allow us to coordinate a sting operation with the DCI, as I'm sure the perpetrators will try to get their hands on this supposed final copy."

As she stood there, smiling at him, Ross couldn't help but smile himself. He rose to his feet and extended his arm. "That sounds excellent Ms. Care. You have the board's full support." Lauren took his hand and shook it. "I will contact the DCI immediately." And with that, she left his office and pulled out her Personal.

As she turned down the corridor to the media room, she sent the DCI a brief overview of her proposal and a query for suggestions. She assumed, rightfully, that they would reply in less than the time it took her to reach her destination. Sure enough, thirty seconds later and halfway through the trip, she received details on how to best word her announcement in order to aid a possible future DCI sting operation. Oddly, they also asked that she absolutely not divulge the bluff to anyone inside or outside the company. Apparently Mr. Ross was under the same orders. Her mood improved significantly with the added support of the organization. Putting away her Personal, she even let herself hope that maybe, just maybe, this plan would work.

- - -

As soon as they were out the backdoor, the adrenaline kicked in, and Stewart let his instincts take over. For the time, that meant blindly and quickly following this crazy stranger wherever he led them.

Their backyard led to a street, both sides lined with houses and apartments. They lived in a relatively up-scale area, so there were rarely any cars—commuters tended to prefer the Diama or, if you were really rich, personal aero-vehicles. One such PAV occupied almost the entire street behind their house, and Jacqueline soon realized what Lucas's plan had been. PAVs were like personal helicopters, minus the rotors and blades. The media dubbed them "the flying cars we've all been waiting for," although, she noted dryly, only the millionaires could afford them. This particular PAV was the size of a large van, and shared many of the same characteristics. Only the futuristic look and giant thrusters lining the bottom edge gave away its true nature. There was their getaway vehicle—complete with driver, from what she could tell.

Lucas opened the side door and motioned for them to hurry. Stewart, still on a rush, clambered in. Jacqueline hesitated, and Lucas went ahead and forced her in, closing the door behind her. As he jumped in front next to the driver, Jacqueline heard a deafening "STOP!" come from their backdoor, and turned her head out the side window to see three men running toward them, pulling out weapons of some sort. For a moment, she was stunned by their speed, and thought they were caught. But the driver had already begun the ascent into the atmosphere. "Put on your seat belts!" Doing as he was told, Stewart looked over Jacqueline's shoulder at the rapidly shrinking DCI agents. One of them held some sort of rifle against his shoulder and fired at the vehicle. The PAV shook frighteningly as the projectile hit its mark. When it settled back into position, there was silence. It was a fraction of a second before Stewart realized just how silent it had become. He overheard Lucas curse about an EMP cartridge. And then gravity hurtled them downward.

- - -

Standing behind the speaker's podium with several cameras and microphones trained towards her, Lauren took a deep breath and signaled to the assistant to start the broadcast. Her announcement was an internal one, meant to address her employees, but there were enough loose lips willing to distort details that they had decided from the start to release a copy to the media.

Can't wait for the headlines, she thought. Oh well, here we go.

"Good afternoon, ladies and gentlemen. It is with great regret that I must inform both you, our incredible and indispensable employees, and the general public, without whom our industry would never exist, that one of our most promising and prized research initiatives has been ruthlessly and thoroughly attacked. Highly encrypted data has been compromised, and physical assets have been stolen directly from our headquarters. The perpetrators have proven to be both efficient and effective, leaving almost no trace and nearly destroying our project in its entirety. The damage will no doubt set our company back a great deal, and more than anything, I am saddened by the nature of the assault. The research initiative in question was based on a desire for a more peaceful and robust human future, a future that has been delayed by what we can only assume were extremist views or hyper-competitive practices."

She paused for a moment before continuing to read the prompter. Here goes nothing, she thought.

"However, let it be known that while this delay will be costly, it will not be long. Although the attackers made every effort to destroy all backups and recovery files, they fell short of their goal. There was one final backup —a master backup, with every bit of our project data—under my strict supervision, which was left completely intact. Rest assured, the initiative will be back online within the week."

With a smile and a short nod, Lauren ended her announcement. And so it begins.

- - -

In the moments immediately following the EMP strike, Stewart realized three things. First, that the DCI was ruthless. Here he was, an innocent man, plunging downward in a PAV from a height he knew would be fatal.

Second, and deriving from his first realization, that despite all the reform, peace, and unity of the Earth in recent history, there was still plenty of violence between men. He forgot all about these thoughts, however, as the third realization took over: his wife was currently in the same predicament.

Before he had a chance to break apart emotionally, the PAV came to an abrupt halt and jolted him to attention. The sudden change brought with it a dull pain and he realized just how badly his body had been shaken. But why were they still alive?

He could see Lucas shouting into some sort of device but couldn't make out the words. What was going on? The PAV was intact—they hadn't crashed. He glanced up into the window and saw clouds moving... downward? Somehow, they were ascending again, but not on their own— the vehicle was pitched nose-down, forcing his weight against the seat belt. He took another glance out the window. "Holy..."

A much larger aerial vehicle was towing their PAV by a wire. During their descent, it must have fired a magnetic hook line onto their hull. The larger vehicle didn't seem to struggle with the weight—an indication of quite a powerful machine. For a moment, he was prepared to congratulate Lucas on a masterful escape plan. But when he turned his eyes to their would-be savior, he was still shouting into his device with desperation. The driver was speechless as he craned his neck to see the craft towing them. Stewart's momentary elation was replaced with dread. It was the DCI. Humane after all... but also perfect.

Then Lucas was done shouting, and had unstrapped himself and entered the back. While his driver began to assemble some large packages, he made his way over to the couple, holding himself up by a brace on the interior. "Listen: we cannot, under any circumstances, let them take us in. I understand that in the past two minutes I may have turned your life upside down, but right now, you're going to have to trust me, or it will get a lot worse." Coupled with the pacing and absurdity of the situation, the plea in Lucas's demeanor was potent. Despite an overwhelming sense of doubt,

Stewart nodded. Lucas sighed and looked back at his driver, who gave him a thumbs-up. "We're going to have to jump."

"What!?" Stewart turned to look at his incredulous wife, whose yell was deafening. "You must be insane, we can't jump out here! There are no fields or flat lands! Just buildings, roads, and the Diama!"

Lucas turned to her. "We have no choice. Each of you will jump with one of us, and we will control the landing. I can assure you we have practiced landings like this."

"Why? Why have you practiced landings like this? I was right wasn't I? You are the ones they want! Of course you can't be caught – by all means, jump! But leave us alone! We are innocent, and sooner or later they will realize this!" Her anger was reaching a peak.

Lucas considered her words carefully, despite the activity around them. He did not break eye contact, facing her fury with a look of disappointment and weariness. "You're right, they would. But we can't let them." Without giving her a chance to respond, he slammed his hand against both of their belt latches, grabbing Stewart before he fell away. The driver, apparently at constant attention, had his arms open to catch Jacqueline, and dropped the other pack next to him. With Stewart in one arm, Lucas let go of the brace and they both slid down to the backsides of the front seats. The driver had immediately pinned Jacqueline against him, her back to his front, and was already strapping the pack's harness to both of them. Lucas wasted no time in following suit, and Stewart was quickly reminded of the man's physical strength as he was jostled into the proper position.

A hand slid into his pocket and pulled out his Personal, throwing it to the ground. He didn't even have time to protest: three hooks snapped, and three belts were tightened. The driver took a glance back and Lucas gave him a quick nod. He kicked open the side door and air rushed in with a tremendous whoosh. Only then did Stewart realize just how silent the PAV had kept the interior—they were moving at quite some speed. There was a split second of hesitation, and then the driver and his wife were gone. Lucas shuffled forward, leaned out for a quick glance, and jumped.

- - -

Staring out at the complexity of the city in front of her, Lauren couldn't help but smile at her own ingenuity. She had decided to take the open glass elevator up to the sky terrace for a breather, and found herself oddly at peace despite the current situation. To be sure, the company was still in a crisis, but she couldn't help but feel optimistic that her plan would work.

Her Personal was flooded with queries from the board, asking why they hadn't been told about this secret backup, and if it was real. Per the DCI's orders, she did not immediately respond, but they were alarmingly persistent. Hopefully they would assume she was busy with the crisis.

Making her way back to the elevators, Lauren tried to comprehend how such an operation would have been carried out. Fenix was a small campus of sorts, with five or six buildings interconnected by wide, gardened paths. These buildings compromised administrative offices, media relations, a showroom... along with a gym, pool, and cafeteria. But the robot assembly lines? The prototype storage? All part of R&D, all underground, and all incredibly secure. How in the world did they manage to walk out with them?

There was a soft chime as the elevator door opened, and she stepped inside. What now? There was nothing left but to pursue any and all leads with the DCI. But first, she'd have to find them. These agents were investigating the physical theft, meaning they were probably in the lower levels where the Bluestone prototypes were kept. That was all fine and good except R&D was notoriously complex and she was typically guided by other employees. She reached the main lobby, walked out of the glass container, and made her way towards an exit.

For now, she decided to go to the R&D lobby, the only part of the department aboveground. Along the garden path, Lauren had an irksome realization: while it might end up being a nightmare finding the agents unless she contacted them, she had a strong impulse not to do so. Between the whispered stories she heard and her previous encounter with their analysts, she had no wish to waste the time of the DCI, even as a President in the middle of a massive investigation of her own company.

Shows how much psychological power they have, she thought. So she opted for the next best thing, and shot a message to one of the upper managers of R&D, asking where they were. Quickening her step, she reached one of the outside doors and pressed her hand against the panel. "Lauren Care." So much security, she thought, and for what?

The door swung quietly open and she walked inside. She stepped out into a large expanse—the R&D lobby had no offices or labs, just rows upon rows of servers, and elevator shafts to take incoming workers to their respective floors. Like the supercomputer port, everything was a sparkling white with hints of black, and for a moment she wondered how on Earth the department kept everything so clean. Robots, of course. She looked around at the pristine surroundings and secretly hoped that the same cleanliness would help the DCI find any smudges, fingerprints, hair follicles… anything.

Her Personal hadn't indicated any reply from the manager, so she made her way to the main entrance, hoping to find an info desk or module. Weaving through the aisles that nearly reached the ceiling, she noticed she couldn't hear a single person. Was she alone on this floor? She had to admit she didn't remember the last time she was in the R&D lobby, but there had to be people here on a regular basis, right? At least a robot? Was it because of the attack? She turned a corner at the end of a server row and saw the main door. Thank goodness, she thought. She may have been wrong about there being a front desk, but she saw two men, doing what seemed like forensic work on the door. One was kneeling, with a Portable in his hands, wires running into the handprint scanner next to the door, while the other was spraying some sort of chemical along the wall on the other side.

Weird, she thought to herself. They look more like Fenix scientists than DCI agents. The kneeling man glanced up from his work. He shot upwards and yanked his cables out of the scanner. The partner noticed what had happened, saw Lauren approaching, and both men bolted into the nearest aisle of servers.

Lauren's heart skipped a beat. No... no no no... Lunging behind the nearest server wall, she ripped out her Personal and called security.

"Yes ma'am?"

"Put R&D lobby on lockdown immediately—DCI override only."

She could feel the tension skyrocket on the other end of the line.

"Yes ma'am! Done."

There was a short pause before the man spoke again.

"No presidential override?"

She thought for a moment about the potential implication of the decision she was about to make.

"No."

She ended the call and immediately dialed the DCI.

"They're still here. Two agents in R&D lobby. The floor is on lockdown except for DCI override."

"Are you there?"

"Yes."

"Are they armed?"

"I don't know."

"Can you still see them?"

"No."

"Remain on the line as we monitor their movements."

"Okay."

She realized they had patched into the R&D detection system, a combination of cameras, motion detectors, and thermal and noise sensors. These men had underestimated their target. Wait, what was she thinking?

If the detection system were working, they would have been stopped during the original heist.

"Can you detect them?"

"Yes."

"Why weren't they detected during the original theft?"

"They had disabled your system. We have since reinstated it."

"Are they close?"

"No. Please remain in place, agents will be there in approximately one minute."

One minute? Lauren had gotten so accustomed to lightning reaction times, even a minute seemed like an eternity. But she quickly realized the reason for the delay – the agents downstairs weren't field agents, they were forensic agents. A new batch had to be sent in. Surely all of their personnel were cross-trained? Then again they had said themselves this was potentially the most masterful breach they had seen... at least they weren't arrogant.

"Ma'am?"

"Yes?"

"Please stay calm."

Before she could ask what they were talking about, the lights cut out.

- - -

The air rushed into Stewart's face, forcing him to close his eyes. He saw one glimpse of a sprawled-out metropolis before shutting them, and now had no idea how Lucas was going to pull this landing off.

He moved his hands into the braces near his shoulders, and Lucas yelled into his ear, "Arch your back!" He did as he was told, realizing just how much faith he was putting in this man, despite his lack of free will in the decision made just seconds earlier.

"Prepare for a jerk!"

Huh? What did that mean? Suddenly, Stewart shot backwards and upright, and his crotch jammed downward into the harness. It was extremely unpleasant, and he let out a string of obscenities.

"Sorry."

For all this man was putting him through, Stewart still appreciated the hint of guilt in the statement. He realized the chute had caused the jolt, and they were now cruising comfortably enough for him to open his eyes.

Well, he thought to himself, hell of a way to knock skydiving off the bucket list. He glanced downward and wondered where Lucas was planning on landing. Then it hit him: where was Jacqueline? He scanned frantically around them and saw another parachute to his left. The distance between them was surprising—the DCI must have been dragging their PAV at quite a pace. He watched the other parachute maneuver left and right and prayed that the driver was not only skilled but proficient.

His attention returned to their landing as Lucas pulled on a handle to bank right. He scanned the rapidly approaching buildings, wondering where this man planned to land them. Stewart's house was in the outer-city, but the DCI had managed to pull them nearly to the edge of the inner-city. Diama lines crisscrossed above the low rises, increasing in density as the buildings increased in height. The system had been built over most of the old infrastructure, so a good way of telling if you were in an older district was to see if the Diama was on the ground or above it. The newest sectors didn't even bother to build roads, but many inner-city residents still opted for their cars. The hardest part of the landing, Stewart thought, would be avoiding those magnetic tracks and still hitting a flat area.

Another bank right. Now Stewart saw a suitable spot—a rather large slot between three Diama lines with a four-lane road beneath. That's odd, he thought. No cars on the road. What was this place?

As they got closer Stewart observed dozens of wires weaving between the buildings on either side of the street. What in the world? Aboveground wires were almost unheard of nowadays—the Cloud handled communication and related networks while other wires such as power had moved underground. Despite being somewhere between his home and the inner-city, Stewart was completely unfamiliar with this area. Wires and no cars, he thought. This place has to be abandoned. Sure enough, as they dropped within a couple hundred meters, Stewart noticed boarded windows and cracks in the asphalt.

He tried to look at his wife again but he was facing the opposite direction. Lucas banked slightly left. They were going to hit soon—the Diama lines were maybe 100 meters away. Another adjustment, and they were aimed dead center of the lines with their slight forward drift. Stewart was growing concerned with the apparent density of the cables—there were no visible holes large enough to fit them. They passed the Diama with a light whoosh and were headed straight for a tangled mess. He saw a few holes now but there was no way they would maneuver there in time, they were dropping too fast. His body tensed as they rushed onward— what was Lucas thinking?

"Grab the harness!"

Lucas pulled down hard on both handles, slowing their descent to a crawl. They were centered over a particularly thick series of wires, and before Stewart realized what was about to happen, it did: Lucas cut the chute about a dozen meters from the wires and kicked his feet up to keep Stewart above him. There were a few seconds of freefall, then a collision. They bounced a bit with the varying tension, and Stewart heard a few snaps. Lucas quickly grabbed a wire and pulled them both downward, in between the cables. They slid feet first and swung back, Lucas holding onto the wire, supporting both of their weights. Stewart looked down— they were about 10 meters off the ground.

A whirr broke his attention. He glanced up to see the DCI craft in the distance, heading back in their direction, PAV still in tow.

"Great, just what we needed right now."

Lucas didn't seem to have a plan at this point. Jumping down attached by the harness would be a complete mess, and there were no soft objects anywhere underneath the line of the cable. And while Lucas was strong, Stewart knew he couldn't hold them both up like this for very long. His thoughts were interrupted by his body swinging side to side—Lucas was shifting them left, towards a building. He glanced toward their destination. There was a broken window relatively close to the end of the wire. If he were alone on this wire, Stewart knew Lucas could manage that swing into the building. But with a man dangling from him on a harness?

They reached the edge of the wire and Stewart saw Lucas trying to judge the best way to swing them into the window. It was about two meters tall and one meter wide, with the top edge slightly less than a meter below their dangling feet. The biggest issue, however, would be the two or so meters of horizontal distance between the wire and the center of the window.

Lucas turned them around so the window was in front of them, to their right.

"Okay Stewart, listen. There is no way I can get both of us through that window at the same time. You're going to have to take the wire, unhook yourself, and swing, grabbing the bottom ledge with your hands. Do you think you can do that?"

A cold chill spread through Stewart's body. He could feel his heart rate increasing dramatically.

"I—I don't know."

The whirr of the DCI aero-vehicle was now a dull hum.

"Stewart, we don't have time to think about this. Grab the wire."

Lucas lifted himself into a pull-up, and Stewart half-heartedly took the cable into his palms.

"Hold on."

Lucas let one arm drop, and Stewart's grip tightened instantaneously as he felt more of his own weight. With each belt being undone, the strain increased considerably, and on the third and final strap, Lucas let him go.

Fear swelled through him. The adrenaline from the skydive was nothing compared to this. If he missed the windowsill, he would probably break his legs. Meanwhile, he was having trouble holding himself up, let along swinging. What was happening? Thirty minutes ago life was calm, normal.

"Stewart, go!"

There was anger in Lucas's voice. The DCI would spot them any second. He kicked his legs to get some momentum. The coarse wire burned into his palms, but the overwhelming rush of adrenaline numbed his hands. His swing reached a good speed, and he eyed the target below him. Now or never.

He let go of the cable right before the front end of the swing. The next three seconds felt like three minutes. As he fell, the cool air ran along the contours of his body. He felt a thin film of perspiration that he hadn't noticed before. Was it from the activity or the fear? It didn't matter at this point. The tips of his fingers prickled with anticipation as he approached the windowsill. Mere centimeters separated him from his goal. His hands hit the ledge, and his fingers clamped down onto the smooth surface. The flood of relief entering his system was almost immediately replaced by dread—he was slipping sideways along the bottom of the window from his momentum. In the split second that followed, Stewart pulled himself upward just enough to throw his left arm into the rapidly approaching left edge of the window, breaking his slide. He didn't wait for the perspiration to get the better of his grip—he hauled himself inside with strength he thought beyond him, and collapsed onto the floor within. Safety at last.

3. Capture

True darkness was a rarity these days, and Lauren found herself unable to remember the last time she had experienced it with such totality. Her thoughts turned briefly to a vague memory of camping with her father. She yearned for the peace of her childhood, especially now. This was not the type of hide-and-seek she wanted to play.

When her ears finally adjusted to the silence, she heard a distant but distinct series of thuds and clatters. Were they trying to escape? Why were they still here? Tying loose ends? Or already after her fake backup? She wondered, for a moment, if her office was safe...

The noise came to an abrupt halt. What now? She strained to hear something, anything. Coupled with darkness, the silence emphasized her rapid pulse. It was at this moment that she realized just how terrified she had become of the situation. What if they had heard her announcement? Would that make her a target? Why did she feel the need to come down in the first place?

As her eyes adjusted to the darkness, she took an opportunity to scan her general vicinity. Part of her wanted to look around the corner of the server row, but she dared not make a sound and reveal her position. Where was the DCI?

The soft sound of multiple elevator doors opening answered her question. Ambient light from the shafts filled the vast expanse, but the server towers prevented her from seeing anything. At least a dozen pairs of shuffling feet took command of the room's acoustics. For all intents and purposes, it sounded as if an army had entered the building. It was obvious the DCI was taking this very seriously.

The shafts closed, and darkness fell a second time. Her Personal vibrated—a message from the DCI, letting her know they would avoid her position until further notice. If anyone tried to grab her or talk to her, it wasn't an agent. Good to know, she thought.

"DCI! Stop!"

Lauren jumped in surprise. Almost immediately, there were a series of electrical hums and screams of pain. She cringed at the sound, but it was over in an instant, and silence returned.

- - -

Stewart did not have time to relax after making his leap of faith—not a moment had passed when Lucas landed firmly on his feet into a squat right beside Stewart's head. How had he managed to pull that stunt off? Before he had time to ask him, Lucas snatched his arm and pulled him onto his feet.

"Not bad, Stewart. But we have to keep moving."

Panting from physical and emotional exhaustion, Stewart looked at Lucas in disbelief.

"What? Why?"

"They don't know where we jumped off, but they know their flight plan. I'm sure they've already called in ground-based search parties for every kilometer they covered. To make matters worse, I left my parachute out there, and I'd bet they're going to spot it sooner rather than later. We could have cut through those wires and landed on the ground but I'm betting they're going to be searching for a landing site and this bought us some time. Of course, it's the DCI we're talking about, so that means probably less than half an hour."

He couldn't believe what he was hearing. They just fell out of the sky to buy maybe 20 minutes. Did it ever stop?

"Well what the hell's your plan then?"

Lucas seemed to ignore the tone, if only because he was so focused on escaping.

"We've called in another PAV, but they're at least a half-hour out, and if the DCI spots them, we'll be out of options. We have to get far enough away that it's worth risking a pickup. Right now, that's going to be at least 5 kilometers. Please, we really shouldn't be standing here talking, let's go!"

With that, he took off into the adjacent hallway, giving Stewart barely enough time to realize he was supposed to follow.

- - -

Her senses heightened by the scuffle she had overheard, Lauren felt as if seconds had turned into minutes and minutes into hours. She couldn't understand why she didn't hear anything else. There was a brief confrontation, and now a painfully long silence. Why wasn't anything happening? If the DCI had stopped the criminals, shouldn't the lights be on and the agents be busy apprehending them? And if the unthinkable reverse had occurred, wouldn't the criminals be busy continuing their escape? She sat frozen, leaning against the wall of servers, not daring so much as to move her head to increase her peripheral vision. It was a torturous eternity.

The vibration of her Personal sent her into a full-body spasm. She knocked her head against the server tower, sending a dull, echoing clang through the surrounding abyss. Whispering an abundance of profanities, she placed her fingerprint on the screen to unlock it.

"Ms. Care."

She nearly hit her head against the wall again—the voice was coming from around where she had heard the tussle.

"We are going to turn on the lights and approach your position."

She glanced down at the message, which repeated the verbal announcement. Before she finished looking at her screen, light flooded her vision, and her eyes slammed shut. Goodness, she thought. No wonder pure darkness was so rare. As she tried to open her eyes, faint footsteps grew louder. Blinking rapidly, she managed to adjust her senses.

"Ms. Care?"

She turned her head to the right to see a figure standing at the far end of the server row.

"Please do not be alarmed. We have apprehended the suspects and determined there are no more threats in the vicinity. May I approach?"

"By all means."

As the man proceeded toward her, she stood and tried to gain her composure. Embarrassing as it was to be found almost in the fetal position, she had started to perceive the DCI as emotionless, and was therefore less perturbed by how the man had initially seen her.

Brushing off her outfit, she faced the agent. This was obviously not one of their analysts - in place of an immaculate suit and tie were numerous thin black plates of body armor. Most of his body was covered in these dark scales, each one uniquely shaped to protect a pectoral or a knee. Wherever she saw gaps, Lauren noticed a flexible black mesh with gray lines crisscrossing its surface. A black dome hung off of his back, and Lauren was glad he had had the decency to remove the formidable helmet before confronting her. The serious disposition, however, was unchanged.

She ran through a list of questions in her head and chose one.

"What did you do with them?"

"The suspects are now in DCI custody, taking a PAV to the closest containment center as we speak."

"I will be updated intermittently?"

There was a small hint of offense in his reply. "Ma'am, you will be updated immediately."

"Why were they here?"

"Our forensic analysts are on their way to examine the area. Initial assessment indicates an attempt to hide evidence."

"How did they get in?"

"We do not know at this time. Most likely, they have been here since the original heist."

Fantastic, she thought. Then she remembered the most important question.

"Are there any more in the building?"

"Probably." A slight hesitation betrayed the man's discomfort.

Lauren took a deep breath and braced herself for bad news. "Probably? Please elaborate."

"Ma'am, we have determined that this incident involved planted operatives."

A knot formed in her stomach. "Planted operatives? Are you saying an employee was involved?"

There were fleeting hints of growing discomfort in the agent's expression. "Most likely more than one."

"Why? Couldn't one person feasibly carry this out?" She was pleading with him, but it was of no use. He was just being honest.

"Everything had to be carried out instantaneously. There would not have been enough time to remove the hardware, the software, clear them through, and clean up the evidence with just one person. In fact, we originally suspected a high number, but the fact that two of their operatives were still actively removing evidence nearly an hour after the theft indicates they were likely understaffed."

"Those two men were employees?"

"Yes."

The knot tightened, and she sank into a sulk. It made sense, of course. Their systems weren't at fault—people were. If this truly began at the project's inception, the perpetrators had four years to infiltrate the ranks, gain clearance, and create backdoors. Were their background checks not thorough enough? What had they missed? But these were the easier questions to ask. What if it was someone she knew? The company wasn't necessarily large on the administrative side, and she had managed to meet most of those employees in her short tenure.

"If others are still here, would they be cleaning up evidence as well?"

"No. We've dispersed more agents to all sensitive locations in R&D."

As intimidated as she was by the organization, Lauren was starting to see gaps in their performance.

"Why wasn't this done sooner?"

"Our understanding of the incident has changed. Before you ran into these men, we considered the possibility of planted operatives, which is why you and the Chairman were asked not to explain the bluff. However, we had since come to the conclusion that all of these operatives would be gone within minutes, if they did indeed exist. That was a severe miscalculation, and we take full responsibility."

The respectful tone of the super solider calmed her irritation.

"Why are agents only in R&D? What about potential operatives on the administrative side?"

"They have no evidence to clean up in that area—all of the thefts were in R&D, the administrative clearance would have helped clear a path for escape and gained access to some of the backups, but nothing more. We have an agent in your room, however, following your announcement, and are actively monitoring all video feeds in that area to prevent any more miscalculations. If you'd like us to increase our presence, we can, but we do not recommend it."

They had a point, she thought. Their presence in R&D was expected but having them walk the halls of other departments would create enormous tension. Productivity, already plummeting due to the commotion, would stop.

"No, thank you." She paused, trying to remember why on Earth she had come down here in the first place. "Have the forensic agents found anything?"

"Yes, but not enough. Certain halls of R&D have experienced heavy loads recently, not in accordance with anticipated load movements by any sub-department. We have therefore determined certain parts of the path that all of the missing hardware took on its way out, but these parts are sporadic and small—there are as of yet too many gaps in the evidence to determine where it was headed."

Not surprising, she thought. R&D was immense; there were plenty of ways to move about. But how did no other technician or scientist notice? Most confounding of all, how did no robots notice?

"Why is it that no human or robot noticed these movements?"

The soldier made a slight frown. "We do not know yet. Even if the operation took place at hours of minimum traffic, and took the most efficient route to exit, they would have encountered, by our estimates, at least ten human and/or robot entities. We are working on an answer."

She sighed with resignation. The most powerful investigative force on the planet was stumbling to figure out what had happened right under her nose. It wasn't worth the stress caused by the answers to continue asking questions.

"Thank you, sir. I understand I will be notified immediately of any and all leads, both from the forensic agents and the interrogation of the suspects?"

"Yes ma'am."

As she turned around, the agent added "One more thing, ma'am."

She turned back towards him. "Yes?"

"Now that we know we are dealing with potential inside agents, I need to know if you have spoken to anyone about the secret backup, and whether it exists."

"No."

"Thank you, ma'am. Your Chairman has not either, so there is still hope that your plan will work."

"Right." With that, she gave the man a dismissive nod, and made her way back to the doorway that brought her into this mess.

- - -

Lucas had led Stewart rather quickly out of the abandoned building and into the street opposite their landing site. The hum of the aero-vehicle echoed against the surrounding structures. With no more than a look and a gesture, he directed his unwilling partner to walk briskly, as close to the walls of the edifice as possible. Stewart could see the street continue well into the next dozen blocks, but was more absorbed with the state of it all

—shrubs emerged from cracks in the asphalt with an unprecedented will to live, ignoring the man-made barricade by blasting right through it. There were wires everywhere: between buildings, along their walls, and on the ground, apparently ripped or fallen. Their criss-crossing canopy created quite a mangled shadow along the ground, which it was obvious Lucas meant to use to their advantage. The buildings themselves stood with solemn facades, alone and abandoned for what must have been a few decades, if not more. Some had collapsed partially, others had been smeared with rainbows of graffiti, and at least every other window was broken or boarded. What was this place?

"Where are we?" He asked Lucas in a near whisper, unaware if he should even be talking.

His guide didn't bother to look back as he led the way forward. "Old industrial district. Mostly housing. When the robots started snatching up jobs in certain industries, the corresponding districts would crumble. Even if some industries were unaffected, the mass exodus among other occupations caused a domino effect."

Wow, Stewart thought. If this was during the Robotic Revolution, the place wasn't a few decades old—it was a century old. Why in the world was it still abandoned?

"Why hasn't it all been torn down?"

A flash of anger appeared on Lucas's face. "This is our history—our heritage. We shouldn't destroy it."

Stewart noticed the man's agitation, and proceeded carefully. "Yes, but then why hasn't it been preserved? Why is it abandoned?"

Lucas stopped for a moment, and looked at the surroundings. His eyes scanned the deteriorated buildings, the knocked over signs, and the shattered glass. Something in his gaze gave an impression of loss, or even defeat. Bowing his head, Lucas gave a sigh. "It's complicated." With that, he picked up the pace, forcing Stewart to cut his questioning short.

They reached the next corner and Lucas pressed himself against the wall, motioning for Stewart to do the same. He stood close to the wall and watched Lucas slowly peek his head around the corner. After some surveillance, he turned back to Stewart and motioned to follow.

They hustled quickly across the expanse, and behind the building they had just shadowed, Stewart caught a glimpse of the DCI aero-vehicle, hovering somewhere over their landing site. When he turned his attention back to Lucas, he had cut halfway across the street toward the other side. Struggling to keep up, Stewart maintained his focus on the direction the man was heading, and not on the inevitable emergence of the DCI agents from behind.

In less than half the time it took them to reach the first corner, they were cutting around the next corner on the opposite side of the street. Once Stewart had gone around, Lucas pressed himself against the wall and looked back the way they had come. He held this position for barely three seconds before whipping his head back and tensing against the wall. "Agents—they just came out of our building... faster than I expected. We need to hurry." Turning his attention to Stewart, he pointed towards the end of the block. "Around that next corner, come on!"

As he picked up the pace, Stewart realized he was likely getting more exercise today than he had in the past month, and he was starting to feel it. From Stewart's position, Lucas seemed to sprint effortlessly, but the labored breathing at every stopping point hinted at his fatigue. Clearing several plant growths didn't help—these were not flat roads but uneven surfaces riddled with debris. It was mostly pieces of asphalt, but Stewart noted the occasional bizarre trinket, and wondered if it was abandoned here recently or nearly one hundred years ago. A butcher's knife, a wooden chair, splintered into a dozen pieces, and a child's doll, gray with dust. How could this place be so abandoned? Why did no one come through here?

They made it around the next corner. Lucas stopped and looked around. Did he know this area? That would be awfully coincidental, Stewart thought. A small device came out of his pocket. Lucas pressed a button, and it emitted a quick beep. Two seconds later, it beeped again, and lit up with some information.

"They are 21 minutes out, and we still need to cover over 4 kilometers to reach the extraction point. We need to start running."

"Running?" He made no effort to hide his exasperation.

"Yes." And he took off down the street.

- - -

Lauren paused at her office door. An agent? In my office? She felt uncomfortable, as if someone was violating her private space. It was amazing how much simpler her life had been just this morning.

She opened the door gently, not knowing what the agent's orders were, and irrationally expecting him to pounce on the first person that entered. With her neck tense she slowly poked her head into the room and looked around. The usual arrangement in her office was interrupted by an imposing figure against her left wall—another solider-type, but with his helmet on. A chill ran through her body, the man was a jarring sight.

"Good afternoon, ma'am."

She examined her bodyguard with a mix of gratitude and apprehension. Oh well, she thought, I guess he didn't pounce on me. Her muscles relaxed and she closed the door behind her.

"Hello. I assume nothing unusual has occurred?" She walked around to her chair but kept her eyes on the agent. She couldn't help her intimidation —no wonder the DCI was so effective.

"You are the first person to enter since your announcement."

"Good. Now what is the plan when someone else tries to come in?"

"That depends on their manner of entry, ma'am. If they are unannounced, and seem even remotely threatening, they will be stunned immediately. But all visitors will have a weapon trained upon them while they are in the room."

Sitting in her chair behind her desk, Lauren raised her eyebrows with skepticism. "Is that entirely necessary?"

"Yes." There was an unwavering certainty in the answer. So be it.

She placed her Personal on her desk and the entire surface lit up. A thin, blue circle of light drew itself around her Personal, and a series of thin lines drew right-angle turns to other, filled-in circles popping up across the desk. A small bar popped into existence, hovering near her Personal's circle, filling itself up with color as her workstation verified the identification and made sure all content was synchronized. Within seconds, the process was complete, the lines erased themselves, and there was a faint click as the Personal was magnetically locked to the desk. Then the entire apparatus tilted downward towards her, creating a beautiful canvas of light for her to work on. The circles rearranged themselves and floated slowly around the expanse of the desk.

She pressed a sapphire-tinted one lightly with her finger, and the color spread across the surface, pushing the other circles past the edges. The words "Project Bluestone" burned in bright white text across the top, wiping in and wiping out in a matter of seconds. Normally, there would be a traffic jam of information on the screen, with updates and progress bars zipping past messages and charts. But their data had been wiped clean. There was nothing but blue in front of her.

"Send DCI correspondences into Bluestone."

A soothing male voice answered, "Yes ma'am" and small white circles exited her Personal into the surrounding blue abyss. Each one drifted randomly for a handful of seconds before slowly expanding into a shimmering collection of dots that faded into the background. It was quite a display for such a simple task, but Lauren enjoyed every moment.

As each circle vanished, a thin black rectangle emerged from the background, creating a small tile with 'Messages' emblazoned across the middle. It was a far cry from the barrage of information that previously occupied the space, but it gave her a degree of comfort.

A green circle emerged violently from her Personal, taking center stage on her screen. 'Franklin Ross' had sent her a package.

"Open package."

"Yes ma'am."

The green circle moved upwards and to the right, opening into a large green rectangle of data. A voiceover from her Chairman emanated from her worktop. "Ms. Care, here is a collection of current press releases regarding your announcement. I've also attached a follow-up investigative query by the BRA. Stock trends are not looking good, but it could be much worse." There was a pause, a search for the right words. "And Ms. Care, I understand there was an incident in the R&D lobby involving you and some of our attackers... please be careful, we can't afford to be too cautious."

Lauren tapped lightly on a small box that read 'BRA Correspondence' and the entire surface went green. There was text, video, and audio of their initial report to the agency, which gave almost no information, followed by their second, full report of the incident. Ross had managed to secure permission from the BRA to only divulge their full report to the agency's Director and Vice Director, preventing the leak from potentially reaching Fenix's competition. Lauren wasn't entirely sure if this was legal, but she didn't care. In any case, the BRA wanted updates on the DCI investigation. Why hadn't they contacted the DCI directly?

Her suited companion turned to face her. "Ma'am, do not answer that message."

She looked up from her desk, confused as to what he could be talking about. "Excuse me?"

"The BRA did not send that message to your Chairman, it is a fake."

She looked down at her workspace then back up at the agent. "How do you know what I am looking at?"

"We are monitoring any incoming and outgoing information to the entire company, including your workstation and Personal."

"You are monitoring my Personal?"

"Yes, ma'am."

Lauren frowned. This was unexpected, and rather disturbing. But she was digressing.

"Who sent this message?"

"We do not know. But the BRA has already contacted us about the investigation and we can confirm that they are unaware of this message. We have tracked the origin, and have sent an agent to speak with the employee who may be responsible."

Insider agents in the BRA? This was making less and less sense. She returned her attention to the workstation. "Announce a second emergency board meeting in 15 minutes with approval from the Chairman."

- - -

Twenty blocks later, Stewart's pace was slowing. They had been running for no more than five minutes, but between the skydiving, the cable acrobatics, and the uneven terrain, it was five minutes too many for someone who was not exactly an athlete.

Lucas took notice. Each corner they passed, Stewart took longer and longer to catch up. He stopped at the end of the block, in the shade of a Diama line, and turned his head back towards Stewart. He had barely made half the distance! But that was the least of his problems. At first, the volume was too subtle, but now he was sure: the sound of the aero-vehicle wasn't fading away—it was getting louder. They were searching. And he was running out of ideas.

He removed his transmitter, and beckoned the PAV. The display read "3400 m, eta 15 min" and an arrow flashed in the direction of the extraction point. There was no way... not with this pace. Stewart caught up, and leaned over, bracing his arms against his legs as if about to vomit. This was obviously not going to work as planned.

Lucas scanned their surroundings. They had continued a zig-zag pattern, never going two blocks in the same direction. The streets here were thinner, the buildings smaller. Taking shelter in one was not an option—the DCI would sniff them out within the hour. He cursed the EMP that brought them here.

Stewart stood up, still breathing heavily. "What... happened? ...why are... we stopping?"

Lucas turned to him. "I don't—" He let the rest of the sentence drop as his eyes locked on the nearest support column for the Diama line above them. It was insane, but they didn't have much of a choice.

"Follow me!" He made a beeline toward the column—it seemed to be no more than 500 meters away, although it took them off their zig-zag. He tried to come up with a feasible plan as they approached. Every support column had access, but it might be a ladder. The Diama line here was a good 100 meters above the ground, and climbing the ladder would expose them to the aero-vehicle. But what else were they going to do? That damn thing would probably tow their rescue PAV if they tried to be picked up now anyways.

They rounded another two corners and Lucas cautiously peeked his head around the edge of the building, looking away from the support column and towards their old landing site. They were still a few blocks from the original street, but he knew the agents had long since fanned out. Nothing. Clear. He spun back and ran towards the column, the bottom still obscured by buildings.

At the next block, Lucas hid himself around the building, and beckoned Stewart to come around behind him. It was slow moving, but he had to be sure the DCI weren't on the same street. Still clear. No sign of the aero-vehicle either. He wondered why it hadn't ascended, but realized it probably had to do with the poor visibility caused by dense Diama lines and even denser wiring. Thank Earth for old technology.

They made the next three blocks in a similar fashion, all down the same street, always checking for pursuers. At the next corner, Lucas paused to take a look at the column. He saw the faint outline of a white ladder on the white background. The occasional whirr of a pod was now audible. It seemed as if the foundation would be around the next block, and once he knew it was still clear, they went for it.

Rounding the next corner, Lucas saw the foot of the support column splashed into the street below. Stewart, upon making up the distance, was surprised at the centrality of it - Diama columns did not typically block streets... but then again, this place seemed abandoned.

The base of the column was hexagonal, and the entire thing spread from about a 10 meter diameter to a 20 meter diameter in the bottom 20 meters of height. The foot seemed to be secured to a separate foundation from the street and buildings—there was a slight crack around the edge, as if they had blasted a hole in the ground. A maintenance ladder, with no surrounding cage, shot upward along one face of the hexagon.

Stewart looked apprehensively at the structure. "What are we doing?"

Lucas ignored his comment and ran to the edge of the base. He made his way around the large foot, towards the side hidden from view. Stewart watched as Lucas jogged around the structure and stopped. Immediately, the concern in his face turned into relief.

"What is it?"

Lucas smiled—the first time Stewart had noticed—and said, "There's an elevator. Come on."

Stewart made his way toward the man but was still lost on the plan. "What are we doing? This is a maintenance shaft, we can't get on a pod from here!"

Lucas approached the recess that held the door and eyed a small panel on the right. "We're going to do what we can."

Stewart didn't like the sound of that. He watched his captor rip off the small panel and unplug some wires. "What about the PAV?"

Lucas continued to fiddle with the wiring. "We won't make it in time. And if you haven't noticed, the DCI are using their airpower on us—that thing would notice our PAV and snatch us up all over again."

Unfortunately, he was right. Stewart took the opportunity to catch his breath while Lucas worked the door. "Why do they even have these shafts and ladders anyway? Don't robots do the maintenance?"

Lucas didn't look at him. "Yes, but how do the robots get up there? Did you think the ladder without a protective shell would be for humans?"

Touché. His hand reached idly for his pocket, forgetting over the course of his adventures that it had been discarded. "Why did you throw away my Personal?"

"Tracking." That was that. Before Stewart could retort, there was a hiss as the door slid open. Lucas dropped the panel, now dangling from the wires, and walked into the elevator. For a second, Stewart wondered if he should run. Not from the DCI, but from Lucas. He could make a lot of noise and head back in their direction, it would only be a matter of seconds before they found him. He would be captured, sure, but he could prove his innocence quickly enough. Lucas would probably even have a chance to escape. Everyone would win...

"Stewart! We don't have time for this, come on!"

And yet, something compelled him to stay. The sincerity in the man's voice, the guilt and apologetic tone throughout the day. Not to mention, he had to admit, the adventure of it all. But his real concern at this point was Jacqueline. How was she? Where was she? And when would he see her?

"Stewart! I'm sorry but we have to go, NOW!"

As he made his way into the elevator, he decided to find out. "Where the hell is my wife?"

The door hissed closed behind them, and they began to climb. "I don't know. I cannot communicate with my driver, in case either of us gets captured."

Lovely, Stewart thought. Just what I wanted to hear.

Their ascent was over quickly, and the door hissed open. Before them was a small platform, maybe 5 meters to the tracks and 15 meters from left to right. Two Diama lines ran in front of them, with another small platform on the opposite side, although with no elevator shaft. There was a constant hum coming from the tracks. They stepped out on the small expanse, and Stewart noticed no railings. Of course not, he thought, robots don't need railings.

A burst of wind nearly knocked him over, and his heart jumped as he got precariously close to the edge—a pod had zoomed by. He scrambled back to the center of the platform and sat down. This was too much for one day.

Lucas had almost lost his balance, but was now fixated on the DCI aero-vehicle, visible down to the right. It was hovering below the height of the Diama. He could even make out a few agents on the streets. It was odd to see that much activity in a place so deserted.

Another two quick gusts had him breaking a fall with his arms. Good Earth, those things go fast! Trying to grab or catch one would be instant death. He suddenly felt as if they were in no better shape than they had been on the ground. He looked over to Stewart, sitting in the middle of the platform. What were they going to—

"How in the world do robots do any maintenance out here?"

That was it! Maybe they could manually stop or block the tracks! Lucas turned back to face the shaft they had come through. To the right of the door, there was a large box. On the outside, a small opening hinted at the complexity inside. It was a connection for a robot—most likely a specific type of maintenance robot. They didn't open the box, they simply stuck a finger in and ran some commands... Lucas didn't have anything to mimic this. Could they break it open?

He approached the box and looked for seams. None to be seen. He was starting to lose faith in the idea... even if they busted it open, he had no idea how to wire the Diama maintenance. Keypads were one thing, but a complicated system like this?

Another pod whizzed by. The hum of the Diama was starting to mix with the hum of the aero-vehicle, and Lucas frowned. He turned back to Stewart and the tracks, and examined the lines in front of them. There were two, wide blocks of guiding track, one for each direction. Both were about 6 meters wide, enough to fit two pods across the width, for passing or when forks came along. In the middle of the tracks was a trench, but from Lucas's position, he could only discern the width of the lip, which seemed to be a little less than half a meter. He couldn't see how wide it became or if there even was a floor, although the column probably formed one.

Out of the corner of his eye, Lucas noticed a dark blur, and turned his gaze to the left, towards the inner city. "Oh no..." Another aero-vehicle was approaching their position. He turned to Stewart, who had been sitting silently, watching the Diama line.

"Stewart, wait here."

Stewart looked up at him, confused. Where in the world was he planning on going?

Lucas approached the tracks, and stood right next to the edge. He looked right, and didn't see anything in the distance. He looked left, and— whoosh! Another pod flew right by him, knocking him onto the ground. For Earth's sake...

Lifting himself back onto his feet, Lucas scanned both directions once more. A small white dot appeared on the right, far away, closer, whoosh! He barely had time to register that he had seen one before it passed them. This was not going to be easy.

He looked both ways once more. Third time's the charm? Nothing. He ran across the tracks, and threw himself into the trench, feet first. He vaguely wondered what would happen if there wasn't a floor, but his feet quickly hit the bottom. It wasn't very deep - he had to crouch to keep his head under the lip, but it got much wider. There was about a meter of width to work with. Lucas looked down the track and smiled.

"Stewart?!"

Stewart had bolted to his feet as Lucas ran across—what was the man thinking!? He thought Lucas had slipped through and fell to the street below, and was enormously relieved to hear his voice. "Yes?"

"There's a trench in here, with floor all along the track. We can walk along this."

Stewart tried to comprehend what that would require. "You want me to run across the Diama track?"

Before Lucas could answer, a pod's rush of wind knocked Stewart back on his rear. The answer came, timidly. "Yes..."

This was ludicrous. Where did he draw the line? Sure, he had just convinced himself to follow this man, but now he really was in a position to escape. Well, escape to capture. Neither option was tempting. No matter how often he reminded himself of his innocence, and how he could explain himself, Stewart did not want to end up in the hands of the DCI. There were too many stories, too many rumors... the damn organization had shrouded itself in mystery and spread a culture of fear. Here he was, about to risk his life, all based on that fear... even when he knew he had done no wrong!

Well... not all based on fear. Stewart was all too aware that his wife was in the hands of this man's companion. If anything, she was worth all the risk he was taking.

Three more pods, in rapid succession. He looked down at the buildings below. The agents were spread across many streets, but their distribution was denser along one particular zig-zag line. Damn. How were they being tracked?

"Be careful." Stewart looked back to the trench and saw Lucas's head poking out cautiously, constantly looking left and right. "If you even think you see a pod, wait until it passes."

Right. He approached the tracks carefully. To his right: nothing, and although he wasn't going to reach the other track, he didn't want to be knocked down while crossing. To his left: nothing.

"Now's the time!" Lucas watched him apprehensively, then continued his back and forth scanning. Was that a pod in the distance?

Stewart sprinted down the 6 meters and saw Lucas duck his head out of the way. As his feet entered the lip, he noticed a white blur to his right, and he instinctively clamped his eyes shut. With his hips sliding into the trench, Stewart felt a gust of wind slam his body against the edge, and then the pressure was gone, and he crumbled onto the floor beneath.

4. Motive

Lauren tapped her foot against the floor of the board room and kept her eyes fixed on her Personal, sitting on the table in front of her. The meeting was supposed to start 5 minutes ago, but one board member was missing. The others were terribly impatient, no doubt angry that she had not answered any of their messages regarding the secret backups. In fact, she would currently be facing a barrage of questions had it not been for Mr. Ross coming in beforehand and keeping them all in line. For once, she was thankful that he was here...

The door opened, and a flustered Rubger walked in. He gave a weak smile to Lauren, and sheepishly took his seat, avoiding the eyes of the other board members.

Mr. Ross spoke from across the table, "Ms. Care, please proceed."

As you wish. "Ladies and gentlemen, there have been some updates to our crisis that warrant our attention. As all of you know, I witnessed firsthand that there were insider agents cleaning up evidence in R&D. And as you also know, they are currently being interrogated by the DCI."

The board all nodded in agreement. She had their full attention, likely anticipating an explanation of their backup situation.

"In addition, you all heard my announcement about the secret backup. Unfortunately, the DCI is asking that I do not discuss the situation with anyone under any circumstances. This is why all of your messages have gone unanswered."

They looked at each other, then back to her. Confusion and frustration spread quickly among their faces.

"What?"

"Why?"

Mr. Ross spoke up. "That is currently privileged information. Please do not try to convince our new CEO to break the law."

She almost smiled at him. Her plan must have really won him over. "What I want to discuss with you all is a new and disturbing incident. Mr.

Ross forwarded a follow-up inquiry from the BRA to my office. The DCI has kindly informed us that this message was sent by an inside agent."

"Another one?"

"Yes, but this time in the BRA."

There was a collective gasp. This was unprecedented.

"Now, members of the board, your reaction was similar to mine—this is unheard of, and takes the crisis to a whole new level. But it begs the question—why? Why in Earth's name would anyone coordinate what might be the most sophisticated heist since the Robotic Revolution just to take down Project Bluestone? Originally, I considered corporate espionage, but at this point, that is nearly impossible. Would any company really think they could get away with bringing out our software, even in the next decade, after such a massive undertaking by the DCI? This reaction had to be foreseen, even the compromising of the BRA insider had to be a possibility. That makes corporate espionage, quite frankly, a silly hypothesis."

They were all ears—Lauren realized she had never quite had all of their attention so completely.

"Then why was it done? What is the goal? To set back robotic development? We're all aware of the general public disapproval of robots, but this is absurd. That same public has been pushing for hard-wired robotic altruism, and Bluestone was the single-most promising leap forward in that direction!"

She sighed, averting her gaze from the board for a moment.

"Ladies and gentlemen, while the DCI does not deal in hypotheticals, I cannot sit around idly while a foreboding possibility dominates my thoughts. As far as I can tell, this must be an act of terrorism."

No one made a sound, but the tension in the room elevated—she could feel it. Lauren returned her gaze to the seven executives in front of her. Eyes darted around apprehensively.

"If I'm right, then the world of robotics has changed dramatically. I brought you in here not to answer any questions, but to warn you. Until the DCI has solved this case, please exercise extreme caution. Do not divulge any information to curious parties, especially over the Cloud. If you have any specific questions, the DCI has been supremely gracious in offering their support. Do not hesitate to speak with them, and rest assured, their communications are secure. I will be sure to—"

A knock, followed immediately by the door opening. A DCI agent stepped into the room.

"Ma'am, my apologies for the interruption, but we need to speak with you in your office immediately."

She glanced over at Mr. Ross, who nodded. "I'll take it from here."

She snatched her Personal off the desk, and walked into the hallway. The agent followed, closing the door behind them.

"Ma'am, we have updates with regards to the suspects in custody for you."

"Shouldn't we share that information with the board?" She didn't bother hiding her agitation—the man had interrupted an extremely important meeting.

"We are still operating under a need-to-know basis. This information is too sensitive for anyone but you and the Chairman."

They reached her office, and he opened the door for her. She nodded at her guardian, still alert against the wall, and sat behind her desk as the agent closed the door behind them. He didn't aim his weapon at the other agent, she noted.

"In case the thought occurred to you, ma'am, don't worry, your building is not under surveillance by the attackers—we have already made sure of it."

I guess that counts as a win, she thought.

"The reason for our discretion is simply our need to keep information in trusted hands. As you know, we have asked you not to explain the situation with the false backup to your employees or the board, and we thank you for your cooperation in this matter."

She nodded. *Now tell me why in the hell you removed me from a board meeting,* she thought.

"The suspects we apprehended earlier this afternoon were clearing both the log memory for the lobby door and any residual forensic evidence on or around it. This in itself we deduced immediately, but were unsure why. If they or their accomplices had removed all physical assets and then proceeded out of the building, they would not have used that door - it would take them right through the main entrance, in clear view of security, even at empty hours."

That's odd, she thought. *If they couldn't have feasibly used the door, why clean it?*

"However, it turns out that the perpetrators who committed the physical theft did in fact use this door."

Lauren eyed him incredulously. "What? You just said they would have been seen if they tried to haul the seven prototypes out that way."

"That's right, but they did not. They exited that way, but only with the recovery disks, which were small and nondescript. Any witnesses would have no idea what was actually being removed."

She paused to digest the meaning in his words. "Then... what? They took the prototypes out somewhere else first, doubled back, and tried to cover their original tracks by taking the recovery disks out through the main lobby?"

He shook his head. "No ma'am. They did not have the time for that. They did not take the prototypes out a different way. In fact, they never took them out at all. All seven of the prototypes are still in this building."

- - -

"Stewart, are you okay?"

Sprawled out on the floor of the trench face down, Stewart groaned. There was a dull pain pulsating through his lower back.

"Don't move just yet."

Thanks, he thought. Wasn't planning on it. He felt his shirt being pulled up slowly, then Lucas's hands were on his lower back.

"Ow!" Pressure, right where it hurt.

"I'm going to slowly turn you onto your back." Lucas took his arms and legs, gently lining them up. Stewart felt him grab his shoulder and hip, and gradually push them over, controlling him all the way until he was on his back.

Lucas looked at him. "Any new pain from being in this position?"

"No, the same."

Lucas took one leg and slowly bent the knee, bringing it up towards Stewart's chest. "Nothing?"

Stewart shook his head. They repeated the process with the other leg.

"Okay, let's try to get you sitting."

Lucas helped him get up into a sitting position, leaning back on his hands.

"Still okay?"

Stewart nodded. The pain had subsided a bit, but the area was still tender.

Lucas sat down across from him. "You should be fine. Nothing seems broken. But we should take a break, just in case."

"Can we afford it?"

Lucas shook his head slowly. "Not really, but we don't have a choice." He pointed down the trench to the right, away from the inner city. "The whole way we go, we're going to have to bend over or crouch. If we try that now you won't make it five minutes."

He pulled out his transmitter and checked the status of the PAV. They were now 3600 m away, no doubt from backtracking and elevating. The vehicle was 11 minutes out. None of that mattered—protocol had it leaving after 20 seconds if they weren't there. He pressed a button, activating an abort order, and put the transmitter away.

Stewart watched him. "What happened?"

"We won't make the extraction point. We'll have to find another way."

"Was this all part of the plan? You know, skydiving and all?"

Lucas shook his head. "No. This transmitter works as a one time S.O.S. signal. I activated it before we jumped. Now that we missed our window, we'll have to get there on our own."

"Get where?"

Lucas hesitated. "Home."

Stewart sighed. "And my wife?"

"They had a separate transmitter. We can only hope they reached their extraction point."

"But the DCI was only following us, right? So they are safer?"

Again, Lucas shook his head. "Before we jumped in here, I saw another aero-vehicle coming from the inner city. It's probably on its way to intercept them, but they have a good ten minute head start."

Stewart bowed his head in defeat. It was hopeless.

"Look, a ten minute head start is invaluable. I don't want to deal in absolutes, but I'd be very surprised if they didn't get to their rescue PAV. Try not to worry about it. We need to focus on our own escape, or it won't even matter."

Stewart looked up at him. "How far is this 'home'?"

"Far, but don't worry. Ideally, we will only have to walk to the next Diama station."

"What? Are you planning on—"

Lucas raised his hand to stop him. "Please, I've got it under control. How do you feel?"

The pain was throbbing, but subdued. He answered hesitantly. "Better..."

"Okay." Lucas stood up, bending downward to keep his head in. "Let's go."

Stewart clambered slowly to his feet. Thankfully, he was able to keep his back straight and just dip his head down. "Ready."

Lucas started walking down the trench, with Stewart close behind.

- - -

Lauren let the silence drag for nearly a minute. When she replied, it was slow and methodical, with a hint of disbelief. "The prototypes are still here?"

The agent nodded. "Yes."

She tried to control a desire to celebrate. There had to be a catch. "Where?"

"We don't know."

She cocked her head slightly to one side. "You don't know?"

"We do not know where they are, ma'am."

"They didn't have a more specific answer?"

"No, ma'am, they didn't hide them."

Her eyes betrayed a mixture of frustration and confusion. "What?"

"I'm sorry ma'am. Let me explain everything we learned. The two suspects we apprehended were only involved in the physical theft. Therefore, we have no new information on the removal of data, or the deletion of backups and saved versions, although it looks like most of that happened through the insecure links we explained to you earlier today."

We? You mean your three analysts? She had never seen this agent before. The DCI had an eerie way of referring to itself as one entity.

"As you know, the physical theft involved two things: the recovery disks and the seven prototypes. This was done by four inside employees: our two suspects in custody and two others, who walked out with the recovery disks. First, this means we do not have access to the recovery disks, and the suspects do not know their whereabouts. Second, it means there are two more R&D inside agents."

She sighed. "Okay, but you just said the prototypes are in the building, right?" She was holding on to any hope she could.

"Yes. At the same time as the other inside agents took the recovery disks out, our suspects dealt with the prototypes. Then, when there was a lull in activity, they tried to clear evidence of the movement through the door. They assumed, correctly, that we would not expect any of them to go through that door, and therefore would not examine it until much later, possibly never. Thankfully, you happened to walk by."

"Wait. You just told me the suspects did not hide the prototypes - now you say they did?"

"I'm sorry ma'am, I'm not being clear. The suspects did not physically hide the prototypes. Robots did."

"Robots?"

"Yes. The two suspects had managed, probably over an extended period of time, to reprogram seven robots in R&D to follow their orders under any circumstances. Normally, this would take unprecedented skill, but these are some of your top scientists we are talking about. They have the skill."

Lauren sat, flabbergasted at what the agent was telling her. Robots? Reprogrammed for crime? There were so many failsafes... all designed by these same scientists. And to a robot, hiding another robot was probably not a crime.

"There were only two of them, however, so they were unable to do any significant reprogramming, for fear of being discovered by their colleagues. But the changes were enough: they ordered the robots to conceal all of the prototypes throughout R&D and ordered them to wipe their memory of performing the task. They were also told to do it by any means necessary to prevent discovery or retrieval. Now, the prototypes had enough security features to stop their destruction, but not their deconstruction. They were constantly being worked on in some manner, so it seemed relatively routine. We know they are all in R&D, and that each piece is intact, but they may not be whole."

"What about cerebral units?"

"Disassembled. Remember, these were not production robots, so their units were still malleable."

She sighed. There were no victories here. "Seven robots you say?"

"Yes, ma'am, seven. One for each prototype."

The entire operation was starting to make sense, from a feasibility standpoint. With so many inside agents, and that level of skill, it was a miracle they hadn't done more damage! Of course, Lauren thought, it still didn't answer the real question: why.

"Okay, is that everything you learned?"

"As far as logistics are concerned, yes. The suspects managed to clear enough evidence in the logs that we cannot be sure which employees left with the disks."

"And the suspects cannot identify them?"

"No ma'am, they are unaware of their identities."

"Unaware? How is that possible?"

"During the attack, our two suspects in custody dealt only with the robots disassembling the prototypes and then later cleaning the door. The other two left with the recovery disks, but no one ever crossed paths. In fact, while the suspects probably worked with the other insider agents, perhaps even on a day-to-day basis, neither pair knew the other. These are experts we are dealing with, ma'am."

She realized, then, that as 'expert' as these perpetrators were, the DCI was able to crack them within minutes. She shuddered at the thought of what might have happened behind closed doors.

"In addition, we independently determined the likelihood of recovering your prototypes, but the circumstances are not ideal. The chances of finding and reassembling even one prototype are miniscule. R&D is a massive labyrinth of equipment, and these prototypes are made with parts that are scattered throughout the labs. Robots, as you know, are terribly efficient. Their concealment techniques would rival our own organization's."

"What about the rest of the people behind this? The suspects don't have a boss or a contact?"

"No. Everything was done extremely remotely. They did go into detail on how they received the assignment, how things were coordinated, and how they were pulled into the operation. All of this has been forwarded to your Personal, but is not immediately helpful."

"Thank you, but what about motivation? You've told me all about how they did things, but what about why?"

The agent looked at her with a hint of surprise. "Ma'am, that is quite simple. They are anti-robot."

- - -

They had been walking down the trench for a good ten minutes without incident. Every couple of seconds, a pod would whirr by above them. The dull pain in Stewart's back had plateaued to a bearable level, but his neck was getting sore from dipping his head down.

"You don't happen to know how far we are?"

Lucas stopped and looked at him. "It's been at least 2 kilometers. Let me see if anything is visible." Slowly, carefully, he poked his head out above the lip. As soon as his eyes were clear, he threw them both directions to check for incoming pods. It must have been safe, because he continued to look for a few more seconds before ducking his head back down.

"I think I see a station, but I'm not certain. In any case, it's still quite far." He turned and continued their walk.

Stewart couldn't bear more silence. "Assuming we arrive at your 'home,' what is the plan? When can we leave?"

Lucas kept heading forward as he responded. "When we get home, we will clean up your mess with the DCI. Once you are no longer a wanted man, you and your wife will leave peacefully."

He rolled his eyes at Lucas's back. "Really? And why couldn't we have done that by just getting caught?"

"Because of why you were targeted in the first place." He stopped, turning to face him. "There was a miscalculation somewhere in the Cloud that led to your Personal. As it happens, that chain of events has an extremely low probability—low enough that the DCI will likely not believe your innocence for quite some time, if ever. However, we have information that proves, in a way, your innocence."

"How so?"

"As you have probably already guessed, I do not exactly operate within the legal boundaries of the DCI."

Stewart scoffed. "Putting it lightly."

"In any case, I had in my possession a blank Personal. Do you know what those are?"

He gaped. "A non-identifiable Personal? Those are extremely illegal!"

Lucas nodded. "Yes, yes, I know. The point is, the way they are able to communicate with the Cloud is by scrambling random identifications of other Personals. Every time it sends a message, a package, or has any outgoing signal, it piggybacks off of a random Personal in the near vicinity. The outgoing data reaches its recipient as if it had come from the unknowing user, but the unknowing user has no log of sending anything. The downside is, of course, you cannot communicate both ways. Blank Personals cannot take any incoming data because they have no identification."

"Okay..."

"Sometimes, this outgoing data might overlap with legitimate data, but usually, they piggyback off of a Personal that is not transmitting anything at the time. In either case, the original Personal, and both sets of data, are unaffected, because they are heading to different destinations. Today, however, my Personal randomly picked your Personal's identification, and tried to send data to Fenix at the same time yours did. Fenix picked up two sets of data from the same Personal, and things got a little fuzzy."

"My credits? Wait, did I make my investment?"

"Don't worry, the content was unaffected, just the method of transfer. The point is, this was highly unlikely, and you were targeted as the source of both sets of data."

Stewart considered the implications for a moment. "In that case, what did you send?"

Lucas turned back forward and started walking. "Do you really want to know? Enough for them to go after you."

Stewart kept up behind him. "Do you have a problem with Fenix?"

"That's one way of putting it."

"You know they're on the verge of robotic altruism. Are you from a rival company?"

Lucas swept around, facing Stewart. The guilt that had defined their relationship up to that point was gone, replaced by a subdued anger. "No! I am not affiliated with robotic altruism in any way."

Stewart looked at him, baffled by the change in tone. "O—okay…"

Lucas searched his face, then turned around and sighed. As he started walking again, he asked, "Do you know the history of robots?"

"Vaguely, yes."

"The military origins? I'm talking about before the Revolution."

Before the Revolution? "Not particularly, no…"

"The common misconception is that artificial intelligence caused the Revolution, but this is only partially true. The evolution of robotics was more complex than that. Before the twenty-second century, there wasn't even a consistent definition for the term robot. A machine precise enough to perform a surgery or construct an automobile was called a robot, regardless of its lack of autonomy or primitive reasoning ability.

"At the time, robots were relegated to niche markets with sufficient demand to maintain their presence. Most of these markets were small, except for one: the military. The military single-handedly drove the vast advancements of the twenty-first century. Many argued that their research was for the wrong reasons, but things weren't so black and white. Frankly, any sort of advancement in AI propelled robotics forward, and boy did the military propel.

"Around 2085, a small company by the name of McRay started purchasing multiple businesses catering to the niche markets that fed off the military advancements. Slowly, almost secretively, McRay amassed quite a catalog of robotics companies. Most people didn't notice, and those that did were perplexed; why would anyone want such an incoherent jumble? But McRay had hit upon an ingenious, if not highly risky, idea: creating a mass-produced base robot which could be easily specialized to perform any of the tasks currently assigned to the niche machines. And the result, as you no doubt know, was the Charlie."

The name was unmistakable. "That was the watershed model—2096, the beginning of the Revolution."

"That's right. Public response was unprecedented. McRay knew they had a hit, but they could not have anticipated the surge in demand. Pumped with profits, the company made technological leaps in mere months. Within a year, the Charlie had over two thousand specialization builds. That's two thousand different jobs for one robot..."

Lucas let his words fade away before picking back up. "Most people see the Robotic Revolution as a triumph, as a victory. Everything was supposed to be easier, safer, better... but that was not the case. Do you know how many jobs were lost in the first year the Charlie came out?"

"No..."

"Twenty million in the United States alone. Twenty million! Riots erupted daily, and violence skyrocketed. Most of it was aimed at the robots themselves. Soon enough, authorities arrested citizens for attacking the robots that took their jobs. The government took the side of security and profit, and jails swelled with the angry and unemployed. It was a mess."

Stewart began to understand the man's anger. It was true that the immediate effects of the Revolution were staggering, but Lucas's argument was rather one-sided. He decided to press the issue, albeit lightly. Keeping pace with his captor, he chose his words carefully.

"The labor crisis was a disaster, I agree, but I don't think you're giving the Revolution enough credit. Things did get safer and better! I mean, do you think we would be unified as one globe without them?"

Lucas responded without looking back to Stewart. "Of course. The Earth Initiative. That's always the first defense. You know, despite the picture I am painting, I agree with you. I honestly think the post-Revolution crisis was worth the Initiative. But that is not where this story is going. The Initiative took hold on what? The first day of 2128?"

"That's right."

"Well, about a decade beforehand, McRay was out-competed by the new powerhouse, United Robotics. They were the ones that really took the machines globally and presented a threat to the military establishments. And as you no doubt know they were also the driving force behind the Initiative. In fact, by the time of the Initiative, United Robotics became an unstoppable power.

"Within a year of the Initiative, the Legislature founded the BRA. United Robotics was so entrenched in its formation that they devised most of the laws regarding robotics themselves. There were no checks and balances, no ethical committees. Instead, AI was allowed—encouraged, even—to progress toward human levels of intelligence. And this, my friend, was a massive mistake.

"It took almost twenty years for reality to catch up to robotics. The euphoria from the Initiative faded, and people realized that robots were getting stronger and smarter. But the scariest part was that they were everywhere. The Diama was built mostly robotically—the communication and transportation infrastructure of our planet is not controlled by humans alone. The BRA reversed course. Newly elected leaders passed amendments, curbing robotic development. But it was too late..."

Lucas stopped. He turned to face Stewart, his expression curious, inquisitive.

"Tell me—what do you know about robotic altruism?"

Stewart hesitated. "Well... just the common understanding... that it is a hard-wired drive to help and protect humankind." As the words left his mouth, he fought the urge to cringe. Lucas noticed the uncertainty.

"Do you doubt that assessment?"

"Well... now that I really think about it, is altruism really programmable? It seems terribly complex..."

Lucas nodded in agreement. "Most certainly. But what you are describing is not robotic altruism. It is friendly AI. Do you know the difference?"

Stewart shook his head.

"Friendly AI is simply AI that has a net positive effect on humanity. We have friendly AI all around us. Every robot you see is hard-wired to help and protect humankind. But even friendly AI is a nightmare to program. You see, despite my initial nit-picking, a robot is, in the end, a machine. These machines are created with purposes coded into their cerebral units. This programming does not account for vague human concepts—it requires precise definitions and examples. So how does one precisely define a desire to help and protect humankind?"

Stewart did not have an answer for him.

"Let me give you an example. Say we decide to program robots to maximize human pleasure. The first hurdle here is explaining to a robot what 'pleasure' is. Can you give an accurate definition? Scientifically speaking, pleasure is a neurological concept rooted in hormones and biological functions. Okay, let's say we manage to translate that concept into the programming, and we turn our new robot on. What happens?"

"We are pumped full of hormones?"

"More or less. There is actually some intricacy regarding hedonic hotspots, but the end result would be neurosurgery or some sort of drug-induced state of constant pleasure. Now, is this, in your mind, a pleasurable existence?"

"No."

"Of course not. Now what if we flipped the script? What if we programmed a robot to get rid of all pain?"

"Basically the same thing would happen."

"Right. The details would vary, but the result would be the same. In fact, what's to stop this robot from simply euthanizing us? If a human is dead, they cannot feel pain."

Stewart shuddered at the idea. The picture Lucas was painting was not a flattering one.

"You're beginning to see just how complex friendly AI is. But back to the matter at hand. While friendly AI refers to simple, logical restraints, robotic altruism refers to a human-level understanding of the concept. Now, humans aren't hard-wired with these things, we learn them. So then the question is, can we teach robots altruism? Can we teach them the difference between right and wrong?"

"In certain cases..."

"Exactly. Now, we can do a pretty good job with this, and we already have. Almost every ethical advancement in robotics thus far has come from case-based learning. So what's the issue? Well, there's not just one - there are three.

"The first problem is us. Who decides what is right and what is wrong? Every culture, not to mention every person, has slightly or not-so-slightly different ideas. Okay... so let's take an average - a worldwide consensus. Now what's the problem?"

"Too many cases?"

"Maybe, but more pertinently, the teaching process must account for any coincidental patterns. For example, say a robot is shown various examples of a species of green lizard and told that it is a lizard. Then it is shown various examples of a species of blue bird and told that it is a bird. If we then throw a blue lizard at it, will it identify it as a lizard based on shape, or as a bird based on color? You may think this is a silly process, and people would be more careful, but it is only silly because the colors and shapes are well-defined. Ethical principles are not so well-defined, and coincidental patterns may show if the cases are over-simplified."

Stewart raised his eyebrows in surprise. There was much more to this than he realized at first.

"What's the final problem?"

Lucas smiled knowingly. "Ah, yes. The third problem is the one most people overlook. Once a robot is built with strong AI, with human or superhuman intelligence, the world will no doubt change. We cannot predict the future, but we can assume there will be new cases our case-based learning will not have accounted for just by the existence of these new super-intelligent machines. A catch-22, no doubt."

Stewart shook his head in disbelief. He was starting to wonder if the man had it right. Lucas used the pause in discussion to check their whereabouts, peering above the rim of the crevice at the outside world.

"Almost there. Come on, we can't stand around too long."

- - -

Lauren was leaning forward in her chair, eyeing the agent in front of her. "Anti-robot?"

"Yes, ma'am."

She couldn't believe it. "That doesn't make any sense... The whole idea of robot altruism should appeal to the anti-robot sentiment!"

The agent nodded. "We understand, ma'am, but I do not think the perpetrators believe in this solution."

"What do you mean?"

"They would argue that robotic altruism cannot be accurately programmed; the concept is too abstract."

She leaned back into her chair. Too abstract? It was true, the task was tremendous, but even the impossible seems possible with decades of research and billions of credits. Some of the smartest individuals on the planet were working in their labs, and the prototype results were promising...

"What do they want, exactly?"

"They are trying to prevent the human intelligence horizon."

They're doing a damn good job, she thought.

"Out of fear?"

"We cannot presume to know their motives in detail, but anti-robot sentiment is common. They may fear an uprising but it seems as if they are more concerned with the pace of progress—they would have robotics slow down."

Lauren scoffed. Slow down? Did these fools have any idea how careful Fenix was being in their experimentation and development? Did they know how many profits were signed away to the cause? This wasn't a maddening commercial run for the prize—this was a painfully deliberate process. It was a miracle no other robotics corporation had overtaken their progress. Well, a miracle rooted in their market dominance and superior resources. She tried to shrug it off.

"Well then... what now?"

"We have extracted all possible information from the two men in our custody, so they will be forwarded to the Courts. Our forensic agents are still working on the load distribution in R&D to try and figure out where the prototypes may have been taken. We brought in some of our own roboticists to interview your robots and try to find the tampered models. If they learn anything, you will know. In addition, we are still pursuing Mr. Anders."

The name was a vague thought, almost like a lost memory, that came surging forward in Lauren's mind. The events of the day had put it behind her, and she cursed herself for not asking about him sooner.

"The hacking suspect? The Personal you tracked?"

"Yes, Stewart Anders. We are still pursuing him."

Lauren eyed the man carefully. "He has managed to elude capture?"

The agent hesitated the briefest moment. "For the time being."

Before she was able to ask a follow-up question, her guardian swung the nozzle of his weapon up towards the door. The other agent stood up, alert, facing the entrance. A tense silence took hold of the office, and Lauren, feeling suddenly in danger, braced herself in her chair. At least the two agents were there to protect her, she thought.

Three knocks. Was this some sort of game? Who was—

"Madam President? It's Rubger."

Lauren relaxed. She had forgotten the precautions the DCI was taking and realized they would perform the same preparatory ritual for any visitor. At that moment, she knew she wanted this ordeal over as quickly as possible. There was no way she would endure such a series of actions for each incoming guest.

"Come in."

The door opened into the room, and Rubger managed to get inside and close it behind him before locking up, eyes fixed on the barrel pointed in his direction. A frown spread across his face.

"Don't worry, Rubger. It's just a precaution."

His eyes lingered on the gun. He seemed hesitant, despite Lauren's comment.

"Rubger?"

He looked to Lauren, then to the agent near her desk. He took one last glance toward the guardian, still frowning.

"A terribly dangerous precaution, don't you think?"

"I'd trust their skill."

Rubger nodded and moved towards the desk. As soon as he started walking, the other agent made his way past him and out the door. Rubger paused to look back at the man exiting then looked to Lauren.

"Worth interrupting the meeting?"

She nodded as he sat down, and shot a glance over at her guardian. The gun was still very much ready to fire. This meeting would not be as comfortable as the last, she thought.

"How can I help you Rubger?"

He smiled, and Lauren realized for the first time that she found him quite handsome. She wondered if it was just a matter of comparison—not only was he the youngest board member, he was also by and large the most respectful.

"Madam President, first I have to ask how you are doing. Is everything alright? We've been told you were never in any danger but I can't imagine it was an agreeable experience."

She smiled back at him. Any other member would have jumped to business-related discussion. Not due to a lack of decency, but rather because of the urgent and fast-paced nature of the day. It was refreshing to see such a caring attitude at a time like this.

"I'm fine. The entire thing lasted less than five minutes, and the official version is right; I was never really in any danger."

He nodded, giving her another smile. "That's good to hear." Turning his head toward the guardian, he asked, "And this is to prevent future incidents?"

"That, and to protect the secret backup."

He turned back to her and some of the joy had left his eyes. "Yes..." For some reason, the silence was uncomfortable. It didn't help that Rubger was avoiding eye contact.

"If I may, Madam President, I must ask a rather disconcerting question."

Lauren hesitated. The sudden change of tone caught her off-guard, and she expected something terrible. "Go ahead..."

"Thank you. I have to wonder about this secret backup. You see, on the one hand, I'm delighted that we have such a secure failsafe, but on the other, I'm concerned about the implications behind it." He paused and looked up at her. "Only one scenario comes to mind. In it, a CEO and a Chairman realize that a project is so important that a system needs to be in place to account for potential inside agents—not just regular employees, mind you, but board members as well."

Lauren fidgeted in her seat. He was right, this was somewhat uncomfortable, even beyond the ever-present background rifle.

"I understand that this might not have been your choice; it might have been the Chairman's. I also understand that you have no obligation to discuss the details of this decision with me, but I feel as if something is missing from this picture. At the moment, I'm being told that you were surprised by two regular employee insider agents in the R&D lobby while at the same time crafting an entire procedure to address the issue with board members?"

She tried to hide her anxiety—this was not a conversation she wanted to have. The truth would absolve her, but it was forbidden. It wasn't so much that she was worried about offending Rubger as it was that she feared exposing the real plan. Lauren had never been a good liar.

Doing her best to evoke authority, she proceeded. "Even with the security plan, insider agents in our own corporation were not predicted... Just because we prepared for the worst does not mean we expected the bad." She thought to herself for a moment then continued, "And Rubger, this line of questioning is not advisable at this time. If I could tell you everything—all the details—I would. But right now, the future of the company is delicately balanced in my hands and I do not want to risk it."

Rubger straightened in his chair. The discomfort seemed to have jumped across the desk. "Yes, Madam President. My apologies."

She let out a sigh of relief. Smiling again, she tried to dispel his uneasiness. "Please, don't worry. Your concern is well-placed. I promise you all of these discrepancies will be addressed when this is over, for better or worse."

"In that case, I have one more question." He looked up at her reassuringly. "Don't worry, it's not like the first one."

His ability to change tone so abruptly fascinated her. He no longer seemed distant and disappointed, but rather charming. He could be very manipulative if he wanted to, she thought.

"When can we resume progress? I understand we have a crisis to manage, and we should make every effort to continue our investigation, of course. But if we have a backup of all the project data, shouldn't we start rebuilding and reorganizing? The sooner the better, don't you think?"

Lauren hesitated in her reply. She had vaguely anticipated such questions within the coming days but not several hours after the attack.

There was a hint of urgency in his voice that made her uncomfortable. Why was he in such a hurry?

"It is much too early to be thinking about resuming progress, and not just because of the investigation. We need to be absolutely certain of our security before proceeding, as this is a very delicate time. With the help of the DCI, we should be up and running within a week's time."

A hint of the frown returned, and Lauren eyed him curiously. "Rubger, I trust you understand we are doing the best we can?"

"Yes, yes. I know that..." He glanced back at the guardian then stood up from his chair. "I promise my pestering is over. You will keep me posted?"

Me? Lauren was a bit surprised by the choice of words, and faltered a half second in her answer.

"Yes."

He smiled once more—a warm smile she hadn't seen from him before. "Thank you, Lauren." And with that, he was out the door.

- - -

A good ten minutes had passed in hurried silence. The pain in Stewart's neck was growing unbearable, but any time he tried to squat a bit to straighten it, his injured back would flare up instead. It was not the most comfortable of situations. Just as he was about to voice his complaints, Lucas stopped and raised his hand.

"Hold on."

For the third time, he slowly lifted his head above the crevice and peered in the direction they were heading. His eyes had barely passed the lip when he threw himself back downward. A pod whooshed overhead. Lucas tried again.

"Okay..." He brought his head down and quickened his pace. "There's a Diama station less than a kilometer in front of us."

"What are we going to do once we reach it?"

"We're going to take a pod."

Stewart did not hide his skepticism. "How in the world are we going to manage that?"

"Tell me something, what do you do if you lose your Personal?"

Lose my Personal? Despite being in that predicament, Stewart hadn't stopped to think about what it meant: no wallet, no ID, no phone...

"You get a replacement at the nearest Personal Center."

"And how do you get to the Personal Center?"

He shook his head sheepishly. Of course...

Lucas continued, "They tend to keep it under wraps but you can take the Diama without a Personal. It's actually quite easy."

They passed a seam in the concrete beneath them and Lucas stopped a dozen meters past it. He pulled the transmitter out of his pocket and opened an antenna along the side.

"Okay, the hard part is going to be getting out of here and onto a pod undetected." His voice was barely a whisper, and Stewart replied in kind.

"What are you doing?"

Lucas turned a knob as he answered. "This is a surveillance jammer. It won't do any good on the microphones, but it will take care of the camera feeds within 40 meters. That being said, keep absolutely quiet. If they hear either of our voices, they'll lock down the station. Once we exit this trench, no talking until I give the signal. There will be a microphone in the pod as well, so we are going to have to stay quiet throughout the entire ride."

Stewart nodded. Lucas finished fiddling with the transmitter and held it steady in one hand, peering above the edge in both directions. He handed it to Stewart and quickly pulled himself up. After another quick glance in both directions, he reached one hand out for it and used the other to signal Stewart to wait. As soon as the device left Stewart's hand, Lucas bolted out of sight.

Two pods passed within seconds of his escape. Only then did Stewart realize how much harder it would be to get out than it was to get in. Was he supposed to check the area out himself? He started to lift his head out of the trench when Lucas's hand flew into his eye-line, beckoning him to take hold. Locking one hand in Lucas's and pressing the other over the edge, he pulled himself out with a grunt.

For a split second, he almost let himself relax, but the hand kept pulling, and, realizing that he was sitting idly on the Diama track, he leaped into a sprint. A gust of wind rushed against his back as he crossed the other edge and Stewart realized his heart was beating at a terrifying pace. That was one too many near-death experiences for the day.

With the ordeal behind him, he took a moment to examine the station. They had crossed the main tracks and were now walking across the pod lines—the side tracks where pods came to pick up passengers. He had never bothered to look for them, but now he noticed at least a dozen cameras. It was only as they walked onto the boarding platform that Stewart realized the station was empty. No people, no robots. This wasn't surprising—it seemed to be a smaller substation that didn't get too much use. After all, it was on the edge of the abandoned district below.

Six or seven pods sat idly near the platform and Lucas pointed to the third one, a double pod. Sensing their approach, the pod's door slid gently open, and Lucas stepped in. Stewart hesitated, waiting for a signal, and was motioned to follow.

"Identifying..."

Stewart glanced over to Lucas, still holding the transmitter in his right hand.

The pod gave out a buzz. "No Personals located." Where Stewart was used to seeing the keyboard appear, three outlined sentences lit up.

"Try again."

"Take me to the nearest Personal Center."

"Riding without a Personal."

Lucas reached out a pressed into the air where the third option was floating. The door beside Stewart closed and the buttons disappeared, replaced with a keyboard.

"Destination?"

Again, Lucas typed out the answer: USTXHOC121. Once he pressed Enter, the Terminal appeared in the subtitle slot and Yes or No buttons hovered before them. He touched Yes, and the pod began its journey.

5. Trail

Rivers and trees slowly replaced buildings as their pod headed for the northern C zone. Stewart watched it all go by outside, doing his best not to make a sound. He had expected the experience to be more awkward, but the scenery gave him an escape. This would be his first time in C zone, and he was quite curious to see it in person.

C zone was known for an abundance of natural land, or land with minimal to no human development, where nature took precedence. Beyond his occasional vacations, Stewart's only encounter with such greenery was the local artery park, built on an old highway.

When the Diama was built, the roads and freeways it replaced no longer served a purpose. For the most part, the Diama was built above the old infrastructure, in order to ease the transition and free it of any design constraints inherent in the old system. This left large lengths of asphalt out of use, and this asphalt was often ripped off and replaced with local greenery. These 'artery parks' formed the basis of a much larger natural land movement in the late 2130s and through the 2150s. Many parks and preserves were expanded, and local wildlife populations grew. Presently, the areas were typically maintained by robots and free to roam by anyone in any manner, provided nothing was significantly changed by human presence.

C zone itself was once the site of a few large parks and rural areas. During the movement, these were all combined into a large preserve. They were currently passing into that very region, and soon enough, the only sign of technology in sight was their Diama track and the occasional station within the park.

He glanced at Lucas, who was also taking in their surroundings. Once again, he let his mind drift to Jacqueline, and he winced at the thought of her potentially being in danger. Were they all going to meet in some hut in the woods? Was that the base of operations for whatever it was Lucas and his driver and whoever else was doing?

Stewart focused his eyes once more on Lucas. What *was* he doing? Evidently something against Fenix, and evidently something highly illegal. It was clear that he wanted to prevent Fenix from testing robotic altruism, but how far had he gone in that cause?

A frown spread across his face. While the man had been convincing in his arguments, Stewart did not believe these illegal actions were the right choice. Surely Lucas knew he had a good deal of public support on his side, were he to protest legally? Then again, there was some truth to his description of the government and their ties with robotics. Even when the BRA started putting the brakes on robotic research, it did so lightly and reluctantly. Who really knew how well they enforced their own policies anyways? So many of their employees were once employed by the very corporations they policed that it was hard to say where the line might have been drawn with regards to robotic altruism and ensuring a thorough and proper development of the programming.

He tried to clear his head of these thoughts and looked out at the park surrounding them. He wanted to ask the pod how much longer, where they were, or at least to see a map, but he could do none of these things. There must be a way to do it without voice commands, but he was not as versed in the Diama as his co-passenger.

Oh well, Stewart thought. I hope Jacqueline is safe.

- - -

As she watched the blue dot follow the curving white line over the green background, Lauren bit her lip. Where were they going?

She turned to the agent standing next to her. "This is in C zone, you said?"

"Yes ma'am."

The situation had changed drastically in the last fifteen minutes. As soon as Rubger had left her office, she received an alert on her desktop and Personal that the hacking suspect was being tracked in a Diama pod.

The DCI asked her to come to the Chairman's office to be briefed, where they were now viewing a live feed on his wall.

Mr. Ross spoke up from behind his desk. "We can't get a video feed inside?"

"There is still an active camera jammer in the pod."

When she came in, a DCI agent explained that cameras had suddenly malfunctioned at a Diama station, alerting the agency of potential foul play. When, less than two minutes later, a two-person pod left the station with no Personals on board and no voice commands, they were all but certain it was their target.

"Take Ms. Care through the whole timeline," Mr. Ross told the agent.

"We tracked the Personal of Stewart Anders to a house in A zone, where an unauthorized PAV arrived shortly before us. Three suspects exited the house and entered the PAV, and, along with a fourth suspect, attempted escape from our agents. An EMP rifle took down their vehicle, and one of our Cruisers hooked them, but they jumped from the craft with parachutes and landed in an abandoned industrial district. We sent out a search party and managed to find both landing sites. During our search, there was a general malfunction of all cameras in the nearest Diama station."

Lauren was missing a piece of the puzzle. "They boarded the Diama without Personals, and I'm assuming you'd track them if you could... where did the Personals go?"

"Stewart Anders's Personal was left in the PAV. Jacqueline Anders, his wife, who we believe is one of the four, left hers at their home."

She nodded. "Okay... now, you said a two-person pod left the station?"

"That's right."

"But there are four suspects?"

"Yes. Two landing sites were found for two pairs of suspects. We believe two of them are in this pod but we do not know where the others are."

"Are you still looking?"

"Yes ma'am. Our search party is in full effect, and our forensic agents are working both trails, just in case this is a false alarm or diversion."

Good point, she thought. Anything was possible in this fiasco. "What is your plan with the pod?"

"We have a Cruiser on standby just out of visual range. We have sent some undercover agents into the park. This is an opportunity to discover a meeting place or even a base of operations, so we are using it as best as we can."

"What is their destination?"

"Terminal 121, a good ways into the park, and as far as we know right now, not near anything of interest."

She looked to Ross. "So now we wait?"

He kept his eyes locked on the screen. "Yes."

- - -

Twenty minutes into their silent ride, Stewart finally felt some deceleration. They were deep in the park now, surrounded by trees and the occasional meadow. The track ahead dropped under the tree-line, and Stewart could see the terminal between the branches.

As they dipped downward, he glanced at Lucas, who gestured him to stay quiet. As if I needed a reminder at this point, he thought. The pod reached the platform, announcing, "Terminal USTXHOC121." Their braces came up and the door slid open. He looked to Lucas, who motioned for him to exit. They got out carefully and Stewart examined the surroundings.

Oak trees hung over the platform, their branches thick and numerous enough to shade most of the station. Thick trunks multiplied in all directions, save one: straight off the platform, where a paved path with railings pierced through the green, weaving out of sight.

Stepping off the platform and onto the pavement, he decided that he needed to visit C zone more often. It was more than likely his imagination, but in comparison to the city and even his district, the air here was fresh. Instead of hearing a constant hum of activity, there were birds chirping and leaves rustling in the light breeze. Only the occasional whoosh of a Diama pod passing on the tracks above gave any audible indication of technology. For Stewart, the experience was wonderful. Childhood memories of camping trips and long days at the park came to mind. If only Jacqueline was with him.

As they continued down the path, Lucas collapsed the antenna on his device and placed it in his pocket. Stewart looked at him inquiringly, and he nodded.

"It's safe to talk now."

"How far is it?"

"A ways. We're about forty minutes out."

His eyes widened. "Forty?"

Lucas nodded in reply.

By the third or fourth turn, Stewart could no longer see the station. Sunlight danced on the pathway between the silhouettes of the branches. What a beautiful day, he thought. With the breeze and the shade of the trees, it was perfect.

"Are we alone?"

"Maybe. Quite a few people visit this park, but it's very large, and there are hundreds of paths—the chances of running into someone are low."

Stewart nodded. He wondered if some of the park was accessible off the path. Camping here would be lovely.

"Is my wife going to be there?"

"That is where the extraction PAV would have taken her."

Stewart frowned. The noncommittal phrasing did not go undetected.

"Are PAVs allowed in the park?"

"No, they would have taken one to the outskirts then finished the journey by air-bike."

Air-bike? Stewart raised his eyebrows. Air-bikes were small, fast, and typically dangerous miniature PAVs. Those were probably not allowed in the park either, but at this point he realized that probably didn't matter.

Around the next corner they came upon a longer straightaway extending through a large field. At the far end, a couple hundred meters away, two figures walked leisurely in their direction. There was the slightest hesitation in Lucas's step, and he shot a quick glance at Stewart before moving on.

Stewart realized, somewhat anxiously, that this would be the first time he encountered another human being during their escape. A nervous fear took hold of him. Was he now a fugitive? Was he a criminal? His eyes darted to the ground, afraid that even at this distance he would make eye contact with the strangers. But why? Was he afraid they would recognize him? Did he imagine his name and image plastered across the news?

Lucas took note of the man's demeanor and gave him a slight prod, whispering, "Compose yourself. These are just people in a park, not the DCI."

Stewart looked at him and nodded, swallowing. Why was this so difficult? The figures were now about a hundred meters away—two men in casual attire, one in shorts and one in pants, both tall and for all other intents and purposes, average-looking. They seemed to pay no attention to Stewart and Lucas, gazing intently at the surrounding field as they walked.

As they crossed out of the cover of the trees and into the open pasture, Stewart did his best to compose himself. The men turned toward them and smiled, each giving a small nod hello. Stewart smiled back, as best he could, and made a slightly forced nod that felt more like a neck spasm. Thankfully, they were already returning their attention to the park, and they passed one another without incident.

A hint of relief hit Stewart's system, and he relaxed his posture. Lucas smiled at him. "See? No problem."

- - -

When the blue dot had stopped at the white box marked USTXHOC121, the cameras at the terminal had stopped with it. A full three minutes later, their function had magically resumed. It seemed a fair bet to say these were their targets.

And yet Lauren had her doubts. Something bothered her about this—it seemed almost too easy. The most technologically sophisticated attack in recent history and the perpetrators didn't expect their pod to be tracked? Where was the twist?

"Are they taking that path?" the Chairman asked.

The image had gone static ever since the pod reached the station. Lauren noted that the small grey line marking the trail was the only visible way out.

"We will know within three minutes. We have two agents nearby on the path en route to the station."

Ross nodded. Lauren turned away from the map on the wall to the agent. "And if they are following the path?"

"We will pursue from a distance." He motioned to the wall again, which changed into what looked like a recording from inside the park. "This is a live feed from one of our agents." The feed was mobile, almost bouncing, and every once in a while the screen flashed black.

"Why is it cutting out?"

"This is a lens camera on his right eye. The occasional darkness you see is blinking."

Lauren wondered if he could still see through the eye, or if it really mattered. The DCI had a surprising number of tricks up its sleeve. She hoped it would be enough to fix this mess. Just a handful of the backup disks was all they needed to get the company back on track. But what if they were already destroyed? Now that she knew what they were dealing with, Lauren realized that there would be no reason for them to hold on to the disks. In fact, they would probably be destroyed as soon as possible. This hadn't quite occurred to her until now. She had been operating on the assumption that all they had to do was catch the bad guys and everything would be back to normal, but that wasn't necessarily the case. She started to feel cold, and a faint nausea took hold. The hope she was holding onto began to slip through her fingers...

"Are you alright ma'am?" The agent was next to her, gently supporting her and guiding her to a chair.

"I... I need to sit down."

Ross looked at her, frowning. "What's wrong, Ms. Care?"

She turned to him, some of the light-headedness creeping away. "I'm sorry Mr. Ross, it's all a bit overwhelming."

He nodded, and pressed the intercom on his desk. "David? Could you get Ms. Care a glass of water please?"

"Certainly sir."

Lauren smiled at him and mouthed, "Thank you."

"There." The agent pointed towards two spots on the video feed. It was difficult to see with the man blinking and walking but Lauren could make out what looked like two people coming down the path. "That may be them."

She felt anxious—nervous, even—as the agents got closer. Most of the time she couldn't see the suspects—the agents talked to each other or looked at the surroundings—but soon enough dim outlines turned into two men. There was a taller one who walked just in front, and a shorter one who kept looking at the ground. Could it be them? Was one of these men Stewart Anders?

"Once we get a clear visual, we will identify."

A beautiful field filled the screen, and for a moment Lauren pondered her next visit to C zone. Then the frame turned, and there they were.

"Freeze it." The picture froze, and Lauren gasped. The agent looked at her intently. "What is it?"

She pointed to the taller one. "I recognize that man!"

"Do you know who it is?"

"No... he's familiar but I don't know why..."

"We're running their faces now."

Ross turned to Lauren. "You've seen him recently?"

She closed her eyes and tried to concentrate. "I... I can't remember."

"Okay we've got them. The one on the left is Stewart Anders and the one on the right is Lucas Roberts."

"Is the name familiar?" Ross asked.

Lauren shook her head. "No... I don't remember a Lucas..."

The Chairman turned back to the agent. "What do we know about him?"

"Lucas Roberts. 29 years old. No criminal history. Listed as an associate robotics advisor to the Legislature."

Ross shot him a look of disbelief. "A federal employee?"

"Yes. We have forwarded you a copy of his advising portfolio and are analyzing it as we speak, but it's safe to say that Ms. Care recognizes him from an official visit."

Lauren put her face in her hands. How much deeper did this conspiracy go?

Ross spoke up again. "And his job before this?"

"None, sir. He studied robotics history in university, graduating with a doctorate in 2213. He joined the Legislature the next month."

Six years, Lauren thought. And two years before Bluestone. Where did the promising young man end and the terrorist begin? Perhaps more importantly, why?

A knock on the door almost made her jump. Ross said, "Come in, David."

The door opened, and Ross's personal robot David walked over to Lauren with a glass of water. She took it, smiling. "Thank you."

"No problem." The slightly artificial tone stole some of the comment's sincerity, but as David left the room, Lauren wondered if she only detected the tone because she saw the robot itself in front of her. Would a blind person be able to hear if someone was a robot? She remembered the DCI analysts and how they provided a glimpse of androids to come. If they already existed, would knowing they were robots steal from the illusion? Or could a human truly be mimicked enough to ignore the truth?

Ross interrupted her thought process. "An associate robotics advisor would have inside access to the BRA, correct?"

"To an extent. As an associate advisor, he would not have the authority or clearance of a senior advisor, but at the same time he would be doing most of the communication."

Finishing a sip, Lauren looked up to the agent. "Do you know how many times he was here?"

He nodded. "Yes, ma'am. His portfolio, along with your company's own records, indicate thirty-two visits during his tenure, twenty-five of which occurred during the development of Bluestone. We are already looking at archival footage of his visit days, searching for suspicious or unique activity."

"Any ties between him and our two employees?"

"Not yet."

Ross turned back to the image. "Are your agents still in pursuit?"

"Yes, but out of sight. We can put up the thermal feed if you'd like."

"Do it."

- - -

It seemed to Stewart as if every turn brought with it a more breathtaking view. Sure, most of it was the same trees left and right, but fields, rivers, and even a few small waterfalls had graced his vision. Also, the farther they got from the station, the more wildlife appeared. Squirrels scampered among the branches, and birds pecked idly at the grass near the path. The gentlemen near the station were apparently an anomaly—they hadn't seen anyone else in a quarter-hour.

The weight of the day's activities were starting to affect Stewart's pace and bearing. His legs ached from sprinting in the abandoned district and crouching down the Diama trench. His lower back was still a bit painful, and even his arms felt weak for whatever reason. Soon after they had passed the men on the path, he was hit with a wave of thirst. Thank god he had eaten lunch right before Lucas interrupted his day, or he'd be starving.

Lunch... his mind wandered to the wonderful meal of tomato soup and roasted turkey he had had less than two hours ago. What he would give to be back there right now...

"Are there any water fountains here?"

"We've already passed one set—they have them about every kilometer. There are some coming up soon."

Sure enough, as if to answer his plea, Stewart saw a set of water fountains up ahead around the next bend. He walked a little quicker, and Lucas followed suit. If these hadn't been here, he may have jumped the railing at the next creek!

Leaning over to sip the cool water, Stewart noticed Lucas scanning their surroundings. He paused to speak.

"Do you know what time it is?"

He kept scanning as he answered, "About 14:00."

A few more sips and he stood, satisfied. "How long have we been walking?"

Lucas started them off once more. "Nearly twenty minutes. We'll be leaving the path here in a bit."

"Leaving the path?"

"Yes."

"We're going to walk through the park?" Stewart wondered how illegal that was.

Lucas shook his head. "No."

"I don't understand."

"You will shortly." And Lucas veered to the left, carefully straddling over the railing and into the park. "Come on."

Stewart reluctantly followed, mentally ticking off another crime to add to the list of charges. As he followed Lucas into the forest, he did his best to avoid stepping on anything other than grass and made sure not to touch anything - even the trees surrounding them. Less than a minute of cautious walking had gone by when Lucas stopped in front of a small clearing.

In the middle of the shaded opening, a small protrusion elevated the ground. It looked to Stewart as if the grass had simply decided to jut upwards awkwardly into a large, jagged section about four meters long and one meter wide. Then Lucas grabbed one part of this growth and pulled, spraying dirt, leaves, and twigs in all directions. It was a camouflaging tarp, and in front of them sat an air-bike.

Now this, Stewart thought, was much more illegal.

- - -

"Are they off the path?" Ross asked.

"Yes."

Lauren watched the red and orange figures meander between the thick black lines that dominated the screen. "What now?"

"Our agents will continue observing from a concealable distance."

"What about the Cruiser? Is it still following?"

"Yes but we cannot get a thermal lock with all of the tree interference."

She frowned. The recent miscalculations by the agency had eroded some of her confidence in its methods. In her eyes, even the existence of a terrorist Legislative advisor was in some way their fault. This was of course preposterous, especially considering how well he had hid his true form, but she was not as comforted by their help as she had been at the outset.

"Have you tracked Roberts's Personal?"

"Yes. It is showing at the address he is listed under, and a contingent of agents will arrive there in two minutes. We are still awaiting a warrant from the Courts to access the data inside."

Access his Personal? Despite the nature of the situation, Lauren cringed at this invasion of privacy. Then she remembered her own Personal was under surveillance, and grew even more uncomfortable.

"What about Anders?"

"That petition is also underway."

"You are allowed to track them but not access the data?"

"That is correct. Under current criminal law, we can track suspects with reasonable cause, which we have for both men and the wife in this case, but access to Personal data always requires a warrant."

"And my Personal?" She let her discomfort characterize the question. After all, both suspects had their privacy intact and she did not.

"We do not have access to all of your Personal data, but we do have access to all incoming and outgoing communications of Fenix and its employees."

She was not satisfied. "And this did not need a warrant?"

"It did—we obtained it almost immediately."

The answer stunned her into a momentary silence. "What?"

"Under the circumstances, Fenix was our first priority. Since we were dealing with highly-skilled hackers, we wanted to protect the company from any and all possible security breaches and emphasized the urgency of the matter with the Courts."

"The others are not urgent?"

"Technically not as urgent. Regardless, the Courts accepted our warrant on Fenix more readily because there was less room for abuse of power— we were trying to protect, rather than prosecute."

"That doesn't necessarily preclude an abuse of power..." Ross looked up at her. She knew she was pushing it, but she ignored his stare.

"True, which is why the Courts also have logs of exactly which sets of data we access, when, and how often. Ma'am, if there were an errant agent in our organization accessing data unnecessarily, it would most certainly be discovered, and the punishment for such abuse of power is heavy."

There was no irritation in his response, nor frustration. In fact, Lauren detected a hint of empathy that embarrassed her. Feeling Ross's eyes still on her made it all the worse.

"I'm sorry..." She averted her gaze from the agent and her Chairman, but it was Ross who spoke up for her.

"Nothing to apologize for Ms. Care—I had a similar reaction when I found my Personal was also under observation. Trust me when I say that after the barrage of questions I threw their way, as well as a bit of my own research into applicable laws, I can tell you the system is quite effective, and only pertinent information is ever accessed."

A commotion on screen diverted their attention. The agents in the park were running, eyes no longer on the suspects.

"What's going on?"

"Change of plans. They have an air-bike."

- - -

Stewart eyed the machine in front of them and felt a cold emptiness in his stomach. Air-bikes were notoriously difficult to operate, and only the most skilled drivers ever took them under the Canopy—let alone into a dense forest. And one look at the tightly-packed tree branches above them told him that Lucas wasn't planning on taking them upward. If they tried to ride it here, he thought, they would die.

He scanned their immediate surroundings for any sort of opening and saw one, to his right, exactly where the nose of the bike was pointing. While Lucas tidied up the vehicle, he shuffled over and peered down the trajectory. It almost seemed like a viable path, but it didn't extend too far. Something told him they probably didn't clear out air-bike roadways in the park.

Two beeps emitted from the vehicle, then a quiet hum. Stewart's pulse, which had finally managed to settle, jumped once more. Air-bikes were basically two giant ducted fans connected by a driver's seat. There was usually no cockpit or enclosure; drivers always wore parachutes for higher flights. This particular model was fitted with three seats, which was the most Stewart had ever seen—most air-bikes were single-occupancy.

Lucas finished clearing the vents of debris and saddled up in the driver's seat. He turned to Stewart.

"Let's go."

The pit in his stomach grew. Everything in his body told him to refuse.

"I... don't think I can do this..."

Lucas eyed him sternly, then ignited the engine. The quiet hum was slowly overtaken by the growing whirr of the propellors. As they sped up their rotation, leaves and twigs underneath the ducts sprayed outward with increasing numbers and intensity. Within seconds, the bike was levitating in idle.

Lucas looked to him again. "If you want to see your wife, you'll need to get on."

Checkmate. He bowed his head and took a deep breath. So be it.

Stewart walked over to the bike and grabbed hold, stepping onto a small step to push himself into one of the passenger seats. Lucas pointed to a belt apparatus and helped him strap against the back of the seat. He was thankful for the seat back—somehow having something to lean onto made him feel safer.

He got one glance at their route before Lucas grabbed the handles, pitched the craft forward, and revved the propellors. The thrust was immediate, and he was pressed back against his seat. The speedometer hovered around 50 kph, but with the surrounding trees within arms reach, Stewart felt they were moving much too quickly.

Bank left. They were veering away from the path, and for a moment Stewart wondered if anyone heard them. It wasn't the quietest machine, but for the size and proximity of the propellers, the noise level was incredibly low.

Bank right. By now his eyes were closed, and he had no intention of opening them. He gripped the sides of the seat with his hands.

Bank sharp left. He felt his body press against the straps and his eyes opened momentarily. The leaves were less than a meter from his face. The bike pitched even more forward, and thrust increased. What was Lucas thinking?

Without warning, they pitched back to level, sending Stewart forward into his harness, and there was a sudden burst of speed upward, followed by a stable hover. Not feeling the air in his face, Stewart carefully opened his eyes. They had cleared the tree-line, and were maybe a meter or two above the tops of the trees. Before he could ask what was going on, Lucas answered.

"Most of the park is too dense to navigate, but there aren't many spots to break out."

He looked down and saw a small opening in the branches—just enough room for an air-bike to exit.

"Don't worry, we'll spend most of our time up here."

With that, Lucas pitched them forward, and they accelerated away.

- - -

For 43 seconds, they lost them. They had mounted the air-bike and blazed away. Both agents on foot had no way to follow, and occupied themselves with examining the air-bike parking spot. The live feed switched to the Cruiser thermal scan, which searched frantically for a signal. On screen, they saw a large swatch of land, centered on the location of the agents which matched the starting point of the bike. Occasionally, a weak flutter of heat would mark the location of the suspects, but it would be gone in an instant. This gave them a rough outline of their path, but if there was enough of a break between these blips, they would be out of luck.

After a few of these weak signals, the program drew a small blue dot, estimating their position and adjusting for each new data point. As Lauren watched the real blips get farther and farther from the estimation, she started to think they would never catch them. That was when a burst of heat came from the top left of the map and the dot locked onto a strong signal.

"What is that?"

"The signal is above the trees. They broke the tree-line."

Lauren turned to the agent. "They can't see the Cruiser can they?"

"It's a bit far, so they won't know what it is, but this is an under-Canopy no-fly zone."

"So they might know what it is?"

"Yes ma'am."

The signal blasted northeastward, and the feed re-centered around the moving target.

"Did they see you?"

"We can't be certain. They are headed away from the Cruiser, but it may just be their flight path. We are lifting above the Canopy and maintaining a good distance just in case."

Ross, who had been silently watching the video, asked, "Anything of note in their trajectory?"

"Not for a while, sir. They are in the southwest corner of the park, so they could fly in that direction for a good twenty minutes before reaching the edge. They'd pass seven Diama lines on the way, but not much else. Beyond the park, there's farmland for another couple hundred kilometers. Even on a full charge, that air-bike could barely travel that far."

Lauren eyed the screen curiously. Where were they headed? Did they have a base of operations out on a farm? It would be a good place to hide, she had to admit.

"Sir, our agents have arrived at the listed residence of Lucas Roberts."

Ross took his eyes off the screen. "Can you go in?" The talk of warrants had caused some legal confusion for the Chairman.

"Yes. Our agents will be inside shortly."

"No warrant necessary?" Lauren was as lost as Ross. In this relatively new age, where the DCI was the only official investigative body on Earth, criminal laws were not always common knowledge. Part of the issue was a dramatic decrease in crime rates—she couldn't argue against their effectiveness. But she was not naive. Sure, they were effective—but at what cost?

"No, a warrant is necessary, and one has been granted."

His answer only exacerbated her confusion. "This warrant was granted but we still don't have one for the Personal?"

"The one for Mr. Roberts was just submitted, but if you mean Mr. Anders's, which was submitted nearly two hours ago, yes—they are not granted in order of submission. Ma'am, do you know how the DCI works with the Courts on a case file?"

She shook her head. "No."

"Every time we open a case, the Courts are notified. As the case develops, they assign people to the file to deal with warrants, evidence, and other legal matters. They have full access to all DCI information—anything we know, they know. They use that information to decide when to grant warrants, among other things. Right now, they have all our submitted warrants and are actively monitoring all updates on the case. As soon as they deem a warrant is necessary and lawful, they will grant it."

"The Courts do not trust the DCI to make such judgement calls?"

"This agency is still in its infancy, and we are adjusting as we evolve. At the moment, the Courts act as a safety net against corruption and excessive power."

"Is it wise to let so many people know the details of a case?"

"There are no security clearances within the DCI itself—all agents have access to all information on all cases. This is why we have a nearly decade-long application and training process. In reality, there are thousands of agents that could know the details of a case. Beyond that, the Courts assign as few correspondents as possible to a case. Some cases only get one person, some get a team... recently they have been adding robots to cases, as you know."

She did. Fenix, along with other robotics corporations, was testing cerebral unit software, and sometimes fully operational robots, with ethical decisions. They had come to an agreement with the Courts to lend the units and test them against real cases. The Courts would remove all sensitive information and report back on how well the robot's decisions matched with the human's. She knew nothing of how others were doing, but Fenix was having a tremendous success rate in most fields.

Ross interrupted their discussion. "Are they in?"

"Yes sir. Based on an initial thermal scan, no one is there, but we will scour the apartment. We found the Personal on the office desk but..." There was a pause as the agent received more information through his earpiece. "...nothing out of the ordinary, at least not yet. Typical household items showing regular use. Forensic will conduct a thorough search to make sure this is Mr. Roberts's residence and trace any other DNA we can find."

Lauren sank a bit in her chair. "That's it? Nothing?"

They had a federal employee involved in a massive terrorist operation, and they couldn't catch him? Even her plan, which she considered so clever, had not turned up any leads. It had been almost two hours since her announcement, and still no attempts at the fake backup. She was probably being too impatient, but with the fate of the company still very much in doubt, Lauren didn't care for patience.

Ross broke the silence after a moment of contemplation. "You said that based on reasonable cause, you can track either of their Personals, correct?"

"Yes sir, either of theirs plus Mrs. Anders."

"Right. Now, what about older location data? Can you track Roberts over the course of last year?"

"No sir. Reasonable cause grants us live tracking. The Courts have granted us access to location data from the time of the attack on Fenix to the present for all three main suspects, which gives us a window from 11:47 this morning until now."

"And where were they at the time of the attack?"

"Mr. Roberts was in the Legislative offices, Mr. Anders was on the Diama en route to a shopcenter, and Mrs. Anders was in her home."

Ross frowned. He had hoped to gain more information from the answer.

"Remember sir, this attack was not planned to happen at a specific point. The perpetrators had an army of computers on constant watch for your systems to make any mistake, and attack at a moment's notice. The suspects would have no way of knowing this was going to occur today, or even this year."

Lauren asked, "How do you know any of them were actually there? Presumably they could be away from their Personals?"

The agent nodded. "Yes ma'am. Technically you are correct, but in that case only Mrs. Anders would be a mystery. You see, her Personal did not leave the house between the time of the attack and our arrival at their home almost an hour later, so we cannot be sure she was with it. But Mr. Anders was on the Diama going to the shopcenter, and we have the video feed from the stations and the pod itself placing him there at that time. We also have video feed of him going home on the Diama around 12:20. In fact, this feed shows Mr. Anders accessing his Personal and using it in some form at the precise time we were able to trace it sending data into Fenix. As for Mr. Roberts, we have unlimited access to surveillance data of all Legislative offices, and have confirmed he was at his desk at the time of the attack and left the office before noon for lunch, never to return. His Personal went straight from the office to his listed residence and then remained there."

"So he immediately dropped it off?"

"Yes ma'am, or someone did it for him. Most likely, he received word the attack had occurred, and used the lunch break as an opportunity to leave."

Ross frowned. "This is useless. Why are the Courts not granting the warrants on previous location data? I understand the hesitation with the rest of the Personal data, but I feel as if the location data would be very useful, and I cannot think of a reason to withhold it."

"I'm sorry, sir. The Courts have a very strict policy on minimizing privacy violation. Legal precedents have been set regarding usage of Personal data, and they are quite rigorous."

She betrayed nothing to upset her Chairman, but Lauren was relieved to find the standards of privacy set so high.

"What about Diama data? Can you trace all of their movements over the Diama?" He was struggling, trying to extract information in any way possible.

"For two of them, sir. As a federal employee, Mr. Roberts's public transport logs are available to us, but they are almost empty. The Courts have granted us access to Mr. Anders's logs as well, but we have found nothing of note yet."

"And Mrs. Anders?"

"We do not have enough evidence on her. She did not send the message, and we have not confirmed she is even one of the four suspects. We can only live track her Personal at the moment, or flag her if she takes the Diama."

He sighed. Lauren looked back to the screen, where the background continued to flow southwest at a steady rate. If the air-bike led them to some sort of headquarters, would the backup disks be there? Could they dare to hope to recover them? What other leads did they have?

She remembered what the agent had told her about their prototypes— still distributed throughout the vast labyrinth of R&D. It was not exactly reassuring. Then there were the tampered robots to deal with. She thought of David, who had come in minutes earlier with her water. Could she trust the machines around them? It seemed silly to question them, but at least seven had already participated in the destruction of Bluestone. But there was one more lead she had almost forgotten...

"Do we have anything on the BRA insider?"

"Not yet, ma'am. The terminal of origin was identified, but the employee was innocent. Someone else managed to access her workspace while she was away and send the message. Whoever did it was familiar enough with the cameras to completely avoid showing their face. We tried tracking their movements before the activity, but lost them in a surveillance-free area."

"A surveillance-free area?"

"The restroom, ma'am. Before the intrusion, the suspect exits the male restroom, but we have yet to see them enter."

"Could they have changed clothes?"

"Yes ma'am, but all other employees enter and exit. No one is unaccounted for."

That's strange, she thought. "What about after?"

A hint of a frown spread across the agent's face. "The BRA's surveillance system was infiltrated."

Her eyes widened. "Infiltrated?"

"Yes. The attack was short-lived - they only managed to cut the cameras for one minute and 34 seconds, but in that time the suspect disappears."

"Disappears?"

"Yes ma'am. No one with their outfit is still viewable by camera after the blackout. This means that they either found an exit or changed clothes. We are pursuing both possibilities, but have had no matches so far."

She nodded. "Right." So much for that lead. She glanced back to the wall, watching the green background pass by steadily. Her Personal vibrated, and she pulled it out to see a message from her friend Molly. They were supposed to meet that evening for dinner...

Food! Goodness, Lauren thought, I haven't had lunch yet, and it's a quarter past fourteen. Besides, this was a bit too stressful for her at the moment.

"Excuse me gentlemen, I'm going to grab a late lunch before I forget." As she got up from her chair, Ross stood and walked over to the door, opening it. She gave a quick nod to the agent, smiled at her Chairman holding the door for her, and walked out into the hallway.

- - -

While he did not care to admit it, Stewart was getting used to the air-bike. Above the forest, with plenty of space, he had no problem continuing this steady, forward route. His eyes stayed open, and he watched as the occasional flock of birds passed them by.

A fifth Diama line came into sight, and Lucas made a slight bank to the left. They had already flown under four Diama lines, each one causing Stewart to reflexively drop his head. This time, however, the bike was aiming straight for a support column. This had to be it, Stewart thought. He prayed that his driver wasn't planning any more inter-tree maneuvers.

Decelerating on the approach, Lucas began to level out the bike. Stewart watched apprehensively as the column got closer and closer. Couldn't he aim just to the side?

A hundred meters away, and the bike went level, still drifting forward from the momentum. Lucas pitched them back a bit to brake. Fifty meters... forty... thirty... Stewart glanced at the speedometer: 24...22...19. He looked back up at the column. Fifteen meters... twelve... nine... His hands gripped the seat, and he braced himself for impact. Seven... five... four... and a gentle stop.

Just as he started to loosen his grip, the propellors came to a near halt, and they dropped downward. He shot a quick glance underneath them and saw just enough room for them to squeeze through... maybe. The back fan duct smacked a branch aside, pushing them slightly forward, closer to the column. Lucas turned them sideways, pitched slightly away and gave a small thrust toward the forest. Their descent had slowed gradually as more power was sent into the fans, and they came to a stable hover over the ground between the forest and the column.

Now why on Earth did he need to drop them like that? That's enough falling for one day, Stewart thought. While they idled, he glanced at their surroundings. The column to their right erupted from the green earth like an artificial tree—a giant, off-white impostor among the oaks. There were about three meters of grass between the edge of the forest and the edge of the column, and Stewart noticed one opening that looked big enough to fit the air-bike. Other than that, the trees were actually denser here, and he had a hard time seeing through the maze of trunks. He peered over Lucas's shoulder, and saw him fiddling with his transmitter.

"Where now?" His voice was almost lost in the noise of the fans, but Lucas heard him.

"We're here."

Stewart looked around again. What?

- - -

Lauren took some stairs down one level to the main floor. Thank goodness Fenix's cafeteria was amazing, she thought. As soon as she had left the Chairman's office, her stomach ached with hunger. She ignored the occasional stares of her co-workers and made straight for the food. She couldn't remember the last time she was this hungry.

The stairs opened right into a large expanse of tables and chairs. To her left and right were buffet aisles, with employees putting together their own meals. Others sat down and were waited by helpful Cafbots—cafeteria robots that moved around on roller-blade-like feet. It was a wonder they never spilt any food or drink as they served. A wonder, that is, combined with immensely sophisticated coordination programming. Lauren made her way towards the trays.

"Can I help you, Madam President?" One of the Cafbots joined her walk.

"No thanks, I'll grab my own today."

"Of course." The Cafbot rolled away to another employee.

She grabbed one of the trays and made her way through the selection. As usual, there was too much to choose from: salads and vegetables of all types, berries and fruit mixed and matched, chicken, turkey, and a variety of fish... all with complimentary sauces and sides. She threw a little bit of everything onto her tray, asked a Cafbot to bring her a glass of water, and turned to face the tables.

About a third of the chairs were taken, and about half of those were staring at her, averting their eyes if she made contact. Lauren realized this was a good move—employees would hopefully assume things were going well if the President had time to come eat lunch, even if it was a bit late.

"Lauren!"

She turned to the call, and saw Rubger approaching from the grand hall. He smiled at her.

"Care if I join you?"

She smiled back, and waited until he was next to her. "Please—you'll save me from this." And she pitched her head slightly to indicate all the watchful eyes.

He smiled again. "Of course. Let's sit, I'll order."

- - -

Stewart looked around one more time. What was Lucas on about?

"Where?"

Lucas turned his face enough for Stewart to see him smile, then pointed at the forest to their left. What, the trees?

"Got it." Lucas took the transmitter and pressed another button. He placed it back in his pocket quickly, and they pitched forward toward the opening. A sharp left brought them in line, and they drifted into the forest.

Stewart tried to find their destination among the vegetation ahead but saw nothing more than trees. Every couple of feet, Lucas had to adjust their trajectory. It was a narrow and tricky path, and Stewart noted that it was the first time Lucas had kept them at a slow speed.

After about three minutes of meandering, they made a sharp right and thrusted forward out of the pathway. They were in a small clearing dotted with some of the biggest trees Stewart had ever seen. Slightly to their right was a large building with three air-bikes parked in front. Above them, the large trees expanded into giant umbrellas of branches and leaves, covering almost every inch of sky from view—Stewart noted that even flying right over it, he had not seen the building. Lucas pulled up next to the other air-bikes and let the machine fall gently to the ground.

"Welcome home."

6. Home

As he unstrapped himself from the bike, Stewart took a closer look at the building in front of him. It seemed to be rather well-constructed, indicating the handiwork of robots—something that surprised him, given their earlier conversations. It looked one or two stories high, around thirty meters wide, and based on the line of trees in the back, probably a good hundred meters long. The roof was covered in smaller trees, projecting upward to create the canopy overhead. What was this place?

Lucas stepped down and motioned him to follow. They took a few stairs up to the front doors, which slid open before them. Stewart took one last glance at the four air-bikes, and prayed that one had brought Jacqueline.

They stepped into a long, tall corridor that seemed to reach all the way to the back of the building. Doors lined both walls, and there were paths protruding from each side on the second floor. Gray and black dominated the interior, but there was a long skylight that ran down the middle of the ceiling, bringing light into the chamber. A dull, low hum reverberated through the walls, as if the structure itself were a giant machine. Most noticeably, there was not a soul in sight.

"Are we alone?"

"No, the others are most likely in the conference room. It's the first door here on the right."

As Lucas spoke, he led Stewart in that direction. Where was that hum coming from? More importantly, where was Jacqueline?

Lucas held open the door, and Stewart's heart skipped a beat as he walked in. The room was slightly elongated, with a dull gray table occupying the middle and a series of screens on the far wall. About a dozen chairs surrounded the table, of which seven were occupied. He recognized two of them: their PAV driver and Jacqueline, who jumped from her seat and ran to embrace him.

- - -

Sure, her hunger probably had something to do with it, but Lauren felt as if this lunch was the best meal she had had in months. Every bite was incredibly satisfying, and it wasn't until she was near the end of her plate that she noticed her rather impolite silence towards Rubger.

She shot a glance up at him, and was relieved to see him eating, looking rather famished as well. The Cafbot brought his order out almost immediately, and thank goodness—she could barely hold off for the minute or two it took to arrive.

"How are you?" he asked. She looked up to see him smile at her. "I hope I can take you eating here as a good sign?"

Lauren nodded. "I almost forgot about lunch."

"That would be rather inconvenient." He smiled once more before taking another bite. She took the opportunity to finish her plate.

"Lauren..."

The slight hesitation in his speech amplified her attention. She tried to catch his gaze, but it was elsewhere, searching... pondering the right words to say.

"I don't really know the best way to phrase this, but I wanted to make sure you know how much your employees appreciate you, especially now. You've been President here for no more than a month, and you are dealing with this situation flawlessly. Honestly, if I were in your shoes, especially down in the R&D lobby, I would be a mess by now."

She laughed; his comments were quite flattering. "Thank you. I'm doing a good job hiding it." A Cafbot rolled up and took her tray. "How have you been? I'm sure dealing with the Market and the media has been a bit stressful?"

"That would be an understatement." He smiled again. "The media response could have been worse, although the BRA has already received transparency petitions on the details of the incident, and the Courts are processing them."

She raised her eyebrows. "Transparency petitions? From the media?"

"Maybe. Or another company."

"Will they pass?"

He shook his head. "Not for some time. They ask for a full disclosure of all investigation data, and I'm sure the Courts will side with the DCI on keeping it under wraps until all suspects have been accounted for."

"A full disclosure on the same day? That seems aggressive."

He shrugged. "This is a unique situation, and they can't be penalized for the petition. They might as well over-shoot and wait until the Courts approve it."

Finishing his last bite, Rubger shot a look to one of the Cafbots, which quickly rolled over to take his plate. "Anything else, sir?"

He replied, "No, thank you," smiling, and watched the robot roll away. His eyes lingered on the machine for a bit, then his demeanor shifted, and he glanced around suspiciously before leaning over their table a bit.

"Are you aware that the DCI is monitoring our Personals?"

She mirrored his lean, bringing her voice down to his level. "Yes..."

"Is this necessary?"

She couldn't help smiling. It was the same conversation she had just had with the agent upstairs. "Yes, to prevent any more attacks on our data."

Rubger shook his head. "It seems a bit far for me. I mean, access to my Personal? I understand the need to protect our computers, especially in R&D, but a Personal is nearly impossible to hack. Why monitor them?"

Lauren shrugged. "The DCI knows better than I do, but I suspect it has to do with the fact that nearly impossible is not the same as impossible, especially given the sophistication of our enemies."

He held her gaze for a moment before nodding, as if in reluctant agreement. "You're right. I'm just bitter because I feel like I have to censor all of my communication right now."

She smiled. "Are you transmitting controversial messages?"

Rubger gave her a matter-of-fact look. "No, but I assume any messages sent to you would be thoroughly screened."

"So?"

He locked eyes with her, and Lauren felt an excited nervousness take hold. Something about his gaze had strengthened, and she noticed, with a hint of alarm, that her mild interest in the man in front of her had evolved into something more. She tried to look away but couldn't. Why was she suddenly so attracted to him? Was it his earlier flattery? Was he really this manipulative? More to the point, was she really this weak?

Finally, the enduring gaze ended, and he stood. Her eyes followed his hand, which clasped around her own. She felt a warm tingle in her cheeks as she struggled to say something, but it was Rubger who ended the painful silence.

"I'm glad we got lunch." As he let go, Lauren felt a sliver of paper fall into her palm. She looked up, but he had already turned around, walking back into the grand hall. What was going on? She looked back down at the piece of paper in her hand. It was folded over, its message hidden, and Lauren felt the nervousness return as she flipped it open. There, in neat handwriting, it read 'A228.'

- - -

Relief was not strong enough a word, Stewart thought, for the overwhelming feeling that accompanied his reunion with Jacqueline. The events of the last few hours were a blur, and the people around him—even Lucas—faded into a sea of background noise against his island of joy. She started explaining how worried she had been, how she heard their pickup had been aborted, how they had arrived safely and then waited, and waited, and waited...

It was then that Stewart realized how the constant activity had been a blessing in disguise—a distraction from his separation. He couldn't imagine the thought of sitting in a room, waiting for Jacqueline with no way to communicate and knowing she was over an hour late... it was a miracle she wasn't more of a mess.

While the couple talked, Lucas joined the other six and explained their ordeal in detail. He was just reaching the Diama stop at the park when Stewart interrupted him.

"Excuse me." Lucas stopped and met his gaze. "You told me that once we got here, we would clean up my mess with the DCI and be free to go. When can we do that?"

"I'm not entirely sure. We are awaiting updates from other operatives, which will give us a clearer picture."

"A clearer picture? Of what?"

A woman to the right of Lucas responded. "Of our progress." She smiled at them and motioned to the chairs. "Please, sit. Would you like some water? Are you hungry?"

Before irritation was able to take control of his reply, Jacqueline pulled him lightly to the seats around the table. He knew it was best to follow her lead. "Yes... water, please."

The woman smiled once more and got up from her chair. She made her way along the wall and out the door. Stewart turned back to Lucas.

"What exactly is going on?"

The other five, including the PAV driver, gave concerned looks to one another. Lucas sighed and addressed the others. "Look, at this point we have them here and we owe them an explanation." He turned back to Stewart and Jacqueline. "I can only hope that once you understand you will spare our identities, if it comes to be necessary."

Stewart knew it was useless to promise anything, but he felt himself nodding nonetheless. Lucas gave him a weak smile.

"After years of preparation and effort, we have managed to wipe out Fenix's robotic altruism program. The operation occurred, quite unexpectedly, right before noon this morning. As I have already explained, your Personal got tangled into the mess, and we made a real-time decision to take you under our protection for the time being."

"You wiped out their entire robotic altruism program?"

He nodded. "Yes."

"But... why?"

The others smirked, and Lucas gave one more weak smile. "Because it was the right thing to do."

Stewart did his best not to seem appalled. "The right thing to do? Wait, because of the complexity? The case-based learning? Do you really think a company could skip any steps on a process so thoroughly scrutinized by the public?"

Lucas answered patiently, methodically. "Well, yes, but that's not the real problem here. The real problem is strong AI. As soon as we build a robot as smart or smarter than a human being, we cannot ensure our own programmed morality, sophisticated as it may be, will prevent an impeding disaster."

"So it's not worth the risk?"

"Of course not. Let's go back to my earlier example, where we program these robots to bring humans pleasure. Let's also posit that they have a remarkable ability to learn. These robots go about their business, and one day, one of them realizes humans just won't be happy all the time. They are always a little unhappy about something. Another robot chimes in, explaining how no dead human is ever unhappy. Then a third one notes that a human knowing of his impeding end is quite unhappy. Their collective solution? Euthanize humanity without ever giving away their intentions."

A chill ran down Stewart's spine at the thought of all of the robots he saw, day in and day out, concocting this mass-murder plot.

"Admittedly, this scenario is rather far-fetched, but it is a simplification of a complex problem that remains grounded in truth."

While Stewart mulled this explanation, Jacqueline joined the conversation. "Why did you decide to bring us here?"

Lucas looked to her and pointed at her husband. "Did they explain about his Personal?"

"Yes—that your blank one used his identification. So? Doesn't the DCI deal with blank Personals all the time?"

"Yes, but it's a bit more complicated. Usually, a blank Personal will use a real Personal's identification and send data to a third party. The real Personal has no log of this, and the DCI is able to examine the third party and determine the data did not come from the real Personal. In our case, however, both Personals tried to send data to the same third party at the same time. This is highly unusual, and the DCI would most likely not be able to tell that our data did not come from Stewart's Personal."

"Why not? He has no outgoing log of it?"

"Oh, but he does. We aren't really sure how it happened, but his credit link was mixed up with our hacking link, even in his outgoing logs. We've never seen this happen before, but then again we've never had a blank Personal send data to the same place at the same time as the real one it randomly selected."

She frowned. "So as far as the evidence points, we are guilty?"

He nodded. "In a way. Look, as far as we know, they could let you go right away, we just don't know. But speaking from personal experience, I doubt that would be the case... when we learnt of the mismatch, we scrambled a rescue operation to bring you here."

The door opened, and the woman came back in with a large glass of water. As she set it in front of Stewart and sat down, Lucas continued.

"Anyways, we are trying to find a way to let the DCI know what happened without putting ourselves in danger, and then letting you go."

Stewart gulped down half the glass before placing it back on the table. There was sincerity in his voice—the same hint of guilt that came into his house when he opened the door on this stranger. For all the hell he had put him through, Lucas was actually trying to help.

"What is this place?" Stewart asked.

Lucas looked to the woman, who answered. "This is our main operational node."

Main, he thought. Were there more of these nodes?

"The DCI doesn't know about it?"

"As far as we know, no."

"What is that noise?"

"The hum? Computers. Other than this conference room, a set of restrooms, some bedrooms, and a kitchen, this building is devoted to them."

"They're for the attack?"

She winced at the word. "Yes."

And there's potentially more than one node? Where did the money come for all this, he wondered.

Jacqueline looked around and cleared her throat. "I'm almost afraid to ask but... why are you trusting us with this information?"

The woman smiled. "We have already decided to let you go. At this point, we have nothing to hide. Besides, our work is done, our goal accomplished. Even if we are captured, Fenix cannot resurrect Bluestone."

"Bluestone?" Stewart did not recognize the term.

"That was the name of their robotic altruism project, initiated four years ago."

"The one you erased?"

"Correct."

He decided he didn't need to know the details. "Well then... what do we do now?"

"We'll get you a room and make you as comfortable as possible. For the time being, we have to deal with the immediate aftermath of the operation. Ethan? Could you take them to the green room?"

The man at the end of the table rose from his chair and motioned for them to follow. As Stewart got up, Lucas reminded him, "Don't forget to rest your back."

Concern flashed across Jacqueline's face, but Stewart gave her a reassuring smile. There was going to be some explaining to do, he thought. Ethan opened the door, and they stepped out into the hall.

- - -

Lauren took the stairs back up to the second level and looked around. To her right was the Chairman's office, where Ross and the DCI agent awaited her. She had felt her Personal vibrate three times during lunch and had yet to check it. No doubt there had been some updates—at this point the air-bike would have stopped or run out of power. But when she reached into her pocket, she didn't pull out her Personal.

A228? She looked at the small, crinkled slip and frowned. The designation belonged to a room: building A, floor 2, room 28. Clearly, Rubger was trying to be secretive about it, but why? All sorts of explanations ran through her head, none of which made much sense. Was he propositioning her discreetly? What sort of proposition needed to be this discreet? No, no, that was just too out of line... But what if he was one of the attackers? An insider on their own board? Then why would he send her to this room? A trap? In her own building?

She glanced at the door to the Chairman's office. Should she tell the DCI? Her gut told her not to—that she was wasting time, she needed to find this room now... But it also reminded her of how manipulative Rubger seemed, how effortlessly he set the tone of an interaction...

The paper went back into her pocket, and Lauren headed left with purpose. Hesitation be damned, curiosity had won this round. She decided to trust Rubger, for better or worse, and had a feeling he had been meaning to pass her that note for a while. Perhaps he had tried in her office, but felt the scrutiny of her bodyguard? Why else would he have popped up in the cafeteria at the exact same time as her?

She veered right at the end of the second floor lobby, passing the media room where she had made her announcement two hours prior. What was room A228? The second floor was home to mostly executive offices—the Chairman's office, along with offices for each of the board members. But A228 was not Rubger's office—those were all between A201 and A210, back near the stairs. Media was A220, and as far as she could tell, A228 had to be at the end of the corridor, against the edge of the building.

The next few rooms were miscellaneous media offices and lounges, then a set of restrooms. Despite her relatively new status in the company, Lauren thought she had explored every part of the main building... what was this hidden room off to the side?

A227, Media Archive, came up on her right, and then, finally, A228. Media Storage. She had reached the end of the corridor, a glass wall giving a glimpse of the city outside. The room itself had no view in, but this was not unusual. In fact nothing about this seemed unusual except for Rubger sending her here.

She stood in front of the door for a good minute, staring at the handle, as if waiting for it to open itself. If nothing seemed out of place, why was she so hesitant? She took a deep breath, closing her eyes for a moment, then let her hand grasp the handle. Whatever was inside, she thought, it couldn't possibly hurt her. Or so she hoped.

She turned the handle, and pushed it open. The room in front of her was a little bigger than her office, with shelving along the sides and back. Various cameras, microphones, and other media gadgets lined the shelves, and a few larger devices occupied most of the floor. There were no other doors, just a large window on the left, giving the same view as the end of the corridor. But that was it. No one was there.

She walked in a little farther, scanning for anything out of place. Something didn't click... why had Rubger sent her to this room? There was nothing special or unusual about it...

Her Personal vibrated again, knocking her out of her trance. This time she pulled it out to take a look. It was Ross, asking her to come back to his office. She glanced at the other three messages, then back up to her surroundings. She was missing something, but it would have to wait. Walking back out and closing the door behind her, she headed back to the Chairman's office.

- - -

For all intents and purposes, the green room did not fit its moniker. The walls were the same gray as the large hallway, with white accents replacing the black. A large bed dominated the interior, but despite the industrial setting, the room itself was rather accommodating. There was a pair of comfortable seats and a small coffee table. In fact, it would probably pass as a hotel room were it not for the glaring lack of a private bathroom. Those, Stewart learned, were out in the hall.

They had been shuffled in here about 10 minutes ago with their escort, Ethan, explaining that they were free to do as they wished, but to please not interfere with the computers. The police bearing of their captors put him at ease, but the thought of escape did occur to him, if only fleetingly. He sat in one of the chairs and listened attentively as his wife gave details of her journey to the base. It was not nearly as dramatic as his own. They had reached the extraction point on time, where a PAV weaved its way through the streets and out of the districts. Somewhere along the way, they had switched to an air-bike and made their way over the trees in a similar manner.

As he started to explain the differences between their two adventures, there was a knock on the door.

"May I come in?" It was Lucas.

"Yes," Stewart replied.

The door opened and he walked in, giving them a quick smile. "How are you feeling?"

"Fine, both fine. My back is still tender and my legs are sore but it's nothing too painful."

He glanced around the room. "I hope this is enough. I'm sorry to keep you here for even a minute, but we really don't know how long this might take."

"Do you have any idea?"

He shook his head. "Sorry... it could be a few hours, it could be a few days—I just don't know." The guilt in his demeanor had doubled, and Stewart did not feel the need to press it any further. "Anyways, I wanted to say goodbye, as I may not see you again, and I hope you don't hold everything that has happened against me."

Stewart looked up, confused. "You're leaving?"

"Yes, I have to get back to my job... this whole ordeal with you two was unexpected, so there will be some explaining to do, but we've worked out a solution."

His job, Stewart thought. This wasn't it? "What about the others?"

"Most of them will stay, some might come and go... this place will be relatively busy for the next couple of hours, and you won't be left alone at any point, if that's what concerns you."

"Where should we go if we need something?"

"Ethan showed you the kitchen?"

They nodded.

"Well you're free to go in there and use whatever you want. If you have any questions or concerns, ask anyone, they will all be aware of who you are and why you are here—even the newcomers. If all else fails, find Mina."

"Mina?"

"The Indian woman who spoke to you in the conference room? She is always here. Her room is three doors down the hall on the left."

Stewart nodded. Something about Lucas leaving made him slightly uncomfortable. This was his man, so to speak, his connection to the others. After he was gone, it would be a building full of strangers.

"When will you be back?" He couldn't help himself.

"Back?" He smiled in a way that gave Stewart the impression that his question was silly. "I won't be back, but if there's something you need from me, Mina will be able to contact me."

Stewart stood and extended his hand. "Thank you for helping me. I may not agree with your cause, but I appreciate your honesty."

Lucas shook it, smiling. "I'm glad."

With one last look around the room, the man who had quite literally shoved his way into Stewart's life walked quietly out the door.

- - -

They were looking at an enhanced thermal scan of a section of the park right where the air-bike had disappeared. Lauren had been told of the intricate arrangement of trees that covered the building, which was now clearly visible as a rectangle of heat. The Cruiser had drifted over, above the Canopy, and taken photos during its pass. They had opted not to stop, so as not to raise suspicion or be spotted. Before she could praise their luck, however, the DCI agent made sure to temper any enthusiasm.

"I must remind you that this could be one of many facilities, or even an elaborate decoy. We can not be certain that it is a building until we have a visual."

"Can we get one?" Ross asked.

"Yes sir, we will shortly. We have agents at the nearest Diama station and park pathways, as well as another Cruiser en route for support. We're sending in the ground agents first to see if they can get a visual."

Lauren frowned. The agent was probably right about other facilities—that would explain the link traces all across the southern United States. Then it hit her. Why hadn't she thought about it before?

"Have the traced locations been investigated?"

The agent turned to her. "My apologies, ma'am, but what do you mean by traced locations?"

"The insecure links? Your analysts spoke of older links being used to infiltrate our system before today's attack, and each one originated somewhere in the southern United States."

"Yes. There were three: one just west of Orlando, another above the Mexico-Arizona border, and the third 72 kilometers southeast of El Paso. We have forensic crews at each location. So far we have found clear evidence of small-scale deconstruction, typically associated with robotic disassembly of temporary structures."

Temporary structures? Was this some sort of traveling, terrorist circus? "Could this be one of those structures?"

"Yes ma'am. We will know when we have a visual. Since each of these links occurred months apart, it could very well be one structure."

"Wait..." Ross looked to the agent with skepticism. "Robotic deconstruction? Aren't they anti-robot?"

Lauren answered for him. "I'm getting the feeling they are strictly against robotic altruism." The agent nodded in agreement.

Ross scoffed. "Wonderful."

She eyed the image carefully. Even if this were a base of operations, what were the chances that the recovery disks were there? And if not, that they even existed any longer? Oh well, she thought. It's the only hope we've got right now.

She turned to the agent. "How long until your ground agents are in visual range?"

"Approximately eight minutes, ma'am."

Her eyes returned to the picture. When she had checked her Personal, two of the three unread messages were from the DCI. One was about the air-bike ending its journey and surveillance shots of a possible base. The other was a summary of developments, including the fact that the trail had gone cold for the other two skydivers, indicating a PAV pickup.

"Do we have any way to trace the PAV of the other two suspects?"

The agent nodded. "Yes ma'am, but it will take some time. Normally we would try to use private or public surveillance footage, but the district was abandoned with no functioning cameras. Since they did not want to alert our Cruiser, they had to maneuver between buildings, which kicked up a good deal of dust, leaving a forensic trail. We are following this trail until we reach a functioning camera."

Lauren nodded, finding herself oddly apathetic to their escape. Sure, they probably had lost them, but did it really matter? They didn't have the recovery disks. In fact, she wondered how any of it mattered—the structures in Orlando and Arizona, the insider BRA agent... even the two employees they had caught in the R&D lobby. The future of the company was her number one priority and at the moment, that meant the future of Project Bluestone. Everything came down to the recovery disks.

"There is an air-bike exiting the tree-line." The image transformed into a live feed, hiding the building under a sea of green but pin-pointing the new craft with another blue dot.

"Do we know how many are on it?"

"Yes ma'am, one. Our Cruiser is too far to properly identify."

"Where is it headed?"

"Currently back to A zone."

Lauren could see it was not heading back the way the other air-bike had come. But at this point she knew the DCI would deal with it in some way, and she refocused her attention on the matter at hand.

"Are any of your ground agents carrying the eye cameras?"

"Yes ma'am, all of them. Would you like a visual feed?"

"Please."

- - -

Stewart's eyelids grew heavy as he stared at the dull grey ceiling. He was aware of his wife's warm hand, grasping his wrist as she lay next to him on the bed. A gentle breeze of cool air ran across his body, keeping him at a comfortable temperature. He wasn't sure if the accommodations were spectacular or if he was just that tired. As soon as Lucas had left, Stewart felt the adrenaline of the day flow out of his body, and an overwhelming fatigue took its place. It was time for a well-deserved nap.

The cool pillow underneath his head sank just enough to put his neck in the perfect position. I'm probably just that tired, he realized. But it didn't matter. He was comfortable. And sweet, warm sleep was embracing him...

An urgent knock jolted him awake. Had he fallen asleep? He turned to Jacqueline, then to the door. He had barely managed to get one leg off the bed when it opened.

"I'm sorry, but we have a situation, and we need you back in the conference room."

It was Mina, but not the same calm and collected Mina from before. She was nervous—afraid, even.

"What happened?"

"We're not sure. Our perimeter sensors went off. Please, come with me."

Quickly but reluctantly, the pair followed Mina out of the room, across the hall, and into the open conference room. They could hear the voices from the corridor, and they walked in on an orderly but tense debate. Ethan and their driver, along with a woman who had been there earlier, were all sitting along the table, each with the same anxious look in their eyes. What was going on?

"Aren't we overreacting?"

"Not necessarily. Did you see the spread?"

"It could still be a herd - have any more gone off?"

"Not yet."

Mina took her seat among them, at the head of the table, while Stewart and Jacqueline sat off to the side. The screens on the far wall, which were blank before, were alight with activity. Everyone seemed to focus on the largest one, showing what looked like three circular arrangements, one within the other, of widely-spaced white dots. Towards the bottom, two of the outermost circle's dots were red, along with five more above them in the next circle.

Mina addressed them directly. "Those white dots on that screen are our perimeter motion sensors. The red ones have been tripped."

Ethan chimed in, "Usually it ends up being deer or a cougar, but we can't be too careful today."

Stewart nodded. So they thought it might be the DCI?

"Do you have cameras?"

"Unfortunately, no." Ethan turned to Mina. "Should we send someone out?"

"Not yet. But we need to expedite the erasure process just in case. Jason, can you go help them?"

Their PAV driver nodded and made his way out. As he watched him go, Stewart asked, "What's going on?"

"We're wiping all of the computers, just in case. We were almost halfway done when you arrived, but we need to jump-start the process if the DCI is at our door."

There was a sharp beep, and everyone turned to the screen. One of the white dots on the inner circle had turned red. The discussion picked up immediately.

"Are we going to wait for another?"

"Right now, this could still be a small herd."

Mina nodded. "True but we want to be ready just in case. Michelle, can you fire up the air-bikes?"

"Yes, of course."

She was out in a hurry, leaving Mina and Ethan with Stewart and Jacqueline. While the couple looked at each other nervously, their hosts were fixated on the monitor.

Stewart turned to them. "If it is the DCI, what is the plan?"

Without taking her eyes off of the screen, Mina answered. "We ride the air-bikes out, and make way for our emergency rendezvous point."

Stewart fidgeted uncomfortably. He knew what it was like to try to fly away from the DCI. Why didn't they have cameras? Michelle marched quickly back into the room.

"Air-bikes ready."

Ethan got up. "I'm going to help them finish." Before he could make it out the door, another beep pierced the tense atmosphere. A second dot on the inner circle was red, two dots away from the last one.

Mina shot up out of her seat. "Go take a look. If you see anything, sound the alarm." He sprinted out of the door down the hall with Michelle right behind him. Once they left, she turned to the couple. "I'm going to activate our robots just in case. If you hear an alarm, head to the air-bikes." Then she was out the door, leaving Stewart with more questions than answers.

For a moment, he wondered what robots she was talking about, but the thought was soon replaced by another. If it really was the DCI, what would they do? When he had arrived, there were three air-bikes parked in front—one single bike and two double bikes. Even if Lucas had taken the single bike, there would be a total of seven seats for at least eight people.

- - -

On the wall in the Chariman's office, Lauren watched one of the DCI agents slowly transversing the wilderness. There was sound coming from the feed, but the agent's breathing was louder than his footsteps, which to her made no sense whatsoever—she could see twigs and leaves on the ground... how was he not making any noise?

A sudden halt in forward motion grabbed her attention. The feed turned left and right, as if the agent were searching for something. Then the camera panned a full 180 degrees, and started to march back the way it came.

Lauren's focus darted from the feed to the agent standing in the room. "Why did he turn around? What's going on?"

"We are being monitored."

Ross turned to him as well. "What? How?"

"Motion sensors, sir. Well hidden, but one of our agents has spotted one."

The Chairman was not satisfied. "Can't you jam those?"

"Sir, we can only jam wireless transmissions. We scanned for any before approaching, but there are none. These sensors must be hardwired."

She turned back to the screen. "Do they have cameras?"

"It is not certain, ma'am. We do not know the sophistication of their monitoring system. However, there has been no indication of evacuation at this time."

"They don't know it's us?"

"We can not be certain. In this dense foliage, their motion sensors cannot distinguish a human from another large animal, in which case they will not know it is us. Even if they had cameras, it would be hard to notice our agents in this cover."

"So what can we do?"

"We will approach from a new angle."

Ross shot the man a look of frustration. "A new angle? Can't you just capture them?"

"No sir. We anticipated an element of surprise, and an opportunity for surveillance. We do not know how many people are there, whether they are armed, and what sort of escape measures they have available."

Lauren maintained composure for the both of them. "Won't they have motion sensors fully across the perimeter?"

The agent gestured to the screen, which switched back to the map. "Not fully. The Diama column where the air-bikes travel in and out is closer to the building than our agents are at the moment. They may have sensors there as well, but it is a better approach given this new knowledge."

Ross continued his line of attack. "And if they sense you there?"

"We have two more Cruisers en route. Our last resort is full infiltration from above."

This last bit seemed to appease him, but Lauren eyed Ross warily. The Chairman was getting a bit too caught up in their capture. The DCI was right—if they stormed the castle, so to speak, there was a higher risk of losing the recovery disks. That is, if they weren't gone already.

"How long until your agents reach the new angle?"

"Approximately five minutes travel time, but we cannot go so quickly. We will approach again in twenty minutes."

"Twenty minutes?"

"Yes ma'am. This gives our Cruisers enough time to fly in and prevents unreasonable suspicion—if they do have sensors near the column, and they go off now, they will probably evacuate."

She sighed. Fair enough.

- - -

Stewart sat with Jacqueline in tense silence for what felt like an hour. Not this again, he thought. They had already managed to escape them once, and he doubted their luck would last much longer. How did they track them? The Diama? It was possible, but they hadn't used their Personals. More importantly, they had crossed tens of kilometers via airbike, how could they have tracked that?

Their eyes were fixed on the monitor, waiting for another sensor to go off. What if more sensors were tripped? Would the alarm go off automatically?

Another beep pierced the air, and husband and wife jumped in alarm. His heart rate soared, but something wasn't right...

"What changed?" He peered carefully at the screen while asking his wife.

"Nothing..."

"What does that mean?"

"Maybe one was set off again?"

He hoped she was right, but he saw the screen himself—there were just as many red dots as before.

A second beep went off, again with no visible change. They heard approaching footsteps, and turned to see Michelle hustle into the room.

"More sensors?" she asked.

Jacqueline responded, "Yes, but nothing changed."

Michelle nodded. "That's a re-trigger. Whatever it was, it's leaving now."

Stewart glanced back out the door for Ethan. "You didn't see anything? Where's Ethan?"

"Not yet. He's still scanning, but our visibility through the tree wall is very low. Unless they get within the last ring of sensors, we usually cannot see anything." She relaxed a bit, and took a seat. "He'll stay out there for a few more minutes, but unless we have any new triggers, we should be safe."

Jacqueline hadn't let herself relax just yet. "What if they just spotted your sensors?"

Michelle did not look convinced. "That's possible, but unlikely. If it was the DCI, and they spotted our sensors, why back down?"

She nodded. That was a valid point. Stewart let a bit of tension go, but kept his eyes on the screen. "Do they reset? Red back to white?"

"Yes, after five minutes of inactivity."

"How often do you have animals set them off?"

She paused to think. "I'm not sure. You'd have to ask Mina, most of us aren't here regularly. But I've seen it happen three other times, although they've never reached the inner circle."

"Why is that? Why is she here but no one else?"

"Well she's never alone, as far as I know, but Mina runs this place full time."

Stewart tried to comprehend what she was talking about. "And the rest of you, what? Part-time?"

Michelle laughed. "You could say that. We couldn't possibly stay here. We have jobs, families—our lives are not tied to this operation."

He was growing more confused by the minute. Lucas had come off as the secret agent type—with experience in everything from camera jamming to skydiving—and yet this did not seem to be some giant criminal organization... or any organization at all.

"That's why Lucas left..."

She nodded. "Yea, he had to go back to work."

His curiosity got the best of him. "Where?"

Her smile washed away and Michelle grew uneasy. He could tell he had asked a sensitive question. "Oh, right... sorry."

"It's okay. I don't really know where we are drawing the line with you two, you'll have to ask Mina. At this point, that sort of information probably doesn't matter."

A third beep drew their attention back to the screen. Again, no change.

Michelle stood. "I'm going to let them know nothing's changed. If you'd like to stay here you can but I'm pretty sure it's safe to go back to your room."

Stewart glanced at Jacqueline and felt a sense of mutual understanding with his wife. He knew they were thinking the same thing. "We'll wait until they go white."

Michelle nodded and made her way out the door.

After she was out, Jacqueline looked at her husband. "What do you think?"

He shook his head. "Honestly, I don't know. I think it's the DCI, but how? And why did they go away? It doesn't make much sense."

A double beep. This time, one of the closest sensors went white.

Jacqueline motioned to the monitor. "If it is the DCI, they're leaving..."

He wondered why he was so afraid of their approach. When he was with Lucas, he had to follow him in order to get back to Jacqueline. But now? Sure, there was some sort of incriminating evidence on his Personal, but at some point, the DCI must be competent enough to determine what really happened? Maybe it would be better for them to be caught... Honestly, even if these people managed to prove their innocence, the agency would still take them in for questioning. On the other hand, their captors had been more than accommodating, and unexpectedly honest. Something about their actions and attitude had Stewart rooting for them, despite what they had done.

Another set of footsteps turned their attention back to the door, and they saw a much calmer Mina take a seat next to them. She focused her attention on the screen as another beep signaled a re-trigger, then addressed the couple.

"As far as we know this was a false alarm..."

It was clear that Mina was not satisfied with this assessment. Her eyes lingered on the screen for a few more seconds, as if searching for an answer among the sensors. A double beep interrupted the silence, making the inner circle totally white. She turned back to them and continued.

"You know, I'm not one to readily accept coincidences, but when I replay everything that Jason and Lucas told us, I can't seem to figure out how the DCI could have found us so quickly."

Stewart remembered his earlier thoughts. "What about the pod we took? Could the DCI have tracked us on the Diama?"

Mina shot him a look of surprise. "Of course they tracked you. No Personals and that close to the landing site? Not to mention the jammed cameras... But then what? So they know you got off at C121. Even given the possibility that those two gentlemen in the park were agents, they did not have air-bikes on hand to follow you."

Stewart's eyes widened momentarily at the thought of his potential brush with the DCI. He tried to remember the encounter, but among the rest of the day's events, it was a blur. Could it be true? Could those two have been agents?

Mina sighed. "And then of course if we presume they did in fact manage to locate our building and those were in fact agents..." She turned their attention to the monitor once more. "...then why on Earth did they fall back?"

That's exactly what Michelle said, he thought.

"Michelle says she's seen false alarms before—how often do animals set off the sensors?"

Mina shrugged. "Maybe once a week on average? Sometimes they might come three times in one day, sometimes nothing passes by for a week. The real pain are the ones in the middle of the night."

Another double beep. "Do you live here?"

She nodded. "Yes. I'm in charge of running this building, but maintenance isn't much work. I'm glad the operation is finally over, it's been a rather dull last few months."

"There wasn't any preparation?"

Mina peered at him curiously. "This operation has spanned the better part of four years - there was quite a bit of preparation. The last few months, however, have been a waiting game."

"A waiting game? For the attack?"

Another wince. Stewart almost started apologizing, but she was already answering, her arms sweeping around in a gesture toward their surroundings. "These computers? They have been constantly searching for vulnerabilities in Fenix's supercomputers via the Cloud, and one was finally found."

Stewart didn't know much about Fenix, but he knew a bit about networks, and this last bit seemed far-fetched. "Fenix's research project was connected to the Cloud?"

Mina smiled. "You're right—it's not that simple. Most of Bluestone's data was held within the confines of R&D, totally shut off from the Cloud. But those years of preparation bought us quite a few advantages, including agents within the company, who were able to remove all physical hardware."

"They weren't caught?"

Her smile dropped away immediately. Apparently Stewart was asking all the tactful questions today.

"Not all of them."

He looked away, a bit embarrassed. "Sorry..."

Jacqueline watched another two red dots go white, and joined the conversation. "I'm sorry, but if they caught any of your agents, wouldn't that explain how the DCI could find this place?"

Mina shook her head. "No. In fact, only one Fenix agent knows where we are, but he has not been apprehended."

"The others don't know?"

"Information compartmentalization. Inside agents were at higher risk of capture, so their knowledge was limited."

And yet, Stewart noted, ours isn't. He wondered if that was due to the operation having already taken place.

"What's going to happen to them?"

Mina sighed and leaned back in her chair. "Well, if they followed protocol, they would have cooperated fully with the DCI, mostly because at this point it doesn't matter. They're being processed at the Courts, pending updates on the DCI's investigation. Their fate is at the Courts's discretion."

Michelle and Jason walked into the conference room and joined the table. Jason updated Mina on the computers.

"We're about 60% done. We've gone back to regular pace, but it should be done by 18:30."

She nodded. "Good. The robots are on standby, so be careful not to set off the order."

Jason nodded, and Stewart looked to Mina with a lost expression. "Excuse me, but you have robots?"

"Yes, this facility is a robotic construction. We use them to assemble and disassemble the building when necessary."

"So construction robots are okay?" He thought they must see the irony in their statement, but their reply was quite matter-of-fact.

"If you're referring to our ideology, we never claimed to have any problems with robots in general. It's robotic altruism and strong AI that we are against. Robots, particularly the less intelligent ones, are extremely useful."

Particularly the less intelligent ones? Stewart decided not to press the matter further.

"So they are on standby to disassemble the building?"

"Correct. If we need to evacuate, we will initiate the deconstruction order. At this point, even if there is no threat, we will leave them on standby until our scheduled departure."

"Our scheduled departure?" This was the first he had heard of such a thing.

"At the moment, we are following a twelve hour plan, meaning that twelve hours after the operation, this area will be clear of this building, us, and any residual evidence. Our original plan called for forty eight hours, but your rescue and the potential DCI presence in this park have sped things up considerably."

"Twelve hours? When was the operation?"

"11:47. We are leaving in about eight hours."

Eight hours? They were leaving in eight hours? Stewart did his best to digest this new information, but he found himself growing frustrated. He had been under the impression that they had reached the finish line, that there was no more running. They would stay here a while, things would get sorted out, and they'd be free to go. Now they were clearing out?

He shot a glance to the screen and saw that only two dots on the outermost circle were still red. Did this escape ever end? Irritation crept into his system, but he did his best to maintain composure.

"Where are we going?"

Michelle and Jason grew visibly attentive. They eyed Mina curiously, as if waiting to see how much she would reveal. Stewart noticed the hesitation in her speech.

"To a friend..."

His irritation grew. "A friend? Thank you for being so specific." Agitation crept into his voice, and Jacqueline placed her hand on his arm.

Mina sighed. "You're right, I'm sorry. You deserve the truth." She paused, giving the couple a look of resignation. "We are going to Senator Laskin's house."

7. Evacuation

The live feed on the Chairman's wall was back to a DCI eye camera, this time inside a pod full of agents. It slowed to a stop over the desired column, and she saw a first person perspective of gear preparation.

A decade of training, she thought. The DCI was the equivalent of any armed forces, and she knew from her history that such training was similar in the past. Still, it was a mighty sacrifice. Could their families know? She didn't know of any friends or acquaintances who claimed to know a DCI agent. How could that be possible? Even if it was supposed to be a secret, surely someone would slip somewhere?

The pod doors opened, and the agents piled out in one neat line. They spread across the column edge, attaching some sort of anchor to the wall. She watched as the agent broadcasting their image placed his anchor on the top of the column near the edge, with a small wire running out of it and into his belt. The wire held him as he positioned himself over the edge, his feet on the wall of the column, back towards the ground. There was a quick glance down, a small click, and then the whirr of the wires as they all rappelled down the side. At the time, she counted four, but there may have been more in another pod. They were on the ground in a matter of seconds, and another click let the wire run back up to the top. How did they get back up, she wondered.

The view turned around to the tree line, just behind them. The agents advanced much more slowly this time, scanning all around them as they entered a small opening in the trees. Lauren strained to see any sign of a device in the environment, as if hoping to alert them.

Her Personal vibrated, and she pulled it out to check. It was a message from Rubger. She couldn't help but shoot a glance at the agent in the room, but he was focused on the screen. What was she thinking? The DCI already knew what this message said. She clicked it open.

"Fun lunch! See you soon!"

Her heart rate increased involuntarily. See me soon? What did that mean? Her mind drifted back to room A228. Had she missed something? She tried to picture it in her mind, but nothing stood out.

Ross broke the silence. "Any sensors?"

"We have not identified any yet, no."

"How much farther?"

"They should have a visual in three minutes."

- - -

Stewart found himself gaping at Mina's revelation. Senator Laskin? One of Houston's most loved Senators, and Chair of the Robotics Committee? Surely this was a joke. This man could never be involved in the most anti-robot operation in the history of robotics?

Michelle and Jason were clearly unsettled by Mina's honesty, and seemed to be holding back their disappointment. It did not go unnoticed.

"I understand your concerns, Michelle, Jason, but keeping it a secret was pointless. If they didn't find out now, they would find out in eight hours when they arri—" A beep stopped Mina mid-sentence, and everyone's eyes shot straight for the monitor. A dot had gone red in the top right area of the inner-most circle. Stewart barely had time to register the change on the screen when Michelle and Jason were up, running out the door.

"I knew it." Mina stood and looked at them. "You need to go, now!" The couple bolted out of their seats and followed her out of the room. She turned right but pointed to the front doors on the left. "Get to the air-bikes!" They didn't wait for an explanation.

Outside, the air-bikes were still hovering, ready for launch. Michelle had already managed to strap herself into the pilot seat of the three-person bike that had brought Stewart. She made a quick nod for them to get on, but they were too busy running down the steps towards her to notice.

When they hit the ground, they heard a harsh buzzing coming from the building, and Stewart realized the alarm had been activated. As he hopped on and strapped in, he wondered if that's where Mina had gone. He clipped in his belt and made sure Jacqueline's was secure. And what about the robots? Were they going to take apart the building? He tapped Michelle on the back to indicate their readiness, and glanced one more time at 'home'. Jason and Ethan were running out the door. So much for safety. He looked at the other two double bikes parked next to them and his previous concern returned: how were eight people going to fit in seven spots?

Michelle punched the throttle, throwing them upwards towards the trees, that camouflaging umbrella above. Wait, was she planning on—

Before he could finish the thought, branches were smacking his head and shoulders, leaving cuts and scratches in their wake. A larger limb hit his shoulder with alarming force and he let out a yelp of pain. He did his best to curl up with the straps on, but by the time he had brought his head down, it was over. They cleared the tree-line, turned a bit left, and shot forward.

- - -

Chaos replaced calm and order. One moment the agents were proceeding cautiously, the next moment they were plowing through the foliage. The agent in the room had kept a cool tone when he announced that the targets were evacuating, but she could tell by his demeanor that things were getting out of hand, fast.

"What's going on?" Ross sat up anxiously.

"We must have tripped a sensor, sir. Our agents hear an alarm. The Cruisers are descending." The video switched to the map again, and a blue dot showed a new air-bike jettisoning out of the tree-line and heading for the city. "Three people have evacuated." A red dot appeared on the map.

"We are dropping an air-bike to follow, we cannot afford to commit the Cruiser."

Lauren clutched the armrests of her seat. No... this was all wrong. How would they ever get the disks now?

"Our agents have crossed into the clearing." The video feed switched back to an eye camera and Lauren watched as two more air-bikes shot upward into the sky. "Four more people have evacuated."

"Do you have enough air-bikes?"

"Yes sir."

She noticed the agents didn't bother watching the bikes fly - they knew their colleagues would handle it. As they made their way to the front steps, Lauren caught glimpses of weapons in their hands and hoped she would not have to witness a tasing. As far as she could tell, all the air-bikes were gone. She focused her attention on the large structure in front of the agents.

"Is this the building?"

"Yes ma'am. It is a temporary robotic construction, but we do not know yet if it is related to any of the other temporary structures we are investigating."

Lauren watched the agents inspect the door. "Is there anyone inside?"

"It is hard to tell, ma'am. The building is dissipating a lot of heat, most likely from computers."

"Can you get in?"

"We are trying."

Ross did not have the patience for this. "Put up the bikes."

The screen changed back to the map. They saw one blue dot, followed by a red dot, and then a pair of blue dots, followed by a pair of red ones. All of the bikes were headed toward the city, and they seemed to be almost equally spaced.

She wondered how far apart they actually were. "Are they aware they are being followed?"

"We have to assume that is the case."

"Where is the first bike?"

"Are you asking about the bike that exited thirty-eight minutes ago with one passenger?"

"Yes."

"We did not trace it, ma'am."

It took Lauren a moment to absorb the reply. "What?"

"At the time, we were aiming for minimal interference and an element of surprise. We could not afford to let our Cruiser follow, and if we had sent an air-bike, it may have been spotted. We are keeping an eye on all camera feeds at the edges of the park."

"Would it have entered the city by now?"

"Based on its trajectory, yes, approximately five minutes ago. However, it could have turned or slowed down. We are monitoring every camera. When we see something, ma'am, we will notify you."

Her attention returned to the bikes on the map. "What is your plan of action?"

"Pursue them until they stop or run out of fuel."

Fair enough, she thought.

- - -

A few minutes into his second trip on the air-bike Stewart realized how much Lucas had been holding back. They were flying so aggressively that he had trouble keeping his eyes open, and wondered how on Earth Michelle was managing to direct them. It was no use trying to communicate—the rush of wind combined with the turbines made yelling difficult to hear. Besides, the last thing he wanted to do was break her concentration. He tried to strain his neck and see the speedometer but the air denied his efforts. Jacqueline had her head bent down, eyes shut tight, and hands grasping the sides of the seat. Stewart frowned. He hated that she had to go through this.

A slight bank right jolted his attention. Clearly they were heading somewhere, but where? With the speed they were going, there had to be someone in pursuit. He only hoped it wasn't another one of those enormous aero-vehicles. Honestly, he was surprised they hadn't been hooked yet.

Were they en route to the Senator's house? That would be absurd— they would implicate him in the plot and they would all be arrested. Although it was a hard story to believe regardless. Laskin? Anti-robot? Sure, the Robotics Committee was responsible for many of the recent guidelines surrounding robotic morality and paving a careful path towards altruism, but they were still paving the path. Why would he risk his career for something like this? Did he believe the stuff Lucas had mentioned?

"Can you hear me?!" Michelle was yelling to them.

Stewart glanced over at Jacqueline, who kept her head down and eyes shut but gave the smallest of nods. "Yes!"

"We are going to get on a PAV! We have to be fast! When I stop, you get off! I will warn you!"

He hesitated, but realized it was foolish to ask follow-up questions. "Okay!" What was she planning? If they reached the city, surely the DCI would catch them. There was nowhere to run, nowhere to hide...

"One minute!"

That was quicker than expected, he thought. They showed no signs of slowing down. He tried to peer into the horizon but the wind worked against him. How was a PAV going to be any better? The last time he got in one, he had to skydive out.

There it was! It came down from above far quicker than he would have imagined, stopping above the tree-line well ahead of them. At least, it was well ahead of them for a few brief moments. In that minute window of time, he realized what was about to happen, and braced himself as best he could.

Michelle threw their nose up, basically slamming the brakes at full speed. Their bodies struck the belts with tremendous force, knocking the wind out of both of them. Although his eyes stayed open, darkness crept into Stewart's vision as if they were slowly shutting. It lasted all of five seconds, and then the pressure was gone.

Time seemed to creep a little slower than usual, and even though Michelle was shouting instructions at him, Stewart could not understand a word she was saying. Everything was blurred, hazy. What had she told him to do? He saw her grabbing at his straps. That seemed odd. A chill ran down his arm. Something cold had grabbed him, and now he was up, out of his seat, being pulled like a rag doll. There was ground underneath him. The cold let go, and he crumbled onto the floor. A sharp pain pierced his back and right side. The darkness was back, trying to take away his sight. For a fleeting moment he tried to fight it, but his body had had enough for the day, and he let it take over.

- - -

"What do you mean it's beyond your reach!?"

Lauren's eyes were glued to the map on the screen, trying to ignore her Chairman's blaring questions and the agent's increasingly tense answers.

"There is not enough oxygen, sir."

The simple fact that this stone wall of emotion was showing signs of cracking was alarming enough. Her eyes were locked, she refused to move them.

"What about the Cruisers!?"

The first blue dot vanished, disappearing without a sound, leaving a lonely red dot in its wake.

"They are on their way, sir."

She shifted her attention to the other two dots, but she knew what was coming. In a few seconds, they would be gone too.

A violent slam seized her attention and she turned to Ross. He grabbed his hand in pain and cursed fiercely. Lauren looked back to the screen, but all the dots were gone. They had escaped.

It all happened so quickly, she scarcely had time to process it. Escape... she didn't even entertain the possibility. The DCI had made a massive miscalculation, and seven fugitives were out of range. Based on the tone of the agent's reply, she could tell the Cruisers would come too late to track them. These terrorists had outwitted an agency she considered beyond outwitting.

As this thought process ran through her head, the screen changed. Lauren recognized the flutter and activity of an eye camera—they were back at the building in the park.

"Our agents have reported a significant drop in heat levels inside the building, as well as sounds consistent with deconstruction. No openings have been made—the robots must be dismantling from the inside out to prevent access to the computers. We were about to force an entry when we noticed a heat silhouette, now clear without the background noise. Someone is inside."

Someone left behind? Maybe all hope wasn't lost. "Why did that stop you from making an opening?" Lauren asked.

"The individual inside would be able to recognize an attempted entry, and may destroy the evidence. At the moment, the computers are dismantled, but they remain intact."

Lauren almost scoffed. As intact as our prototypes, she thought. And look where that was getting them. What were the chances the disks were still there? Did setting off the alarm lead to their immediate destruction?

"So we just wait?" Ross, while no longer fuming, seemed annoyed by the prospect. In his defense, there had been quite a bit of that already.

"Based on the size of the structure, the deconstruction should take between 10 and 20 minutes, and an opening will be made at some point before that."

To Lauren, this was fascinating. "10 to 20 minutes? How is that possible?"

"The building is designed for quick assembly and disassembly. The robots themselves are designed for this specific building. They have a set pattern of movements, and some of the building itself is mechanized. All of this contributes to the speed of the process."

She had never heard of such a thing before. An entire building stripped to pieces in what amounted to the blink of an eye.

"The roof is opening."

She tried to see the deconstruction in action but the ground agent continued to scan the section of wall in front of him.

"What if they have an air-bike inside?" Ross did not want to lose another one.

"Our Cruisers are now directly above the building, sir. In addition, there is no heat signature that indicates an air-bike."

Lauren replayed the evacuation in her head. "If your Cruisers can stop air-bikes, why weren't the original bikes stopped?"

"They were on descent from above the Canopy, and thus too far to hook the bikes. We also did not follow any of the bikes because we did not know how many people might be left in the building - our thermal readings were not clear due to the computers."

"What about the extra Cruisers you sent for the PAVs? Are they still on their way?"

"Yes ma'am. Even though we lost signal, we will attempt interception via likely routes. As always, we have cameras primed to alert us if they are spotted."

It wasn't much, Lauren thought, but it was something. She pulled out her Personal to check the time. 15:51. Only four hours had passed since the attack on R&D, but it felt like four years. What had her plans been for the day? What had her plans been for the weekend? The dinner with Molly flashed in her memory once more, and she realized she hadn't yet sent her friend a cancellation. Was she hoping she wouldn't need to? They were supposed to meet in three hours. Frankly, if things kept happening at their current rate, three hours could decide the fate of her company.

The screen changed once more, and the wall now showed Lucas Roberts, marked and labeled among a small crowd on a busy street.

"What is this?" Ross's irritation seemed to vanish with this development.

"A camera feed outside of the local Legislative offices, sir. Lucas Roberts has been positively identified."

Lauren ignored the fact that they were supposed to catch him on the way into the city. "Where is he going?"

"Inside, ma'am. This was seven minutes ago, he is now in his office."

In his office? This made no sense to her. Did he know he would be monitored? If he managed to evade them from the city limits to the steps of his office, why show his face now?

"What are you going to do?"

"Monitor him closely. We have undercover agents in the offices, as well as access to all video feeds and, thanks to our identification in the park, a warrant for monitoring of all incoming and outgoing transmissions from his work station."

"Why aren't we capturing him?" The irritation was creeping back into Ross's voice.

"As long as he does not know we have identified him, he may lead us to other suspects."

He was right, Lauren thought. For all they knew he might even lead them back to the seven hackers they had just lost. Frankly, she only cared that he lead them to the disks.

"He is not aware he has been identified?"

"So far, he has not done anything to indicate such knowledge except evade all camera exposure up to this point. All of the transmissions to and from his work station are routine."

It almost seemed too easy, which made Lauren uncomfortable. She thought back to when they had first snapped his picture. If he had suspected DCI agents, he could have hid his face. But did he even know about these eye cameras? Lauren was vaguely aware of commercial versions of the same product, the possibility must have come into his mind...

146

What if he just didn't care? Then and now. Maybe he knew he was being watched but he didn't mind. The damage was already done, at this point why did it matter? The camera jamming had alerted them in the first place—that seemed like a risky move at the time, too good to be true for the DCI. On the other hand, why run in the first place? Maybe it was their last resort. Maybe it was the only way to get into the park, to get to C121.

She gasped involuntarily. Ross turned his attention to her, but she averted her gaze. C121... of course!

"Is everything alright?"

The Chairman seemed confused, concerned. She looked back to him and answered.

"Fine, yes, fine. Just remembered something."

He peered at her curiously. "What?"

She felt nervous, under pressure. "Nothing... not something about this."

It wasn't convincing because it wasn't necessarily true. She wasn't lying, but she wasn't exactly being honest. The terminal in the park had reminded her of the coincidental equivalence of Diama station numbers and room designations at Fenix.

A228. It was a terminal.

- - -

"Stewart? Stewart?"

The voice was distant, vague. For a moment it was alone in an abyss of silence, and Stewart realized he was waking. His body lay flat, cool metal supporting his back side. A strong hum increased steadily—the sound of a machine. A wave of memory came upon him: the bike, the PAV, his wife...

He opened his eyes and saw Jason and Jacqueline kneeling over him on either side. Before he could say a word, his back flared up once more. He winced at the pain.

"Please, don't move. We're safe."

He saw Jason eyeing him with concern. What had happened? He let his eyes map out the interior of a PAV... was it the one they had pulled up next to? He didn't know. Jason wasn't on their air-bike though.

"Wha...?"

"We got away, sweetie. We're on our way to the Senator's house." Jacqueline grabbed his hand as she spoke.

As if the back wasn't enough, he started to feel dull throbs of pain in his head.

"What... what happened?"

"You were knocked unconscious by the bike."

"How long?"

"Less than ten minutes, don't worry."

Slowly, his surroundings came into focus. He overheard other voices - nearby, out of his line of sight. There were clouds moving outside of the window and two monitors with what looked like maps on the wall to his left. It was clearly a much larger aero-vehicle than their original getaway PAV, but not nearly the size of one of the DCI aero-vehicles. Michelle walked into his frame of view from behind.

"How are you feeling?" The concern and guilt in her expression translated into the question. It reminded him of Lucas.

"Uh, I've been better." He did his best to force a smile.

She frowned. "I'm so sorry."

Jacqueline's hand tightened around Stewart's just enough for him to notice a squeeze. When he glanced her way, he saw a hint of anger— clearly she blamed Michelle for this. He decided to change the subject.

"How far are we?"

"About twenty minutes," Jason replied.

"They won't catch us?"

He shook his head. "Don't worry."

Pain swelled up from within him like a wave, flowing through the rivers of his nerves and crashing all over his back. He let out a yelp.

Jason stood up and walked out of his field of vision. A moment later, he was speaking to him, and Stewart could tell he was still very close.

"We've got some pain medication for you. We had a robot run a quick x-ray and nothing is broken—just very bruised. The Senator will have a medical bot that can take a look at you just in case."

He came back into sight with a small capsule that Stewart recognized from all his childhood crashes and illnesses. There were ubiquitous injectable medications for all sorts of common problems, especially general pain. Inside his body, Stewart had a dozen or so highly specialized nanobots constantly monitoring his health. These bots would recognize the bruising and pain, and once the syringe pierced his skin, allow the proper amount and type of medication through. The bots themselves were placed inside him over the course of his infancy, as with every other child of the last four decades. At first, the system was deemed too invasive and unnecessary, but as the bots became cheaper and their utility increased, they became commonplace. It was something Stewart didn't even think about—he hadn't even considered the existence of those bots since the last time he had to take a capsule, which would have been at least three years ago.

Jason put the capsule against Stewart's arm, and the needle penetrated the skin. As the medicine began to take hold, so did a realization. What if these nanobots were traceable? That would explain everything!

The capsule beeped, and Jason removed it. As he stood to replace it, Stewart voiced his concerns.

"Jason, can our medbots be traced?"

Jason smiled down at him. "Don't worry, they can't. If there's one thing the Legislature has gotten right, it has been honesty and transparency. You can look up the designs of those things, even go see where they are made and watch every step of the process yourself. And even if you don't believe all that, if medbots were traceable, they would have stopped us a long time ago."

Interesting as that may be, it meant Stewart was still at a loss to explain their location of the base in the park. How had they traced the air-bike ride with Lucas?

His mind shifted immediately to the relief the medication was bringing. The wave of pain had lost its force, replaced by a mixture of numbness and warmth. He felt a desire to sleep again, and understood why he hadn't been given the capsule while still unconscious.

"Oh... thank you." It was wonderful.

Jason and Jacqueline both smiled. "Here, let's try to get you up."

While they both stood, Michelle walked around behind him.

"Hook your arm under his, like this." Stewart felt Jason's right arm slide under his left armpit. His wife copied the motion, and they lifted slowly. Michelle's hands provided support on his wife's side, and soon enough he was on his feet. They all let go gently, and he had to admit, he didn't feel too bad standing. Admittedly, any sort of running or strenuous movement would knock him out, but that was not an issue at the moment.

All three remained close by, and Jason gestured him towards a chair protruding from the wall near the monitors. He took gentle, deliberate steps, but had no problems getting there on his own. When he sat, it was more from the presumption that he should than from actual physical necessity. Well, that coupled with the doping effects of the medication.

Now facing the other direction, he saw that there was a second area of the PAV through a narrow archway. That was where Michelle had come from, and where he would occasionally hear more chatter. How many more people were on board? The medication had eliminated the headache, but now his thoughts were clouded. There was something he was going to ask...

"I'm going to see if Laskin got our message." Jason nodded in reply to Michelle's statement. She gave Stewart a weak smile before turning around and walking through the archway. He watched her leave and the question came back to him.

"How did we escape?"

Jason smiled again. All of these gestures put Stewart at ease.

"With a lot of careful planning and just a hint of luck. You see, we never really expected the DCI to locate our main operational node - that's why we only had motion detectors and not cameras, we were more concerned with curious wanderers than government agents - but we made sure to have an evacuation plan, in case of an emergency. That plan consisted of a network of robot-driven PAVs above the Canopy near the node. When the alarm was pulled, a signal went out to these robots, which locked onto our escaping air-bikes and dropped themselves in for interception. Each evacuating air-bike met with a separate PAV and transferred passengers. This was easier said than done, as you know first-hand."

Between the concussion and the medication, his memory was foggy, but Jason's description was ringing a few bells. He remembered stopping, but not getting into the PAV.

"How did I get on the PAV?"

Jacqueline answered him. "A robot. It pulled you in, and then us too."

Jason nodded. "As soon as you were on board, it ascended."

"And the DCI?"

"Oh this was just the beginning. When our air-bikes broke the tree-line, the DCI sent their own air-bikes after us. This is why we needed to go as fast as possible. Those agents have EMP rifles, and their bikes are much more powerful. That being said, they could not use the rifles without dropping us to our possible deaths, so we were at an advantage. I can assure you that they were well within firing range."

Stewart thought back to their original escape plan, and how quickly that had fallen apart. But that was a lifetime ago.

"This is where luck came in. The DCI had two of their large aero-vehicles monitoring our node—something we obviously did not know until recently, or else we may have rethought our escape plan. Thankfully, they did not send those aero-vehicles after us, or we would have been hooked just like before. I don't know if it was because we had three air-bikes to their two ships, but those behemoths did not pursue. Now, our PAVs cannot outmaneuver their air-bikes, but that wasn't necessary. All we had to do was ascend beyond the upper Canopy, and they would be forced to fall back."

His eyes shifted to the window. The upper Canopy referred to an altitude of fifteen kilometers. Typically, the term Canopy referred to the lower limit, although it actually defined the area between the two limits—the lower Canopy and upper Canopy. A few more kilometers up, and they would be in near space.

Jason noted his gaze. "We aren't quite that high anymore. That wasn't the end of the line. As you may or may not know, around nineteen kilometers of altitude you reach something called the Armstrong line. This is where humans need a pressure suit to survive—something the agents did not have. They were forced to fall back, and we continued up to about twenty-five kilometers, then jammed their radars. Remember that at this point we are not talking about one PAV—we are talking about three different PAVs, each with one air-bike's worth of passengers. The problem now is that the DCI has identified these three PAVs and will be on high alert for them. In fact, while their two main ships did not follow us, I'm sure back up was on its way once they realized what we were doing. That's where our main PAV came in."

As he said this, he spread his arms, gesturing at the vehicle they were in.

"All of the robot-driven PAVs rendezvoused with our main PAV up at the twenty-five kilometer mark. We piled on, taking our robots with us, and left the three smaller PAVs on auto-pilot to wander above the Canopy. We took this PAV back down, and now we are on our way to Laskin's in a vehicle the DCI does not know to look for."

During Jason's explanation, something had bothered Stewart, but now he was having trouble putting his finger on it. Damn this medication, he thought. What was it that didn't make sense?

Jacqueline saw his concerned expression. "What's wrong?"

He ignored her momentarily, trying to focus his mind. They went past some line... The agents had to back off... They regrouped in one PAV... Wait, who drove that one PAV? Probably another robot... That was it!

"Wait, so you had an army of robots driving PAVs above your base and here we are trying to destroy them?"

Jason made a slight frown at his statement. "Stewart, we are not trying to destroy any robots. Robots have been incredibly useful for more than a hundred years. We are trying to save ourselves. Every robot currently in existence is less intelligent than the average human. We do not want to reverse that trend."

The conversations at the base came back to him, and Stewart almost felt guilty for asking the question. He was still having trouble wrapping his head around the heavy use of robots by an essentially anti-robot organization. But, he thought, that was just it. They were not anti-robot, they were anti-intelligence horizon. And he was starting to appreciate the difference.

"Can I ask you something?"

Jason nodded.

"So you stopped Fenix's project. Isn't it just a matter of time before someone else starts something similar?"

He looked at Stewart for a moment, then gave him a sad smile. "Unfortunately, you're right. As far as we can tell, no other company was even close to where Fenix was, but that doesn't mean they won't be soon. It might be a decade, it might even be a year, but it is inevitable. Fortunately, society is on our side. Public opinion has steadily swayed against the robots. You've heard of the protests, the stories. People want robots to do the dirty work, and that's already happening. Why risk having them rise up against us, as so many plot lines in fiction have explained? Granted, I for one find that possibility very implausible, but there is more to it. We have established ourselves as the masters of our own destiny. We may be animals, but we are unique on this Earth. Why risk our dominance? Why risk our freedoms? Most of all, why risk our superior intelligence? In the end, even if the robots coexisted with us, or continued to do our bidding, I feel like we would lose a fundamental part of what it means to be human. I don't want to lose that. Do you?"

It was an effective speech, and Stewart found himself well focused despite the medicine. The more time he spent with this lot, the more he agreed with their views. Was he that naive? Or were they actually on to something?

Michelle walked in again, followed by Ethan and two others that Stewart recognized from his first entrance into the conference room back at the base.

Ethan looked him up and down. "How are you? We're deeply sorry, we had to make sure Laskin knew we were coming or else we would have been in here sooner."

"It's fine. Thank you. Jason gave me an injection, and I'm not in any pain."

Ethan smiled. "Good. Laskin has acknowledged our approach, and will be there when we arrive."

Stewart looked at the six people around him and felt a knot form in his stomach.

"Where's Mina?"

- - -

They had looped the video of Lucas for two minutes before switching back to the building. At any moment, the deconstruction would reach a point where the agents could enter. But Lauren was not focused on the screen. She had Rubger on her mind.

Why did he want her to go to that station? Why did he need to tell her so discreetly? Was his message about seeing her soon supposed to mean something? And even if she decided to go, how would she go about doing so?

She looked up at the agent once more. Why did she feel as if she couldn't tell him? Had she not entrusted her entire company to this organization? It was a frustrating conflict, exacerbated by her own feelings of imprisonment—the mere fact that she was afraid to simply walk out of the room and take the Diama to the station said something about the way this investigation was being handled.

"We have made entry."

Her eyes turned back to the screen. There was movement everywhere —the entire building was closing in on itself in a bizarre, orderly dance. Only a narrow corridor, right in front of the agents, was lacking commotion. At the end there stood a woman, watching their approach.

"Have you identified her?"

"We are working on it, ma'am."

The agents reached her in seconds, and she gave no hint of surprise or fear. They must have gestured for her to move, because she began walking down the corridor the way the agents had entered.

Ross grew impatient once more. "Still no identification?"

"No sir. Her face did not match."

On the video feed, Lauren saw the agents stop the woman outside of the building. One of them pulled out a medbot scanner and began waving it around her body slowly. After a few seconds, a light on the back flashed red.

"What does that mean? I've never seen one do that."

"She has no medbots, ma'am. She is completely off the grid."

Lauren turned to the agent, astonished. "Off the grid?"

"Yes."

"But how is that possible?"

"An undocumented natural birth, probably by choice. It is completely legal, although uncommon."

She thought about the implications. No one turned down medbots because medbots were the key to modern medicine. And if she didn't have a picture on file, it meant she definitely did not have a Personal. Again, this was legal, but simply unheard of. No Personal meant no communication, no finances... how could anyone survive without one?

"So you have no idea who she is?" Ross was displeased again.

"No sir. But she will come in for questioning while we analyze what remains of the building and its computers."

"And the recovery disks?" Lauren was almost begging him for a positive answer.

"There's no sign of them at first glance, but they may have been packed away within the building. If they are here, we will find them. More importantly, if this woman knows anything, we will tell you."

She fell back into her chair in resignation. This was getting old, fast. Ross was right to be impatient. Despite everything that had happened, it was as if nothing had happened at all. She had had enough. After a split second of deliberation, she stood with purpose.

"Excuse me, sir, but this is about as much as I can handle. I'm going to go home and try to clear my head."

Ross turned to Lauren and, to her surprise, his frustration with the situation vanished. "You're right. Get some rest. I know the DCI will send you everything. I'll message you if there is any real progress."

She gave a small smile, then looked to the agent. "Is there anything I should be aware of?"

"We have stationed two agents outside your home for protection. If this makes you uncomfortable, you may call them off at any time."

She gave a calm nod, then turned and walked to the door. But she wasn't calm at all. Agents at her house? That ruined everything. How was she supposed to go to A228?

- - -

Stewart's question left an uncomfortable silence in its wake. Jason's smiles were gone, as were everyone else's. It was Jacqueline who responded.

"She stayed behind."

Stewart looked around at them, one by one, ending on his wife. "Why?"

She shrugged, but Michelle was already replying. "There was not enough room on the air-bikes."

Two realizations came to Stewart in rapid succession at this development. First, that they were the reason there was not enough room and second, by extension of the first, that he no longer doubted the words of his captors, their noble intentions, or their selflessness. This silence, he thought, was more uncomfortable than the last.

"What will happen to her?"

"We can't know for certain, although she will be questioned."

Stewart's eyes widened in fear. Michelle waved dismissively.

"Don't worry, she won't divulge our destination or anything along those lines."

He was not convinced. "How can you be so sure? This is the DCI we are talking about."

"Yes, but the DCI is an organization bound by Legislative law. Their agents are absolutely forbidden from violating any basic rights of suspects. The Courts watch their every move and are heavily incentivized to report misdeeds. Mina will most likely answer every question she can without giving us or any of our friends away. After that, she will be detained for processing by the Courts until they can pass a judgement."

As she spoke, Stewart realized just how little he knew about the DCI and the Courts. He was expecting some combination of truth serum and torture followed by incarceration. Maybe the medication was compounding his fears...

"We've started our descent." A robot announced their progress from the other room.

Michelle, Ethan, and the two others turned back and walked out, leaving Stewart with Jason and Jacqueline again. His wife turned toward Jason.

"What do you think will happen to her?"

"In the end? Some technological restrictions. Level two or maybe level three monitoring. All of this means she will be given a Personal and put into the system, so to speak. At the moment she is completely off-grid."

"Off-grid?"

"Meaning she is not on file. She has never had a Personal, or even medbots. Her birth was undocumented."

"How?"

"A natural birth, not registered for medbots. No one seems to realize that it is quite possible to live without these things, and quite legal too. The Earth Initiative was very pro-anonymity, and so our laws allow someone to live in complete privacy, if they wish. The trade-off, of course, is near-total isolation. But the option exists."

Jason was right. Stewart, and Jacqueline by the looks of it, had no idea that this was the case. Of course, they also had no idea why anyone would want to live like that. For a moment he figured that only high-level criminals would follow such a path—and then he realized just how right he was. Then again, criminal now seemed too harsh a term. His world was very much in the grey at this point.

Jason glanced out the window. "We're almost there. As soon as we get inside, I'll get that medical bot to take a look at you."

Stewart nodded. "Thank you."

He looked out the window at a modern suburbia. In his mind, he didn't need to see the medical bot. Another dose of the medication would be all he needed.

- - -

The sun, now making it's way down, made a dazzling display of light on the glass and steel Fenix campus. But Lauren's mind was back in the pitch black lobby of R&D. That same fear gripped her. Fear of her attackers, and this time, even of her guardians. A fear of the unknown that lay before her. As she crossed the garden toward the garage, she began to second guess herself. Originally, she planned to message the DCI and call off the protective service. But going to A228 might be a terrible idea. A trap of some sort. She couldn't know for sure, so why risk it? For someone in her position, it really made no sense. Yes, Rubger had been convincing, but so are the best con-artists, and for that matter, the best serial killers... She shuddered at the thought. Rubger was not a killer. At least, she thought he wasn't. But he didn't have to be one for her to want to avoid him.

Her PAV came to a hover about fifty meters ahead of her. Location sensors in her Personal had recognized her walk to the garage and brought it over. She eyed it suspiciously. If she called off the guards, could the DCI still track her? She had assumed going to the terminal in her PAV was safer than the Diama, but maybe she shouldn't have. Then again, that would probably be crossing legal boundaries, but her paranoia wasn't going to sway under such considerations.

She reached the launch pad and the PAV, recognizing her Personal, opened its doors. She stepped inside, placed herself in the centered pilot seat and strapped in. The door closed behind her, and then there was silence.

Normally, this was the point where she would tell her PAV where to take her, and it would chart a course and take off. The problem was, she wasn't sure where she was going. The Diama station was sounding less and less appealing, but what were the other options? If she went home as expected, she would grow restless, regardless of the thoroughness of the DCI updates.

There were too many thoughts crowding her mind—too many possible scenarios. She looked out the window at the campus in front of her. A slight breeze shook the trees, sending a few leaves into the air. To her right, there was a narrow creek that she had crossed on the way over. Only now did she notice just how delicately the sun reflected off the current. It was a wonderful place to work. Her eyes drifted to the large glass panels of the main hall, and she watched dozens of employees strolling in groups of two or three. There was a slow trickle out of the exits as the day reached its end, some heading for the campus Diama, others for similar PAV launch pads. Everyone, regardless of the level of rumors, was going on with their lives.

Lauren closed her eyes and listened to the beat of her heart. It was slowing now, her mind clearing. What would happen if she went home? Nothing within her control. She would be safe, but helpless. And if she went to the Diama station? Maybe, just maybe, something good.

"Take me to Diama terminal A228."

"Of course, ma'am."

There was the gentle bump of elevation, and she was on her way.

8. Revelations

Stewart hadn't noticed their stop when he heard a door opening. Jason and Jacqueline took their places on either side of him, and he used their arms to help himself up. As his journey to the door began, he realized that even though he felt no pain, he did feel a bit dizzy—akin to a slight inebriation—and was thankful for his stabilization crew.

Passing under the archway, he saw the front chamber of the PAV. There was a cockpit about five meters ahead, accessible from either side but with a wall directly in front of him. On either side, the large doors butterflied up and out, and the edge of the floor sunk down into two stairs. Ethan and the man and woman he did not know had already left—Michelle and a robot were waiting for them outside the left door.

Jacqueline gave him a nudge, and they made their way to the stairs. The opening was wide enough for Jason and Jacqueline to walk down next to him, helping him take each step slowly to the ground.

Michelle watched their progress. "Ethan is sending a wheelchair."

For a moment, Stewart was going to protest, but he realized it had been a painfully slow three steps down. It was for the best.

They waited in a group by the PAV, and Stewart took in the surroundings. They were on a launch pad about ten to fifteen meters up. A path attached to the pad led into a large, three-story complex. The building itself was a large circle, with other launch pads flaring out of it at regular intervals like spokes on a wheel. It had to be at least a hundred meters in diameter, the size of a small stadium. At first glance, Stewart guessed there to be at least thirty units here, more if they were not multiple stories.

Michelle brought context to the sights. "This is the local Legislative house. Four Senators live here, along with another forty to fifty advisors."

Stewart turned to her and noticed a hint of anxiety in her demeanor. Was something wrong? The door at the end of the path opened, and a robot with a wheelchair came towards them. He tried to shrug it off. He probably didn't want to know, anyways.

Jason met the robot a few steps from the group and brought the wheelchair over, behind Stewart. As he sat, Jason spoke.

"Okay, when we cross this path, we will go in two groups. Stewart, you'll come with me and Laskin's robot. Jacqueline, Michelle and our robot will escort you."

This seemed odd. He looked to his wife, who was just as confused.

"Whatever you do, do not get out of the chair. Jacqueline, you need to try to keep an even pace and a straight line. And both of you, please do not speak until you are inside and the door is closed behind you. Understand?"

Stewart understood. They were on public, surveilled ground. His image and voice were active targets for the DCI's eyes and ears. Apparently his wife's as well. With all that that meant, he truly hoped this would be the last stop in their journey.

Jason pushed him forward and they were out from under the shade of the PAV door. The robot that had brought the wheelchair walked sideways, leaning over Stewart, effectively shielding his face. This was definitely going to bring attention, he thought. About ten meters in, the robot quickened its pace, and maintaining its lean over Stewart, looped around the front of the moving chair. Jason, he noted, was doing a surprisingly good job of keeping them at a uniform speed. The door was a few meters away. He wanted to turn around, see if Jacqueline was also being blocked so awkwardly. How was this not going to set off any alarms? Oh well, he thought, I have no choice at this point.

About a meter from the entrance, he heard the door open and the robot stopped in his tracks while they continued inside. What a bizarre dance. Jason stopped them almost immediately and they waited for the second group. Stewart turned in time to see Michelle lead his wife in, their robot presumably also left outside. He looked up to Jason who put his hand up. The robots came in, the door closed behind them, and the hand went down. He let out a sigh, and Stewart could see the tension exit his body. No wonder Michelle had been anxious.

"Are we safe now?"

"Yes, perfectly."

"Would you know if they identified us?"

"No, but I would trust the precision of our robots."

"Won't that set off any alarms? The leaning and everything?"

"Very unlikely, unless Laskin is already under surveillance. The DCI is large, but they don't have the manpower or the computing power to watch or analyze every camera all the time. Your faces would have triggered something, but not the robots blocking the view. In the end, this was less risky than attempting a landing on the edge of the path, which might alert nearby tenants along with the camera system."

Stewart nodded. They were now in what looked to be a trapezoidal waiting room, about ten meters long and tapering from ten meters where they came in to eight on the other end. The walls along the side had two sofas each with a door in between, and the narrower end had a third door between two little gardens of shrubs and flowers jutting out of the wall. Shades of blue and green dominated the interior, except for a wood floor. All in all, it was much more homey than 'home' had been.

Just as he started to wonder if they were waiting for someone, the door on the right wall opened, and a medical bot stood on the other side.

"Please, come this way."

Jason pushed Stewart through the door into another room of the same shape but a few meters narrower. A long, dark gray table with about a dozen chairs occupied the middle. There were three doors here, in the same places as the last room except for where the PAV launch pad would be. Dark purple replaced the blues and greens of the waiting room, complemented with hints of the table's gray throughout. It was a very modern and colorful place, and Stewart was rather impressed. Before he had time to inspect the dining room further, Jason wheeled him right behind the robot, around the table and through the door on the other side.

They were in the kitchen now, roughly the same size as the last room but with three major differences. First, the wall to his right, toward the outside wall of the building, was a good four meters closer. Second, there was no door across from them, they had probably reached one side of the unit. Third, and most noticeably, the narrow end did not have a wall—it opened up into what looked like a small hallway, where all the other narrow end doors had led. He was trying to get a good look at that hallway when they turned through a door on the right.

For a moment, Stewart was stunned by the jarring transition. For all he knew, they could have transported into a hospital. Medical and surgical equipment lined the walls and filled the shelves. Bright white mixed with the sheen of stainless steel, and there was a faint hint of disinfectant.

"I need you to lay here on your back. Would you like any assistance?"

The medical bot gestured to an examination table in the center. Only then did Stewart notice Michelle and the other robot had not come with them, although probably for the best: there was not as much room here, and even with Jason, Jacqueline, and the robot it was almost crowded.

"No, thank you." He stood slowly, and looked to Jason. "What is this place?"

"This is a medical pod. Every Senator has one. Their ability to make rational decisions is rather dependent on their health, so all Senatorial living spaces include one. In the case of emergency, it jettisons to the nearest hospital—hence the smaller size and being on the outer wall."

Stewart lay back on the table and took another look at the equipment all around him.

"So this is all public property?"

Jason nodded. "Technically yes. The entire home is public property. Laskin will have to vacate the premises when his term is up. Of course, anything that is his own, he will keep."

A large rectangular block came down slowly from the ceiling above Stewart's head and the robot turned toward him.

"Please keep still."

He did as he was told, and the rectangle gave out a hum, working its way down his body about half a meter above him. It did three slow passes up and down before returning to the ceiling.

"One herniated disc and significant lumbar muscle strain evident, both incurred by blunt force trauma approximately three hours ago. Mild concussion approximately thirty minutes ago. Blood sugar very low. Recommend significant rest, specifically of the back, for at least a week. The medication you were given ten minutes ago also boosted your glycogen but you will need more."

At this last sentence, the medical bot went over to a small rectangular protrusion on the wall. It placed its finger in a connection, and with a small green light and a quick chime, it transferred the proper medical contents into the robot's digit.

Stewart ignored its movements, focusing on the herniated disc. "Is rest going to be enough?"

The robot answered him as it came over next to the table. "In most cases yes. If you reject my treatment plan and remain active, you may need minor surgery."

Its finger pricked into Stewart's arm, but he didn't feel it. Rest was fine by him. That's all he wanted right now. To be home and relax.

The front half of the table began to lift, raising Stewart's upper body. He looked at Jacqueline. She seemed a rather worried by the robot's diagnosis. She could also use some rest, he thought. It was a shame she had to be dragged into this with him. At least he was the one with injuries.

When the table had finished its movement, Jason put out his arm for support.

"Let's get you back in the chair and take you over to a couch or bed."

He turned, taking his back off the surface and swinging his legs off the edge. With this newfound knowledge, even sitting like this made him nervous. He took Jason's arm and transitioned into the wheelchair as carefully as possible. Despite the robot's prognosis, a herniated disc sounded pretty bad in Stewart's mind. The only major impact that occurred three hours ago was his fall into the trench. He wondered how much the subsequent air-bike rides had exacerbated the problem.

The door back to the kitchen slid open and they wheeled out, Stewart in the lead. Black countertops contrasted sharply with the warm white floors, and the dark gray from the living room accented their surroundings. They passed between a large island and countertop and Stewart noticed specks of food, a dirty plate near the sink, and a pot still on a stove. This surprised him, as most people with advanced robots could get away with having the machines cook. This also pleased him, as he respected someone who could cook his own food. His mind drifted to the scent of roast turkey and tomato soup..

"Where is everyone else?" His wonderfully talented wife asked.

"Right across here in the living room. We're going there now."

They had reached the hallway now, and Stewart realized he could hear Ethan's voice, along with a few others. On his right were three doors along the wall, and on his left was a shorter wall with two doors—the first to the dining room, and the second to the waiting room. The walls opened slightly to the left up ahead into what had to be the living room.

When they rounded the corner, he absorbed it all at once. The space was grand, the size of the dining room and kitchen combined, and took the warm white with dark gray and injected a few doses of the blue and green from the waiting room. The right side wall was covered entirely in vines, and the first meter or so of floor was a garden of dense flowers. An impressive window covered almost the entire far wall, and in the middle of the room, three large sofas formed a wide semi-circle facing the view. At each end of this semi-circle was a chair, pushed somewhat inwards and turned in towards the middle. In one of these chairs, stopping his discussion and looking up towards them, was Senator Laskin.

- - -

There was a click as she pressed the lock button on her Personal, and the screen went black. But Lauren continued to stare at it. What had she done? Her message to the DCI was now on its way: please remove the protective service. She tried to reign in her growing fear. As far as the station went, there would be active cameras everywhere, but even that did not give her solace. Every so often, there would still be a random act of violence, despite the level of day-to-day surveillance. True, most of these acts were almost immediately stopped by robots or the DCI, but every once in a while, maybe three or four times a year, there would be a murder in public.

She trembled. Why was she thinking about these things? If anything she would be a target for kidnapping more than assassination. And what of her original thought process? What if Rubger wasn't faking anything? This truly piqued her curiosity. What could be so urgent, yet so secret?

Her PAV had made a little over half of the journey, and a small timer on the dash read nine minutes and twenty-six seconds. Despite the stress she was under, she realized this had been the only time other than lunch where she was given some peace and quiet since the attack. She thought back to the employees leaving work, and wondered what would happen if they never found the recovery disks. Were the prototypes still an option? The agent in the Chairman's office hadn't mentioned anything about any progress being made with them, or with the roboticists examining their robots. And what of the BRA insider? Maybe they had found something and sent her updates—she had a constantly expanding folder of information on the investigation from the DCI, but she did not bother to check it. Those other Fenix employees had it right. If the recovery disks weren't found, life would go on. It would be difficult, it would be painful, but it would go on. How long might it take to restart a project like Bluestone? The scientists in R&D could answer that question better, although she was sure the answer would not be ideal. The real question was whether the company could overcome such a loss, and whether it could amass the resources for another try. Frankly, she would rather face whatever was at A228 than the answer to that question.

- - -

Even though he knew they were going to his house, even though he had been told that he was a part of their movement, Stewart was still surprised to see Laskin. He was an older man, and in Stewart's mind, embodied the image of a Legislative Senator. His words were carefully chosen, his tone calm but potent. Here in his home, outside the public eye, Stewart saw that he was no different. The way he looked up at them, then stood, projected the self-assured presence of experience.

"Welcome, friends. Please, Jason, have a seat." He gestured to the couch in the middle. "Stewart." Their eyes met and Laskin paused, the slightest of frowns breaking his composure. Stewart saw the undertone of guilt in his gaze—the same guilt he saw from Mina and Lucas—and, before he had even said a dozen words, Laskin no longer seemed to be some strange figure of authority; he was an equal, and he was working to earn Stewart's favor.

"I am so sorry for everything that you have gone through. They have not told me your whole story yet, but the wheelchair speaks for itself. Please, this couch is for you." He gestured to the empty couch on the right. "Mrs. Anders, my apology extends to you as well. Please have a seat next to your husband, and we can begin to tackle what must be the most pressing issue on your minds: getting out of this mess."

Ethan, Michelle, and the others were spread out on the other two couches. Jason pushed him towards the empty one.

"Medic, what was the prognosis?"

The house answered—Stewart realized the robots must be synced with the unit itself. "One herniated disc and significant lumbar muscle strain. Blood sugar very low. Recommend significant rest, specifically of the back, for at least a week. Glycogen has been boosted and pain has been reduced by two doses of medication."

Another slight frown. They rounded the chair at the far end and Michelle came across to help Jason. Stewart took Jason's hand to pull himself up out of the chair and lower himself down onto the couch. He turned, bringing his feet up and laying his head down near the chair where Jacqueline was about to sit. As soon as he had finished, Michelle and Jason went over to the couch, and Jacqueline sat. Laskin stood for another moment, glanced at each of them as if to make sure all was in order, then took a seat.

"Tell me, are you two aware of the nature of your involvement? Have you been told about the blank Personal and the data transfer?"

The couple nodded. "Yes."

"Of course. As you have heard, your Personal now bears the incriminating log of the outgoing packet. The statistics are stacked against you. If I may be frank, up until the evacuation, we had no idea how we were going to get you back home safely. Any attempt to contact the DCI would lead to our immediate unmasking. Fate, however, seems to have favored you."

He paused, and Stewart raised his head a bit. "What do you mean?"

"Mina. She will explain your entire situation to them, I guarantee it. As soon as they have finished questioning her, she will be transferred to the Courts. This transfer notice should be public, at which point you will be free to go."

Stewart was overtaken with a bittersweet mixture of relief and guilt. Their ordeal was almost over, but at what cost?

Laskin noticed his expression and put out a reassuring hand. "Please, don't dwell on her capture. It was her decision and we support it. She is alive and well, and at most she will have to deal with a slightly less private life. It is a price worth paying for two people's absolution."

Jacqueline, whose irritation with Michelle now seemed to be directed at the entire group, answered with a tone hinting at her growing frustration.

"Senator, if I may be so blunt, why was it so important for you to have captured us in the first place? We've been told, over and over, about the blank Personal. The evidence. What of it? Even on the off-chance they never discovered the truth, it sounds like the worst that would happen is a slap on the wrist. So what?"

It dawned on Stewart that she was blaming them for his injuries, and after the recent visit with the medical bot, was on the verge of a breaking point. The Senator met her electric gaze with calm but well-chosen words.

"Your query is justified, of course. But I have over-simplified Mina's fate. In the end, it comes down to your right to privacy. Mina's life will never be as it once was, and not just due to her unusual circumstances. Even if she had had a Personal and the digital trail that comes with it, things would be different starting today. A file has been created on her person in the DCI and the Courts. There is now at least one robot and probably a human assigned to that file for the remainder of her life. All of her purchases, all of her messages, all of her movements across this Earth are being analyzed by and relayed to DCI's vast monitoring system. No, the humans won't look at everything, but that's not really the point, is it? The authorities now have the power to interpret her every decision and potentially punish her based solely on that interpretation. The door for potential abuse has been opened, and it cannot be shut."

Jacqueline pondered his assessment with a light nod. Stewart noticed she seemed at least a bit more convinced, but knew she had more to say.

"Okay, I can see the potential for abuse but in reality isn't it just that? Potential?"

Laskin shook his head.

"Unfortunately, no. There are safeguards, of course. The Courts are always watching the DCI, and a good deal of the reverse happens as well. Assignment selection is randomized, but corruption can't be completely removed. How do you think the Ting Affair came about? If there is enough motive, many safeguards lose their power. Granted, we have but a percent of the problems present before the Initiative, but they exist nonetheless. More to the point, if there was a case on par with the Ting case, this would be it. The destruction of robotic altruism will rustle quite a few feathers, and the DCI may even be forced to provide a robotic escort for Mina's protection."

Jacqueline's eyes widened. "You believe she is in danger?"

The Senator looked at her intently for a moment then turned his attention to the large window on the far wall. His reply was quieter, carrying more weight than his earlier speech.

"We all are."

Jacqueline seemed to accept this explanation, and waited for him to speak once more. With his eyes still focused on the view of Houston, he continued.

"There is one last favor we must ask of you. Mina will exonerate you, but that does not mean the DCI will ignore you. You have been under our care for a good four hours and have interacted with a good number of our operatives. They may not know the extent of your knowledge, but they know that it is worth investigating. We have chosen the path of honesty and disclosure out of respect and goodwill. Our final request is that you honor our operation, whether you agree with it or not, and maintain our secrecy. We do not ask that you lie to the DCI—in fact, we strongly recommend against it, as this may lead to perjury charges. However, we do ask that you refuse to answer questions that would jeopardize our identities, or the identities of other operatives."

Stewart nodded awkwardly. He was taken aback by the level of respect he was receiving from this top-ranking official, and didn't quite know how to react.

"Of—of course."

Laskin gave a small smile, turning his attention back towards them. "Thank you. Now, is there anything else I can do for either of you?"

Stewart looked to his wife, who seemed equally surprised by the nature of the interaction. Before she said anything, he realized he did have a question for the Senator.

"I have to ask you, sir, why you are doing this? Why are you trying to stop robotic evolution?"

He smiled again, and thought for a moment before responding.

"That is a complex question with a complex answer. But, since I am asking you to protect us, I am obligated to argue our case. Understand that this operation has one key objective: preventing the strong artificial intelligence horizon. Fenix, as you may know, was on the verge of robotic altruism. Now this is not the same as strong AI. Strong AI is human or superhuman level intelligence. Robotic altruism is the programmed desire to help humankind. Based on this distinction, you may be wondering why we targeted Bluestone at all—are you aware what Bluestone is?"

"Their project."

"Yes. Now, if Bluestone was an altruism project, and we are targeting strong AI, why did we wipe Bluestone? The answer is quite simple: altruism and strong AI go hand-in-hand. This is not to say that one leads to the other, or that one even requires the other—they are very much separate concepts. However, since the days of the Revolution, when strong AI was first hinted at, these two ideas required integration. Any work on strong AI had to include robotic altruism. It's true that this was the letter of the law, but that wasn't what was important. Any roboticist at a high enough level to be tinkering with these concepts knew the importance of their combination, and it was more of an unwritten necessity than a legal constraint. Which leads us back to Bluestone. Fenix was on the verge of robotic altruism and, as far as our evidence could indicate, strong AI as well."

Jacqueline interjected. "How could you know? What separates the most sophisticated robots today from those Fenix was working on? In fact, what defines this horizon? How do we know when we have reached human-level intelligence?"

The Senator put up a hand to stop her, smiling. "Please, one at a time. Each of those questions is equally complicated."

She bowed her head a bit in embarrassment. "Sorry... What defines the horizon?"

Laskin turned toward the couch on his right. "Ethan?"

Ethan looked at the Senator and then to Jacqueline. "As you might guess, there is no well-defined boundary for strong AI. In the end, it comes down to your definition of intelligence. By some measures, robots have long since surpassed us. This is particularly true if you base your definition of intelligence on reasoning ability. Even before the Revolution, robots were able to reason. The ability to come to logical conclusions, to plan, to learn; all of these things have always been in robotic programming. Modern robots have no trouble learning languages on their own or making sophisticated and spontaneous decisions regarding their tasks. Thus, if you were to define intelligence strictly in terms of reasoning, the strong AI horizon has come and gone."

He paused, then shook his head.

"Well, that's not entirely true. If we are being exact, then some forms of reasoning are still beyond a robot's capabilities. And this leads to the now commonly accepted definition of strong AI, where the focus is on the 'human' in human-level intelligence. Among the characteristics within this definition are self-awareness, sentience, and consciousness. This is why some forms of reasoning are still unattainable—without true consciousness, robots cannot fully mimic human levels of intelligence. Human intelligence is the whole package. Morality based on logical reasoning is not the same as morality based on emotional reasoning. Does that make sense?"

Jacqueline nodded.

"So in that sense, the horizon has not yet been reached. Fenix, however, was on its way."

She cocked her head a bit. "Are you saying Bluestone was going to make robots with a conscience?"

"Theoretically, yes."

"How?"

Ethan looked back to Laskin, who answered.

"With an ingenious solution. Not in the creative sense—the idea has been around for quite some time—but in its application. They were basically copying the human brain. Instead of a cerebral unit full of processors, they pumped it full of artificial neurons. This approach had never worked before because technology could never quite match nature. How does one come up with a programming language for neurons? For lack of a better analogy, Fenix has been playing god.

"But we have digressed from the original question. You asked why we are doing this—or more precisely why I am doing this, although the answer is the same: to protect us, to protect mankind. Strong AI comes through robot consciousness, and robot consciousness is a dangerous prospect. This is where the argument for robotic altruism comes in, but I simply refuse to consider that a viable solution. Robotic altruism is supposed to be constrictive programming on a robot's conscience. The idea is that if we can control how they reason rationally, we should be able to control how they reason emotionally. But what if we are wrong? After all, these conscious robots will have reasoning capabilities well beyond our own. We cannot claim to know where such intelligence will lead them, nor can we claim to program for every possible contingency. Even now, roboticists are surprised by robots' versatility and ingenuity. They are designed to go beyond their original programming. What happens when we add emotional sentience to the mix? It is not a risk worth taking."

It was a much more thorough and accurate argument than mass euthanization, but the message was the same. The fact that it was the Senator saying it made it all the more convincing—he had been a leading roboticist before his tenure in office, as was prerequisite for any member of the Robotics Committee, let alone the Chair. If Stewart had been on the fence earlier, he was starting to climb down on the other side.

Laskin smiled. "Now, I have my computers watching for the transfer notice—it should come up within the hour. Until then, we are at your service." He gestured to the rest of the group. "If you don't mind, we need to discuss a good deal of business regarding the operation and the evacuation. Can we get you anything beforehand?"

Jacqueline looked at her husband. "Some water, please."

The Senator looked over to the hallway, where a robot was standing, and nodded. It disappeared back towards the kitchen. He turned back to Ethan.

"Please continue."

- - -

Her PAV broke the Canopy and made its way toward a small launch pad off the side of the station. She peered downward out of the window, trying to discern any threats in the vicinity. It was a silly endeavor, but it gave her something to do.

A228 was somewhere near the western edge of the A zone, about 60 kilometers from Fenix. It was a suburban, outer-city area, with the Diama at ground level. Lauren could see a school and a large park among the hundreds of homes dominating the landscape. As far as she knew, this must be where Rubger lived.

She was relieved to find a handful of people coming in and out of pods on a regular basis—the terminal was busy, public. Three or four robots walked along the platforms, helping riders and watching over the premises. It dawned on her, at that moment, that she had no idea what to do once she landed.

The PAV decelerated evenly, and a small chime announced their arrival. Some of her fear started to return, and her heartbeat ramped up a notch. She looked over to a large panel on her left that would open the left door, hesitating. Her eyes went back out the window, watching the comings and goings of the Diama passengers. What was she waiting for? Her hand pushed against the switch and there was a light whoosh as the door opened.

She stared at the pad right outside the door—the ground where her feet would soon step. I've come this far, she thought. Her heartbeat jumped again as she exited the PAV and stood on the pavement of the launch pad. What now?

Fear enveloped her for a split second as her peripheral vision caught someone heading her direction. She turned to see her would-be attacker— the embodiment of the monster she expected, her end and her doom. But when her eyes met the incoming threat, she almost laughed at herself. It was one of the robots, not doubt on its way to help her. She realized then just how on edge she was, and worried that a sudden noise would give her a heart attack.

Trying to compose herself, Lauren brushed off her outfit and walked across the path toward the station. She heard the PAV door closing, and waved at the robot coming towards her.

"No thank you!"

She smiled at the humanoid machine as she tried to yell to it, but it continued on its course. It wasn't its fault, she thought. The noise here was a bit high. Every few seconds a few pods would whoosh by, making things difficult to hear. But a small knot formed in her stomach, and the sense of foreboding was back. Something about the way this robot was walking toward her...

It would reach her in about twenty seconds, and there was nothing she could do. If she tried to run away, it would catch her in an instant. She stopped in her tracks, confused and a bit scared, wondering how the President of a robotics corporation could be afraid of a robot—a machine she knew from experience had absolutely no way to harm a human. Even if they could be manipulated to perform small crimes, hiding parts of a robot is a far cry from assault.

When it came within ten meters, she tensed instinctively. A little over a meter away, it stopped.

"Good evening ma'am. Please, come with me."

With that, it turned around, and started back down the path. Lauren watched it for a few moments before following. What was going on?

At the end of the path, the robot turned right instead of continuing towards the pods. She glanced over and saw about six more paths, all leading to other launch pads. Was it taking her to another PAV?

As she reached the end of the path from her launch pad, she saw the robot turn right, towards the fourth pad away, where a PAV was hovering in idle. Then it hit her—public land was surveilled, and her PAV was most likely traced. This was a way to get the DCI off her back... but did she really want that? She turned onto the path after the robot and realized her safety net depended on observation. In an unfamiliar PAV, she had no control over the situation. Now, more than before, she had reason to fear.

The robot reached the PAV and a side door slid open. Lauren had made it about halfway down the path but each step was slower than the last. Her previous dread had been for the most part unfounded, but this new state of affairs warranted hesitation. She noted, rather alarmingly, that the PAV's windows were shuttered. This was wrong. Coming here was a blunder, but this would be a catastrophe.

About ten meters from the PAV, she stopped. The robot remained beside the door, watching her. She wondered if that was the correct word —watching? It saw her, it recognized that she was there, and it maintained a visual hold on her. But did it understand that she was hesitating? And if it did, could it understand why?

She thought of Bluestone, and all its potential. Robots with human-level intelligence, with emotion, with morality. If this robot had been programmed with strong AI, it would surely know that she was hesitating. Would it be reacting now, instead of just standing there, waiting?

Lauren's thoughts were put on hold as the PAV rotated, bringing the open door in her direction. Inside, sitting in the far passenger seat and looking straight at her, was Rubger. Even though she had been expecting to find him here, she was still surprised. He smiled at her, but she could see a dash of anxiety in his expression. The fact that he was not exiting the vehicle, or for that matter even speaking to her, kept her locked firmly in place.

Realizing this, Rubger dropped the smile. But where Lauren expected anger, she saw despair. He gestured for her to come, almost begging. She was about to speak to him when he flashed a shush signal. What was going on? If the DCI was watching her they would already know she was here. What was he worried about?

He looked at her helplessly, gesturing for her to come once more. And even though she really wanted to believe him, her small crush wasn't going to propel her toward a man she knew could be deceptive.

When his second entreaty did not work, determination took place of desperation, and Rubger stood, walking over to the back wall of the PAV. Lauren watched with curiosity as he opened a panel, causing a small shelf to slide out. He picked up a small object from the inside, and turned toward her, lifting it up so she could see.

In his hand, unmistakable due to their unique design and dimension, was a Bluestone recovery disk.

- - -

At first, Stewart had tried to pay attention to the proceedings going on in front of him, but the woozy sensation of the medication was deteriorating his focus. Ethan was going through the events that had brought them there, along with some details that went over Stewart's head. There was talk of alibis for each respective employment situation, and some words were shared regarding the fate of the PAV network in the air. One thing did catch his attention—their air-bikes had apparently self-destructed upon their evacuation to destroy all forensic evidence, and he wondered absentmindedly if the DCI agents were harmed in this process.

Every once in a while Jacqueline would get up from her seat, come over to him, and help him sip some water. This recurring dance was the only thing keeping him awake, and hardly at that. He wondered how much she was listening—maybe beyond the haze of his drugs, the conversation was actually quite interesting. But he didn't mind relaxing. It was about damn time.

Stewart felt his eyelids closing, and thought of his interrupted nap in the green room back at the node. It was difficult to register just how much he had been through that day. Mina, Lucas... would he ever see these people again? It was odd that a stranger he only knew for a few hours could have more of an impact than an acquaintance he'd known for years.

A light tap on his shoulder woke him up from his trance. Jacqueline was standing over him with some water. He reached for the glass but paused midway. The room was empty. Had he fallen asleep?

"What happened?"

Jacqueline went ahead and pushed the glass into his hovering hand.

"They finished their discussion and left. Laskin excused himself to his study and left us in the hands of his robots."

"How long was I asleep?"

"I don't know, maybe fifteen minutes?"

Between his exhaustion and the medication, he had not even noticed.

"What did they talk about?"

She raised her eyebrows.

"Quite a bit. Did you know they had a guy in the BRA as well? There are a lot of people involved in this."

"Yes there were." Laskin's reply drew their attention to the hallway where he stood. "My apologies for the disappearance, there were a few Legislative duties to attend to."

Stewart watched him walk back towards his chair.

"Is everyone else gone?"

He nodded. "Yes, either back to work or home."

Stewart thought back to Lucas's departure, and Michelle's reluctance to divulge his employer. He felt relief for a moment, thinking that his captor had managed to avoid all of the evacuation action, but relief soon turned to concern.

"What happened to Lucas?"

"Lucas Roberts? He is currently at work."

"Weren't the DCI watching the node?" He paused, and his concern turned into dread. "In fact, didn't Mina say the two men in the park could have been agents? They would have seen Lucas!"

Laskin put out a reassuring hand once more.

"Please, don't worry. It's true, those two men could have been agents, but most likely, his air-bike was tracked by the DCI watching our node. If he has been identified, there's not much we can do about it. At the moment, however, he has not been apprehended."

"Where does he work?" Stewart remained curious.

Laskin smiled. "With me, in the Legislature. He is an associate robotics advisor."

This was starting to make sense. "The others too?"

"Most of them, yes. This operation was born in the Legislature."

"Born in the Legislature? What do you mean?"

He smiled once more. "It's a rather long story, although I can't blame your curiosity. Let me ask you something—are you aware of the Robotic Assembly Proposal?"

Stewart shook his head.

"It refers to the idea of replacing the Legislature with a robotic entity. You may have heard it under a different label."

This time Stewart nodded. There had been talk of a robotic legislature since he was growing up, but the public would never allow it. Let the robots make decisions for us? Not a chance.

"Well as you no doubt know that idea has been rejected enough times to make one wonder why it keeps coming back in the first place. What most people don't realize, however, was that it was a key provision of the original Earth Initiative. This was when pro-robot sentiment was at a peak. Decades of corruption and bureaucracy were being eradicated in a matter of months, why leave out the parliamentary systems? Representatives were constantly being bought, if not outright then subtly. Their vices slipped into messy works of law that made many citizens of many countries disgusted with their decisions. Robots, on the other hand, had proven themselves clear of influence."

Stewart interrupted him. "But couldn't a robot be programmed to make decisions in a certain manner?"

"Undoubtedly, but the cerebral scanning would catch these inconsistencies. Without the scanning, your argument would apply to any robot involved in the Earth Initiative."

Of course, he thought. One of the key reasons why the Initiative had succeeded in the first place was the cerebral scanning system, which amounted to an almost infinitely redundant check on every robot's programming. Somewhere along the line between the Revolution and the Initiative, robots had started to use cerebral units. There were many reasons for this standardization, but one of the remarkable results was cerebral scanning—where any robot could quickly analyze another robot's code wirelessly. If another robot detected malicious or simply unusual programming, it would be obligated to alert the BRA (or at that time, the appropriate authorities) immediately. Any attempts to hide or protect code would leave a trace and set off a similar alarm. At first, this process occurred automatically, any time robots were in relative proximity. Now, every robot ever created was always analyzing some other robot's code over the Cloud. To be sure, there were a few inconsistencies—such as older models not understanding some new programming, or deceptive programming masquerading as regular code—but that was what the BRA did on a regular basis: analyze the scan data for the world's robotic population. This was what kept robots clear of influence, as the Senator put it, and what made them so popular at the time of the Initiative.

"Now, proponents argued about the fairness of a robot legislature, the lack of bias, and so on, but they missed a key point. What happened when robots reached human-level intelligence? At the time, as it has been for the last century, strong AI seemed to be right around the corner. There was a small group of people, members of what would eventually become the

Earth Legislature, that opposed the use of a Robotic Assembly on the grounds of humanity's control over its own destiny. In fairness to the proponents, the Assembly would be the least of our concerns if the robots decided to turn against us, but even the idea of benevolent machines controlling our laws was too much for some to swallow. Eventually, the human Legislature won out, and the Assembly Proposal was left to resurface every few years.

"That small group, that opposition—that is where this operation comes from. The more United Robotics and the BRA gained power, the more our predecessors realized that the public was not going to stop the oncoming strong AI horizon. They had dodged a bullet with the Assembly, but the main problem had not been addressed. Eventually, human-level intelligence would be developed. Since then, they, and now we, have been doing what we can to stop it."

And there it was. Stewart imagined a contingent of puppet-masters, driving the events of robotics history. But that wasn't right—they were the minority. They did what they could in secret.

"Does this stuff happen often?" He had gotten a glimpse into a covert world and wanted to digest every bit of information.

Laskin gave him a half smile of surprise. "Often? Not at all. This operation is by far our largest, most concentrated effort. After all, the horizon was finally coming, most of our time before was spent waiting."

Jacqueline entered the discussion. "But how could you know?"

"That it was real this time? We've had friends in the BRA and every major robotics corporation for years. Whispers turned into talk, and talk turned into evidence. We had a vague action plan for an event like this, but as you can expect, every detail needs to be considered. It's been a long four years, but we succeeded. Towards the end, Fenix had been making serious progress, and we almost had to blow our cover, but that crisis was avoided."

"What do you mean?"

"Well, as my associates may have explained, our operation hinged on computer access. Yes, we were taking hardware out and removing prototype models, but we needed a massive Cloud-based infiltration which could not be predicted. In fact, we had been ready to go for almost two years now, but today was the day an insecure link let us through. The problem was, what if that insecure link didn't show? How close do we let Fenix get before we do something drastic? We would have certainly been able to pull it off with our insider agents, but I doubt any of them would have been able to escape punishment."

Stewart cringed at the thought of Mina's capture. All of this elaborate planning and execution, and yet something fundamental remained unanswered. Jason had given him some vague remarks, but nothing substantial.

"But what happens when the next company gets close? Or if Fenix recovers?"

The Senator sighed, falling back a bit into his chair.

"That is the real question, isn't it? If robotics research is allowed to progress, the horizon is inevitable. But one thing has changed drastically since the days of the Initiative. Public opinion of robots is at an all-time low. We've accepted their usefulness, we allow them to run our infrastructure, but people are starting to realize just how scary a robot with a conscience can be. Does the average person think robotic altruism can work? No. Friendly AI was easy. Making robots incapable of harm, make them always willing to help humans—not a problem for a machine based on cold, hard programming. But add emotions? Ethics? Principles? How can these things be constrained? There is an easy example to reference: us. How often have attempts to direct human emotions worked? How often has that gone according to plan?"

Laskin seemed lost in his own thoughts for a moment, then looked back at the couple.

"The point being, we just need to hold out a little bit longer. It may be a losing battle, but I think we stand a chance. At least for now."

- - -

Lauren eyed Rubger warily. He had dealt his hand, no doubt, but was that supposed to make her trust him? All she knew was that he had a recovery disk, which led to a great many hypotheses, but only one conclusion: that he was somehow connected to the attack.

Her heart raced at the sight of the hardware. She had been waiting in her Chairman's office for hours, hoping the DCI would find one, and here she was, two steps ahead of them. The question was, what now?

Their stalemate held for a few seconds before Rubger lowered the disk, still looking straight at her. The plea in his eyes had not diminished, but with each failure, his resolve decreased. If only she could trust him...

He turned to the robot and spoke a few soft words, lifting the disk in its direction. The robot turned, grabbed the disk, and proceeded to make its way over to Lauren. It stopped in front of her, and stretched the disk out in its hand.

For a few seconds, Lauren stood there without moving. She stared at the object being offered to her and tried to comprehend how this was happening, why this was happening. Did she miss something? Was this a trick?

"You may take this to your PAV, if you wish, and send it back as collateral. I need to speak with you."

The words came from the robot, but they belonged to Rubger. She looked over its shoulder into the PAV, where he was still standing anxiously. Her eyes returned to the disk, and she reached her hand out to take it.

There was no hesitation, no ruse. The robot let go of the disk, and it was now in her hands. Having fulfilled its orders, it dropped its arm, turned around, and walked straight back to its original position. But Lauren didn't notice it leave - she didn't notice anything at all except the object in her palm.

She turned it over in her hands, feeling its weight. It was about fifteen centimeters long and four wide, with a small ramp in the middle, making one side about two centimeters taller than the other. Most of the disk was dark gray, but along the right side, etched in glowing sapphire, was the word BLUESTONE. Underneath, in smaller, black lettering, was written Fenix Corporation. While she had seen these disks before, sitting comfortably in R&D, she had never been this close; the level of detail surprised her.

The whoosh of a pod broke her hypnosis, and she looked back up to Rubger. A flurry of questions went through her mind. Was everything still on the disk? They were meant to be unalterable, but she wasn't going to put anything past the realm of possibility. After all, they had to be updated, and that counts as alteration. Should she simply leave with the disk? Maybe cutting her losses was a good idea at this point, given the circumstances. But what was it that Rubger wanted to tell her?

Lauren turned around and started walking back to her PAV. Two possibilities came to mind: either Rubger was deceiving her straight into a trap, or he was under some sort of duress that she was unaware of. After all, what would kidnapping her, or any form of extortion for that matter, add to the equation? She had contemplated the idea that they would ransom her fake backup, but that seemed too brazen for this attack. Not after their elaborate and effective attempts to conceal their identities. And murder? Sure, the primal fear was still there, but it was totally irrational. What purpose would that serve? Which led her to a reluctant deduction: it was, in all likelihood, not a trap.

As she approached down the path, her PAV recognized her Personal's presence and was awaiting instructions.

"Open door."

The door closest to her began to butterfly upwards. She glanced once more at the disk in her hand. Once there was enough room to squeeze in, she stepped inside the PAV. Paranoia took another brief hold, and she glanced behind her down the path. Nothing.

"Close door."

She scanned the various shelves in front of her and found the security drawer. A small button on the right side slid it right out - it was not locked at the moment. Her fingers ran along the contours of the disk in her hand, and she took the opportunity to analyze it once more. The whole situation was surreal, and it was still a surprise to see the disk here, now, in front of her. Especially like this.

It made a light clatter falling into the drawer. Another bit of hesitation, and Lauren closed

it.

"Secure drawer. Open by my Personal or Franklin Ross, with or without Personal."

There was the slide and click of a strong lock, along with a chime and green light to verify

instructions.

"Launch PAV in five minutes, to Fenix. What time is it?"

"16:40, ma'am."

"Notify Franklin Ross of arrival by message at 18:00."

She glanced one more time at the drawer, the small button next to it still glowing green. "Open door."

It was time to figure this out.

9. Betrayal

Rubger had closed his door in her absence, and the robot had disappeared, presumably back into the crowd. When Lauren reached her previous threshold, the door slid open. The look of relief on Rubger's face seemed so genuine that her fear almost washed away. Almost. There was the slightest pause right outside the vehicle, then she stepped inside.

The door slid shut behind her, and Rubger motioned for her to sit in one of the back passenger seats. He took the spot directly across from her, and looked at her intently. A gentle reassurance underlined his words.

"I understand your hesitation, but you are not in danger."

She gave a weak nod. Despite his tone, there was still anxiety in his demeanor, and it made her nervous.

"I'm going to set a course, but I can't yet tell you where. I want to ask you to trust me, and that nothing unfavorable will happen. However, if you do not feel comfortable taking this journey without knowing the destination, you may leave. I know it may seem paranoid, but I do not want to speak any more than I have to here at this station—I would rather explain things in transit."

It was a persuasive gesture, as usual, but was it genuine? She tried to stick to her earlier conclusion, and reminded herself that there was no reason for him to be lying.

"Okay."

He nodded. "Take us to destination four."

"Of course, sir."

Lauren felt the small surge of lift and started to ponder the nature of this trip from a

positive perspective. Assuming Rubger was being truthful, three questions came to mind: what did he have to share with her, where were they going, and why couldn't he tell her—yet?

After his order to the PAV, he hesitated, searching for the right words. She was beginning to think he was more nervous than she was.

"As you have probably concluded, I am part of the operation that occurred this morning." He looked at her, as if waiting for an acknowledgement, but Lauren stared at him blankly. "What you don't know is that, although it appears to be on the contrary, I am trying to save this company."

He paused again. She watched him carefully, but still said nothing.

"I have gone to great lengths to undo the maximum amount of damage that I can, and I

am now in a grave predicament." He caught her stare and held it. "Lauren, I need your help."

At that moment, something inside her clicked. A wall came down and she thought to herself, whatever is going on, for better or worse, I believe this man. She took a deep breath

before responding. "What's going on?"

Relief flashed across his face at her question, and he did not delay his answer.

"Quite a bit. That recovery disk I gave you? As you can guess, it was meant to be destroyed. And while you may be celebrating this change of events, I cannot. I know you probably think I should turn in my friends to the DCI and everything will be fine, but that is not even remotely true. First off, they are exactly that: friends, some of them very dear ones. The failure of this operation will bring them enough despair, I do not want them rounded up and punished. Then, of course, if they find out I was responsible..."

He looked around helplessly.

"But that's not all. What about my involvement from the DCI's perspective? Sure, I gave up a disk, but I was a knowing participant of a massive plot that could be classified as terroristic. An argument can be made that I won't be punished, but that's not the point. Most of the time, this information is not secret. People will know. Do you think the rest of the board would ever dream of keeping me at Fenix? And if I leave, who would take me?

188

"That being said, I stand by my original points. My fate is secondary, but the fate of the others... I do not know what to do."

Lauren attempted to digest all of this new information while Rubger reeled in his apprehension. He was breathing more quickly, and it did not help her disposition. This was a lot to throw at her at once.

"Alex, I'm trying to understand... You were part of the attack this morning?"

He nodded. "I was an inside agent. Not so much this morning as for the past six years." Six years!? She staggered at the revelation. But that was before Bluestone... Never mind,

she had more pressing questions.

"But you gave me a recovery disk. Why?"

He smiled as best as he could given his nerves.

"It feels a bit ironic saying this, but because it was the right thing to do."

She cocked her head to the side. "Ironic?"

"For years, I had been arguing the same reason for the opposite outcome: that stopping

the development of robotic altruism was the right thing to do. But things have changed."

"What changed? Why are you doing this?"

"I've seen the progress firsthand, Lauren. I've interacted with the prototypes myself. Mind

you, they were far from the final model, but there were hints, hints of an emotional intelligence. I used to think that such a robot would bring the downfall of mankind. Not anymore."

That wasn't a full answer to the question, but it would have to do for now. She tried to ignore her own curiosity and prevent a digression. After all, he was in the process of saving the company. The least she could do was focus on him.

"What about these friends? Are they waiting for the disk? What about the other disks?"

He shook his head. "I don't know about the other disks, but I see no reason why they didn't reach their intended destination..." He glanced up to her shamefully. "...incineration."

She winced, but held on to hope. All they needed was one.

"Do they know one is missing?"

"They know I took one. There were two agents tasked with the removal of the recovery

disks from the premises. The plan was to take the disks, connect them to special Portables, deactivate the tracking software, and leave. Before they got out, however, I took one of the disks from them."

"What did you tell them?"

"That the tracking software in that particular disk was still active. Board members can access that information, so they believed it, and I said I would handle it."

Lauren nodded. Part of her was still trying to grasp the consequences of what was happening. Things were maybe, just maybe, going her way.

Rubger continued, "This is where I need your help, Lauren. Your secret backup—does it exist?"

She froze at the question. Despite everything that had happened, red flags went up in her head. The DCI had warned her not to tell anyone for precisely this reason—inside agents. They had even prepared for the possibility of a board member being part of the operation, and Lauren was forced to admire their thoroughness. She had crashed through the wall of doubt between her and Rubger, but now part of it was rebuilt.

"Why would you ask that?"

Rubger frowned. "I understand that such a question raises suspicion, but let me explain. If your secret backup exists, then I am absolved on both counts. With the attack, it wouldn't have mattered if I had intervened. The outcome did not change. Not only that, but if you agree not to use the recovery disk I gave you, the DCI never has to know about our meeting here."

He looked her up and down, then sighed, leaning back in his chair.

"But I don't think that's true. I don't think there is another backup. Why else do you think I held onto the disk? As soon as you made the announcement, I knew it was too good to be true. The others did too—we called your bluff. That's why I came to your office. That's why I was in such a hurry to restart the program. I wanted it to be true, I wanted the weight off my shoulders. If there is a secret backup, then I may have betrayed my friends, but it would not matter. Not as much, at least."

Shaking his head, Rubger contemplated the gravity of everything he had done.

"If I'm right, and there is no other backup, then I have a serious problem. Granted, there is still a chance to sell the story of the secret backup publicly, but what about the DCI? I don't know what to do."

Lauren took a moment to process everything Rubger was telling her. Even though she wanted to help, she was not going to divulge information regarding the veracity of the secret backup. But it wasn't too difficult to get around that obstacle.

"Alex. I understand this is a delicate situation, but I cannot ignore the acquisition of the recovery disk. We are going to use it, regardless of our other options. In this case, yes, it may be possible to publicly announce that we only used our final backup, but as you have pointed out, that is not the key problem.

"Try to understand the position you've put me in. I have to return to Fenix with a recovery disk. Questions will come barreling down on me immediately. Am I supposed to lie to the DCI? More importantly, am I supposed to lie to my company?"

Even the announcement she had made to facilitate a sting had been hard for her. Her generation, and the one before it, had been brought up with the principles of the Earth Initiative, foremost of which was honesty and trust. Small lies could ruin careers, and not just socially—legally too. Even circumventing the truth was a huge crime. The more power you had, politically or economically, the higher the punishment. In this way, robots acted as a sort of police force. Their omnipresence usually had them on the front lines of such scandals, and they would report them without prejudice. Obviously, lying had not stopped altogether—corruption and misconduct were all over the place, but they were becoming almost an art form, reserved for the highly skilled.

He nodded. "You're right, Lauren. I'm just desperate. I've fought for what I consider the greater good, and ended up putting myself in a corner."

Her wall was starting to fall again, and she watched his confessions with pity.

"Rubger, I don't know what to tell you. Surely the DCI will agree to a lighter sentence, given your actions. As for your career, well, you are saving Bluestone singlehandedly. Do not presume the board will ignore that fact."

He gave her a weak smile. "They may not, but trust is a pillar that, once broken, is seldom remade."

No matter how she might argue in his favor, Rubger was right. Given the circumstances, there was little to no doubt that he would be out of a job and ostracized not only from the robotics community but, to some degree, from society in general. It was a byproduct of the culture of honesty, as if once a liar meant always a liar.

"My fate is sealed, but there remains one loose end I must attend to."

Lauren gave him her full attention. His expression changed, clearly preparing to say something of great importance.

"Firstly, you have misplaced your efforts. Stewart Anders is innocent." Her lips parted, the words not quite sinking in.

"In— innocent?"

"Yes. In fact, he was not involved in the operation in any way. A supreme case of bad luck

brought him to your attention and unfortunately, by extension, brought us to your attention. This information will be corroborated by Mina, if it hasn't been already."

"Mina?"

"The woman you found at our node during its deconstruction. If you want the details on why he is innocent, just take a look at your next update from the DCI."

How could this be possible? Lauren remembered there being a mixup in the links, but she did not believe what Rubger was telling her. Of all things, that would be quite a blow to the DCI's investigational prowess. They had the wrong man the whole time? But that didn't make sense either—why did he run, and why did he lead them to the base? The pieces of the puzzle simply did not fit.

"But Anders is not the loose end I was referring to. With Mina's testimony, he will be cleared of charges—I do not need to argue his case. What I need to talk about was the DCI's pursuit. I've been informed that aerial support was involved in the infiltration, and our best guess as to the DCI's ability to locate our node is that you traced Anders there. That being said, he had no Personal on him, or any other device for that matter. As far as I can tell, the air-bike he took in must have been followed. Am I right?"

For a good ten seconds, Lauren didn't answer. This was partially due to the nature of the question, but for the most part she was still trying to process the idea that Anders might be innocent.

"Why does this matter?"

Rubger sensed her agitation and put out a reassuring hand.

"I'm sorry, let me finish my conjecture before you decide to trust me. So let's assume that

the DCI tracked the air-bike to our node using some sort of aero-vehicle. That means that they were monitoring our site from the time the air-bike arrived until the time of their infiltration. Within that period of time, another air-bike left the site."

The lone passenger, Lauren thought. Lucas Roberts.

"It would be foolish to think the DCI would not follow this air-bike. I have to assume that they traced it and at some point identified the occupant. And that is my loose end. The identification of that occupant."

He looked at her with those pleading eyes again, and she wondered how much longer she could hold her composure.

"So now I'm in another corner. I want to ask you if you have identified my friend, but I cannot give you their name. Will you tell me if you know who I am talking about? Would you trust me enough to let me know that you have identified this person?"

She wrung her fingers nervously. Was this somehow another trap, a ploy for information?

"What would you do if it turned out to be who you thought? Warn them that the DCI was coming? At this point, it won't make a difference, will it?"

He sighed.

"Lauren, it's more complicated than that. He is not just my friend. He is my partner."

- - -

"Stewart?"

It was Jacqueline, her voice distant.

"Stewart?"

He opened his eyes and looked up at his wife standing by the couch. Again?

"Sweetie, Mina told them everything. We are free to go."

Stewart looked past her to see Laskin standing behind his chair with his robot.

"The transfer notice came in?"

The Senator nodded.

"Just now. We are preparing a PAV for your departure."

He looked at his wife once more.

"I feel asleep again?"

She smiled.

"You're surprised? Between all you've been through and that medication, it's a miracle you were awake for that discussion between naps."

"How long?"

She looked at Laskin.

"I don't know, about twenty minutes?"

"Yes, about that. Stewart, if you're ready, we will go ahead and get you back in a wheelchair."

Stewart nodded and slowly pushed himself upright while bringing his feet over the edge of the couch. Laskin made his way over and Jacqueline pulled up the chair. As they transferred him, the Senator began to explain their course of action.

"This PAV will take you to a surveillance-free zone and drop you off. The closest zone to your house is about five kilometers away, but it's not all that important—the DCI will intercept you regardless. If you'd like, we can drop you off closer to one of their buildings, but even then they will take you in by aero-vehicle."

Jacqueline let go of Stewart, allowing him to sit back in the chair, and looked up.

"Then why do you need to drop us off in a surveillance-free zone?"

"So they do not trace my PAV."

The robot opened the door to the waiting room and Jacqueline guided him towards it. Stewart looked up toward the Senator.

"It doesn't matter then. Wherever is easiest."

Laskin nodded, and they walked into the waiting room, turning towards the entrance through which they had arrived.

"Before you leave, I should note that for the foreseeable future, our relationship, along with your relationship with anyone else in this operation, must remain a secret. I do not expect this to be an issue, but if for some reason you see Michelle or Ethan or any of the others in public, do not be offended when they act as strangers. It is the life we have all chosen, in a way. As far as I know, you have agreed to this arrangement, so

I ask that you stick to it. If anything were to change, we would find a way to contact you."

Even though he had thought about it already, Stewart was still amazed by the amount of trust Laskin was putting in them. Granted, in this day and age, trust was a cornerstone of all relationships—whether lifelong friends or total strangers. But this was an exception. This was trust based on dishonesty, or at least trust based on an omission of truth. It was a difficult concept to accept, and he was still busy wrapping his head around it.

They stopped just short of the door, the robot standing in front, and Laskin to their right. He turned to them as he spoke.

"With more resolve, and a touch of luck, we may reach a turning point in the near future where actions such as our own are looked upon as heroic and necessary. I hope you've come to understand our point of view, even if you don't fully agree. Some things in this world are not as black and white as we'd like them to be."

He smiled at both of them, and extended his hand to each in turn. With that statement and pose, Stewart saw Laskin transform into a politician.

"I apologize for the events of the day. We have done what we can to protect you from wrongful indictment. Just a few hours of questions and this will all be behind you."

Stewart wondered if he'd be able to stay awake through the interrogation.

"Thank you."

The door opened and a second robot was waiting outside. Probably to block Jacqueline's face, Stewart realized. He turned to take one last glance at the Senator, who gave them a parting nod.

"Take care you two."

With that, they began their bizarre walk across the strip to the PAV.

- - -

Lucas Roberts. The still photo from the park flashed in her mind, and Lauren tried to remember his face in detail. His partner? She was having trouble with this influx of information from Rubger, constantly asking herself what was going on and who she should trust. The possibility of Anders's innocence still dominated her thoughts, but it was quickly joined by her board member's personal life. Did she owe him this information, since he was saving the company?

Lauren sighed, sinking back in her chair. When she spoke, it was softly, with pity.

"Yes."

Rubger sat up straighter, more anxious.

"Yes what?"

"Yes we identified him."

She looked up at him, and he continued to stare at her, his posture tense and uncomfortable. Some of her fear returned, and she realized she had probably said too much. For a good ten seconds, neither said a word, and Lauren felt her pulse quicken. Finally Rubger interrupted the silence.

"His name? What was his name?"

The question confused her - how did this help him?

"Lucas. Lucas Roberts. The DCI is monitoring him as we speak."

The tension in Rubger's body snapped away and he crashed into the back of his chair with his face in his arms.

"No... no..."

There was a desperation in his voice, more acute than the earlier anxiety, and Lauren realized that all his fear, all his nervousness—it wasn't a product of the recovery disk or the DCI or even most of his friends. It was because of Lucas.

The implications of it all came to her slowly, and as the man in front of her fought back tears, she started to realize the extent of Rubger's sacrifice. With Lucas on the DCI's radar, what would become of their relationship? Would they ever be able to see each other again? But there was something more fundamental she dared not ask. Did Lucas agree with Rubger's actions? How far did his betrayal extend?

"I— I'm sorry, Lauren. I was afraid this was the case."

He sat up, his eyes a hint more red than before, and turned toward the cockpit.

"How much longer?"

"Six minutes to destination, sir."

During their preceding discussion, Lauren had forgotten that they were on a trajectory unknown to her, but Rubger was already answering her unasked question.

"We are on our way to see him right now. We are on our way to Lucas."

She grew uneasy. Lucas? The very man they had been tracking all day? Add to that the fact that they were still tracking him—there was no way Rubger would be able to get close. Not to mention she was now in the mix. No, no, this was not good.

"What? Why? Can't you drop me off at Fenix?"

"I'm sorry Lauren, but I don't have time. For all I know, they could be capturing him now, especially if they're done with Mina. As soon as you got the recovery disk, this was priority number two. Be grateful I put our company ahead of my private life—it was an incredibly difficult decision to make. How do you think I've felt, waiting for you to arrive at the terminal? Time is of the essence."

She frowned. How was she supposed to know?

"But what are you going to do? The DCI is watching his every move! If he so much as steps out of the office, every camera in range will be focused on him!"

He sighed, and when he next spoke, the anxiety was gone. His voice was calm, his manner peaceful. All of his frantic worry was behind him.

"I know, Lauren. Part of me hoped that I was wrong. Part of me wanted there to be a secret backup, for the air-bike to have slipped away. But it was a foolish wish. Even if it were all true, it would not erase what I have done. I cannot hide in the shadows of my actions. My friends will know of my betrayal. The DCI? They will slap me with some sort of oversight. Even Lucas might get off with level three monitoring. That is unimportant. That was never important. But right now, before anyone knows anything, I want one chance to speak to him again. One chance to apologize for what I have done."

With her assumption confirmed, Lauren felt a growing pit in her stomach. At first she did not trust this man, and then she dared question him. But if she was in his situation, would she have gone as far as he went?

"If you'd like, you can take this PAV back to Fenix. It doesn't matter at this point. But the DCI may try to intercept it, unless you communicate with them first."

They were descending now, and Rubger stood up from his seat.

"Thank you for coming out here. In hindsight, all that secrecy was rather silly, seeing how everything turned out."

Lauren didn't know what to say. She wanted to thank him, but how? Most of all she wanted Lucas to forgive him. But based on his words, based on his expression... She was pretty sure that was not going to happen.

He walked over to the door then turned back towards her. Even though there was a sadness in Rubger's eyes, the lack of anxiety comforted Lauren. There was a mutual feeling of coming closure, as if each of their states of affairs were being taken care of, one way or another.

"Thank you for coming out to see me, I was worried I'd have to come up with some new plan."

She nodded, still trying to comprehend everything that was happening. He was thanking her? The PAV came to a hover at its intended destination but Lauren was oblivious.

"Alex, I— I don't know what to say."

He smiled wearily.

"You don't need to say anything. You can always visit me at the Courts."

Rubger pressed a small panel and the door slid open.

"I just hope he will forgive me."

Before she could react, he hopped down to the ground and ran off.

- - -

Stewart and Jacqueline had been riding in near silence for the past eight minutes, absorbing everything they had just experienced. He had expected to fall asleep again, but the seats in the PAV were not quite as comfortable as the couch, and the thoughts swirling through his mind kept him wide awake.

"What are we going to do?"

Jacqueline was looking at him, putting into words the number one question on both of their minds. But Stewart recognized that tone. She already had her mind made up, and was fishing to see if her husband agreed.

"I don't know. What do you think we should do?"

Jacqueline shrugged.

"I'm burnt out, Stewart. I've had enough adventure for a lifetime. Now I'm supposed to lie to the DCI? I never thought I would even entertain such a thought! This whole situation is absurd."

Stewart could tell some irritation remained. But his feelings were more conflicted.

"They treated us as equals, with respect and without secrecy. Think about the risk they were taking. Even they weren't entirely sure it was necessary, but they did it all the same."

His wife sighed in reluctant agreement.

"Yes, but aren't there punishments for holding back information?"

He nodded.

"I'm sure there are. But those should be minor, especially in our case. No one will be physically hurt by our refusal to answer. Besides, we can cooperate with everything but the identities, and still give the DCI quite a bit of information, I'm sure."

Jacqueline shook her head and looked out the window.

"I don't know Stewart. I just don't see it being that easy."

There was a short pause as they both continued to ponder their fate and Stewart noticed a hint of descent—they were getting closer.

"What do you think about what they did?"

Jacqueline turned back towards her husband as she continued the question.

"What do you think about them destroying that project?"

Of course, Stewart had been thinking about it for the entire ride, but as Jacqueline had just said—it's not that easy.

"I— I'm not sure. Laskin and Jason were very persuasive, but are we seeing the whole picture? This whole time, something has bothered me about all of this. Why would Fenix threaten our own existence?"

He frowned as he continued.

"You know the investment I made? The one that got us into this mess? I did quite a bit of research on Fenix before making that decision. There hasn't been an ethical complaint against the company in thirty years! They are run by a seven-member board, five or six of which have advanced robotics degrees. They recently added a president with a doctorate in robot psychology. Everywhere you turn, there's another roboticist. We are talking some of the most brilliant minds in the business, and it's a business of precision. Mina herself said the project took a few years, and I'm sure they would take as long as they had to. But you start to listen from Laskin's perspective and... what? They decided to go with something good enough and close their eyes if the world burned? This isn't the twenty-first century anymore. Profits don't rule all, and definitely not with this margin of catastrophe."

Stewart looked to Jacqueline for input.

"You're right, but don't forget roboticists are still humans. Even though they might try to mimic their creations, they can never be as precise."

He nodded and then smirked, wondering if they had thought about that. If their new robots were meant to be more human-like, wouldn't that make them less precise? It was a mind-boggling question, and he ignored it, seeing as there were quite enough of those on his mind already.

A gentle bump indicated that they had braked to a hover over their landing spot, and Stewart glanced out the window at the small alley. Jacqueline unbuckled her safety belt and looked to her husband.

"So what's the plan?"

He turned to her and thought back to Lucas. While he felt less loyalty towards the others, he couldn't fight the idea that he was somehow in the man's debt. So be it.

"I say we honor our agreement. Are you okay with that?"

Jacqueline looked at him intensely, her mind trying to come up with an answer.

"Yes."

Stewart unbuckled, stood, and walked over to door with his wife right behind him. He put his hand over the panel and looked at her one more time.

"You sure?"

"As sure as I'm going to be."

He pressed the panel and the door swung up. They stepped onto the alleyway and had barely made it ten steps when they heard it closing behind them. With a slight crescendo of engine noise, the PAV begin its ascent back to the Senator's, and Stewart focused his attention on the path ahead.

About fifty meters in front of them along this narrow passage was a road, and they saw a car drive by every couple of seconds. He wondered how many places like this existed, free of surveillance, within the main city. Most developed areas were blanketed with cameras, for better or worse, but there were two options for those who desired privacy. One, underdeveloped areas and parks were, for the most part, not watched. People often opted to live well outside the city limits to be free of these eyes in the sky, although that usually necessitated a nearby Diama or owning a PAV. The second option, of which Stewart had just been reminded that day, was very rare indeed. Undocumented natural birth, which led to true, complete anonymity. Mina was the first and probably last person Stewart would ever know under those circumstances.

But even the average citizen had presumably little to fear for two reasons. Firstly, that unethical or uncalled for usage of any surveillance footage was heavily punishable. The enforcement of these regulations was left to robots, who are always aware of who is accessing what, and are programmed to alert randomly selected reviewing parties—typically someone across the globe, with no known or possible connections. Secondly, as Jason had put it when they performed their awkward dance with the robots in and out of Laskin's residence, there was just too much footage to watch anything that wasn't flagged for suspicion. Of course, he remarked to himself dryly, his face was now one of those flags.

They reached the end of the alley and stopped. Stewart turned toward Jacqueline.

"Are you ready for this?"

She nodded.

"Let's get it over with."

Stewart pointed at a bench to their right just a few steps away.

"Want to just wait there? No reason to walk, they'll come to us."

Jacqueline shrugged.

"Sure, why not."

With that, the couple stepped out of the alley and into camera range.

- - -

Lauren peered out of the door of the parked PAV at the building fifty meters ahead, up whose marble white steps Rubger had just ascended. Somewhere behind those grand columns a very tense interaction was about to take place, and she wondered for a moment how Rubger would be cleared to enter the Legislative offices. Maybe he would simply call Lucas down? It didn't matter. The man had abruptly left Lauren in an odd situation, and she thought about what to do next.

Her Personal vibrated, grabbing her attention, and she took it out to see an incoming voice call from the Chairman. Had the disk been found? She pressed the button to answer.

"Lauren?"

"Yes Frank what is it?"

"Lauren listen. I know you are trying to relax and get away from all of this but something very disturbing has just happened. Alex Rubger has been spotted walking into the local Legislative office where Lucas is working, and he has asked for him by name. Do you have any idea how he knows this person? Did you mention anything to him?"

She smiled, half-amused by the reaction she was about to elicit.

"Yes, I know. Frank, I need you to do me two favors. First, I need you to tell the DCI to pick me up outside of the Legislative office, I am in a shuttered PAV on the launch pad right now, but I'll walk out here in a moment. Second, I need you to open the locked drawer in my PAV, which should be in the garage. Rubger gave me a recovery disk. Everything is going to be fine."

10. Questions

If Stewart hadn't known any better, he would assume that the DCI had decided not to interrogate him. However, despite having the appearance of an office, the room he was in was not meant for leisurely chats. The agent in front of him was quite serious—more serious than anyone he had ever seen—but not exactly threatening, an odd quality shared with the room itself. The solemn entity sat motionless in a comfortable chair behind a desk, with two robots tucked in the corners behind him. Stewart sat across from him, in what seemed to be the same chair, but in the center of the room. His back faced the door through which he had entered, where he had been separated from Jacqueline, who, as far as he knew, was in the adjacent room. Their first encounter with the DCI opened with a long explanation regarding how what they said might be used as evidence and that they were not required to say anything at all. In addition, they had been informed that robots were being used to help determine the veracity of their statements. It was all a bit daunting, but what was eeriest of all was the agents' near-silence. From the pickup point until now, they had only used two phrases: "Please come this way" and "Thank you." A change of pace would be welcomed.

"Good evening. Would you like a glass of water, or something to eat?"

Stewart wondered if this was how everyone was treated, or if the DCI had decided to believe Mina, and was only asking them follow-up questions.

"Water would be great, thanks."

The agent gave a slight nod and a small panel in the desk slid open, allowing a small glass to rise up. A faucet rose up alongside, and poured out enough water to fill the glass before disappearing back in the desk. The robot on Stewart's right came out of its corner, picked up the glass and brought it to him. Something about this procedure made him uncomfortable, and he realized he just wanted to be done with this and go home.

"Mr. Anders, it seems that you have waited for the proper moment to appear. We take this to mean that you are aware of recent developments regarding your case?"

He hesitated, as if one wrong word could mean his doom. He decided the less he said, the better.

"Yes."

"Why did you evade our agents at your residence today at 12:43?"

His heart rate went up a notch—he wasn't expecting this question, although it was perhaps the number one question he should have expected. How could he answer that properly?

"Fear."

"Could you elaborate, please?"

"Knowing I was innocent, and given the stress of the situation, I opted to believe my captors, whose intentions seemed, and later proved, to be genuine."

"At what time did Lucas Roberts enter your residence?"

Hearing proof of his friend's identification tied a knot in Stewart's stomach. Part of him was still holding on to the hope that he was free.

"No more than a minute before your agents arrived."

"Was his entrance into your residence your first encounter with this organized group of individuals?"

"Yes."

"Did you have any knowledge of this group, or anything related to this group, before Mr. Roberts entered your residence?"

"No."

"Did Mr. Roberts or any of his associates explain the reason for your capture?"

"Yes."

"Could you tell us what they said the reason was?"

"Yes. They said it was due to an overlap in Personal data."

"Was this reason given to you at your residence?"

"No."

206

"What reason was given at your residence?"

"None, except to escape capture by the DCI."

The agent paused, still staring, emotionless, at Stewart.

"If at any time these questions make you uncomfortable, or you would prefer not to answer, please let me know."

Stewart nodded. The glass of water in his hand remained untouched.

"Mr. Anders, understand that the willful evasion of the DCI carries a punishment based on the perceived severity of the case. Would you like to explain your action in any other way, as defense, or do you believe you have said enough?"

He frowned. How was he supposed to explain himself? Even he wasn't sure what he was doing at the time, it just seemed like the right thing in the heat of the moment. Reluctantly, he pressed forward with the exchange.

"Not at this time."

"Your decision has been noted. Do you know the names or identities of members of this group other than Lucas Roberts and Mina Bhatnagar?"

"Yes."

"Are you willing to provide any of their names?"

He sighed.

"No."

"Are you willing to divulge any information about any of these accomplices?"

Stewart shook his head. He felt nervous, more nervous than he had anticipated.

"No."

"Mr. Anders, the other members of this group are under investigation for their involvement in the attempted destruction of a high-level robotics project. Failure to provide information about these persons is a punishable offense. Do you understand?"

"Yes."

"With that understanding, do you now wish to divulge any information that you had previously decided to withhold?"

"No."

The agent paused again, never breaking eye contact. Only a rare blink reminded Stewart that he was human.

"Your decision has been noted. Mr. Anders, were you aware of the reason for this investigation at any point during your time with Lucas Roberts and his accomplices?"

"Yes."

"Are you willing to discuss your whereabouts between 15:46 and 17:15, namely the time of departure from the concealed building in C-zone to the time of discovery thirty-five minutes ago?"

"No."

"Mr. Anders, seeing as we do not know your whereabouts or actions between these times, we cannot assess whether or not you were engaging in illegal activity. Currently, there is no evidence against you, and therefore no punishment can be given. However, if evidence were to present itself, and you refuse to provide it yourself at this time, it will be deemed a punishable offense. Do you understand?"

"Yes."

"With that understanding, do you now wish to divulge any information that you had previously decided to withhold?"

Was this an agent or a robot? Come on now.

"No."

"Thank you, Mr. Anders. Those are all of the questions we have for you at this time. Is there anything you would like to say related to this case, for the record?"

Finally, he thought.

"No."

He brought the glass to his lips, taking a sip.

- - -

Lauren eyed the agent in front of her with skepticism. She had been transported to a DCI facility and placed in a bare room with nothing but two opposing chairs, a desk in between them, an agent in the opposite chair, and two robots behind him. It seemed an awful lot like an interrogation room.

"Am I being questioned?"

"Yes ma'am, we are going to ask you a few questions."

She frowned.

"Am I under investigation?"

He showed a hint of discomfort.

"Yes."

"Why?"

"We are still unaware of the details surrounding your encounter with Rubger. If you would provide us with those details, we could pass the evidence on to the Courts to make a judgement on the matter."

She nodded, and realized there was no real reason to be surprised by this. The DCI was charged with investigating every possibility, no matter how far-fetched, and at the moment, they simply had no idea what happened between the time she left Fenix and the time she was picked up outside of the Legislative offices.

"Have you apprehended him?"

"Yes ma'am."

"And Lucas?"

"Yes ma'am."

How had that conversation gone, she thought. How much time did they have before the DCI interrupted? Before she let her mind wander, she focused on the agent patiently waiting for information.

"Well, it started with Rubger wanting to meet me discreetly. He intercepted me during my lunch and passed along a note with a Diama terminal designation on it."

She thought back to that moment, and her temporary infatuation. Had he used his charm on her purposefully? There hadn't been much time to process it, but she began to wonder if she was disappointed in the revelation regarding Lucas.

"What designation was that?"

"A228. At first I thought it was a Fenix room number, but that led me to Media Storage, and I saw nothing out of the ordinary in there. Once I realized what it really was, and there was a lull in activity, I excused myself from the investigation and proceeded to the station."

"Was this under the pretense of going home to rest?"

There was no judgement in his voice, but Lauren looked away. She answered softly.

"Yes."

"Why did you not inform us of your intentions?"

Good question, she thought. It didn't matter in the end.

"Rubger clearly intended to keep our encounter secret. I chose to trust his reasoning and maintain confidentiality."

"Did Rubger meet you at A228?"

"Yes, he was waiting for me there."

"Did anything occur between you and Rubger after your lunch meeting but before arriving at A228, other than his incoming message?"

Lauren had almost forgotten that her incoming and outgoing data were being monitored. She wondered if the recovery disk would speed up the process to restoring her privacy.

"No."

"What happened when you arrived at A228?"

The question surprised her.

"Can't you see that yourself?"

"We have analyzed the footage, ma'am, but would like to hear your account."

"Okay. Once I landed and exited, a robot approached me and told me to follow it. It led me to Rubger's PAV, where he showed himself, still hiding from the cameras, and asked me to speak with him. When I hesitated, he had his robot bring me the recovery disk, which I promptly sent back to Fenix as collateral. At that point I returned to his PAV and entered. Speaking of all of this, has the recovery disk been downloaded?"

"Your Chairman has initiated the recovery process, yes. We are taking measures to ensure the security of the process itself."

"What sort of measures?"

"Your networks are completely off-Cloud, R&D and otherwise, for the time being. In addition, the recovery system has been physically removed from all other systems, and we have already made a copy of the disk and are running two recovery processes at once."

Her unease from the interrogation lightened. No matter what happened, her company was back on track. She also noted that even though she was under investigation, the agent did not hesitate to tell her all of these details. In her mind, that was a good sign.

"Ms. Care, could you explain what occurred during the flight from A228 to the Legislative offices?"

"He explained his actions, to a certain degree."

It occurred to Lauren that in all of the talk about Lucas and the recovery disk, she had lost sight of something: Rubger's motivation. He had never really given her a clear answer.

"Why did he maintain such a high level of secrecy with you, instead of revealing his intentions to the DCI?"

She thought of Rubger's desire to clear his own name, along with his original plan if the secret backup had existed. Should she reveal this information? It seemed more incriminating than his other actions.

"With all due respect, I'd prefer him to answer that question for you."

"Ma'am, please realize that failure to answer may be construed as an attempt to withhold information. Do you understand?"

Lauren felt trapped in the chair, scrutinized by two robots and an almost-robot. Why was she here in the first place? Her company was on the mend, Rubger and Lucas were caught, what else did the DCI need? Whatever it was, she was not going to betray her friend, even marginally.

"Yes I understand. But that does not change my stance, sorry."

The agent nodded.

"Your decision has been noted. Ms. Care, were there any other subjects of conversation during this trip?"

She thought back to the ride in the PAV. It had all happened within the last hour, but it felt surreal and distant, like a film more than a memory. What else had they talked about? He had asked about the secret backup, but that was something she didn't want to share.

"Yes, he talked about his relationship with Lucas. That was why we went there, so he could talk to him one last time."

"Did he know Lucas was under surveillance?"

"Yes, he deduced it and I verified it. This was not until late in the ride, but he must have assumed as much, seeing as he set the course immediately."

"Did he mention anything else about Mr. Roberts?"

She paused, replaying the bits of conversation she still held fresh in her mind.

"Not that I remember."

"Were any other operatives mentioned?"

Lauren shot upright, remembering the most shocking among all of Rubger's revelations.

"Yes! Well, sort of. He said Anders was innocent. Is this true?"

"Mr. Anders was not involved with the operation in any way until today. As far as the targeting of and attack on Bluestone, he is innocent."

She gaped.

"How is that possible? Didn't you trace his Personal? The link?"

"Yes ma'am. Allow me to explain. Are you familiar with blank Personals?"

"Yes..."

"After the attack on Bluestone this morning, Mr. Roberts sent a small data packet through Tier Six to scramble some traceable data that they had accidentally left behind. Not wanting the packet itself to be traced, he used a blank Personal. As you may know, a blank Personal piggybacks off of a true Personal in its relatively near vicinity and uses its identification to send data anonymously. Mr. Roberts's Personal happened to choose Mr. Anders's. Normally, this would not affect Mr. Anders's Personal, even if he were sending data out at the same time. However, not only was Mr. Anders sending data out at the same time, he was sending it to the same recipient. The probability of such a situation is infinitesimal, mostly because of the timing: if one had been sent mere nanoseconds later, it would have been identified as a separate entity. However, based on the fact that Mr. Anders's investment link was garbled with Mr. Roberts's data packet, they had been sent within a margin of a hundred picoseconds. The odds against this are staggering, and such a case has never been observed; in fact, the only reason we are aware of the possibility of such an outcome are controlled tests with blank Personals."

"So... Anders sent a regular investment?"

"Yes."

"And then what? Lucas and company decided to pick him up?"

"Yes. As far as we know now, they were aware of the mixup and its minute possibility, and intervened in an effort to protect Mr. Anders from unwanted prosecution."

"Was there any evidence that he was innocent?"

"No ma'am, not until we received testimony from Mina Bhatnagar and moments ago Lucas Roberts verifying the account."

She had nearly forgotten about the whole affair with Rubger's discussion of Lucas, and now she had a chance to try to play back the last few hours in her head from this new perspective. Anders innocent? All of this chasing... and to think, if they had not traced him, would they have ever found Lucas, or Mina? Probably not.

"Why did they risk their operation like that?"

"Ms. Bhatnagar gave two reasons, ma'am. First, that protecting Mr. Anders was ethically correct, and second, that their operation had already been deemed a success, and therefore they could afford to be caught. They are not necessarily concerned with their capture, so long as the human intelligence horizon is avoided."

Well that didn't quite work out for them, she thought.

"Do they know that we have a disk?"

"Mr. Roberts was told by Mr. Rubger. Ms. Bhatnagar is not yet aware of the development, and presumably all operatives not yet apprehended are also unaware. It was decided with your Chairman that that information will not be made public until Monday for security reasons."

The encounter between Lucas and Alex came to mind once more. Each one had sacrificed so much for their goal... She didn't know Lucas, but it would take a superhuman level of forgiveness to pardon Rubger's actions. The world was cruel.

"I'm sorry for the digression, do you have any more questions?"

"In a way, ma'am. I must ask if there is anything else you know, related or not to your interaction with Mr. Rubger during your flight from A228, that may help our investigation in any way."

Other than what I don't want to tell you, she thought.

"No, that's it."

"Thank you, Ms. Care. Those are all of the questions we have for you at this time. Is there anything you would like to say related to this case, for the record?"

Lauren leaned back into her chair and looked at the agent.

"Yes, yes there is. Alex Rubger is the only reason Fenix will survive. He has sacrificed more than any of us to keep Bluestone alive. The destruction of his personal life is punishment enough. If the Courts hold true to the ethics they are meant to uphold, he will see no more discipline. I'm not talking about sentencing—I expect him to be pardoned—I am talking about collateral effects. Publicizing his involvement will lead to professional and social ostracism beyond need. They would be right to weigh their commitment to transparency with their commitment to morality."

There was a pause before the agent reacted, and when he nodded, Lauren noticed a hint of agreement and respect behind the wall of authority and calculation.

"Your statement has been noted."

It has indeed.

"Is that all?"

"Yes ma'am. We will escort you off the premises and you will be on free parole until your case is processed."

"I'm sorry, what is free parole?"

"Your case is being forwarded to the Courts, but the DCI has deemed you near-certainly innocent of any sort of crime. Until they have officially processed your file, you are still technically under investigation, pending a judgement. Free parole means you have no restrictions of any kind during the time that you await this judgement, which should occur within the next few hours. You will receive notice via Personal."

She nodded.

"What about Rubger? Is he on free parole?"

"Mr. Rubger is currently being questioned, ma'am. Most likely, he will be transferred to the Courts for temporary detainment while his file is being processed."

"And the others? Lucas and Anders?"

"Mr. Roberts is also currently being questioned, and will surely be detained due to his high level of involvement. Mr. Anders has just been granted a level two monitored parole, which grants him freedom of movement but under a medium level of surveillance, again until a judgement has been passed."

Why the next question came to her, she did not know, but Lauren felt compelled to ask.

"Can I see any of them?"

"Mr. Anders is being escorted out with his wife, we can bring you to them if you'd like. You will not be able to see Mr. Roberts or Mr. Rubger until they have been moved to the detainment center."

"How long will that take?"

"As soon as we have finished questioning them, they will be transferred over. At the moment, you are still receiving updates from us on this case, and therefore a message should appear on your Personal when either or both of those transfers occur."

"When might that be?"

"They will most likely be transferred within the hour."

She nodded.

"Where is the detainment center?"

"Mr. Rubger and Mr. Roberts will be taken to the adjacent Courthouse."

Right across the street.

"Will that be all?"

"Yes, ma'am. We may escort you to the Courthouse if you would like to wait there."

"Thank you."

- - -

Apart from exchanging a knowing glance, Stewart and Jacqueline had not spoken a word to each other as they were escorted to the building's exit. Both were wrapped in thought over their encounter with the DCI, which it was safe to say seemed much less intimidating than expected, at least psychologically. But Stewart couldn't fight the feeling that that was precisely their intent.

"Excuse me! Stewart Anders?"

The exclamation came from behind them, and the couple, along with the escorting agent, turned in unison. Jacqueline looked at the young lady heading in their direction and knew right away that she was definitely not a member of the agency. She turned to her husband, who, to her surprise, was wide-eyed and speechless.

"Do you know her?"

The agent answered for him.

"That is Lauren Care, President of Fenix Corporation."

Stewart found his voice just as Lauren came into speaking range.

"Y-yes?"

His mind raced, bouncing a dozen implications as to why she was here and why she was talking to them. Did she want to interrogate them as well? Had she been behind the DCI this whole time? Could he hold back the growing conviction that he now considered her to be working, albeit indirectly and even unknowingly, against humanity?

"I'm Lauren Care, President of Fenix. I'm sorry to startle you like this, but I wanted to apologize in person for the DCI's misunderstanding. I can't even fathom the level of stress you have been under due to all of this, and to add insult to injury, it was all over an investment into our company. Now, I do not want to give the impression that I am being patronizing, but with your permission, I would like to refund the entirety of that investment, at the very least."

Lauren could tell Stewart was surprised by her presence, and wondered if he knew that she was also here to be questioned. The idea to reimburse him had come to her only after she saw him, but now she was wracking her brain to find a more thorough and appropriate way of treating this poor man and his wife for all they had been through. For the moment, she had some time to think, as Stewart could not find the right words to say.

"I— thank you, um... thank you."

Before he could embarrass himself further, Jacqueline stepped in.

"Thank you Ms. Care. And we are sorry to hear about the attack on your company. It is very kind of you to think of us so graciously during a time of crisis."

Lauren smiled.

"The people who support our company are always going to be our number one priority. And not to worry, the crisis is over. In fact, Mr. Anders, while we will repay your full investment, we will not delete it. You will be entitled to all of your profits off of our potential breakthrough."

Jacqueline turned to Stewart, puzzled. Her husband caught the look then focused back on Lauren.

"We were told your project was destroyed."

Lauren remembered that apart from the DCI, a few executives at Fenix, and the other two men in custody, no one knew about the recovery disk or the rebirth of Bluestone. The interrogating agent had mentioned the Monday announcement plan, but there was no reason for secrecy. Not with these two.

"Well yes and no. Due to a particularly fortunate turn of events, everything is back on track. Damage has been done, but none of it irreparable. Don't worry, their attack ended up a failure."

She smiled, but Stewart did not share the enthusiasm. How was this possible? Had Laskin been lying, or perhaps unaware? Or was this all part of the plan, and this President in front of them simply did not know it yet?

"Wh—what do you mean?"

One of the agents interrupted.

"I'm sorry Mr. Anders, but until your judgement has been passed we must advise Ms. Care not to answer your question in more detail."

He looked to the imposing figure. Free to go, but not yet free to know.

"I appreciate the advice, sir, but I believe this man's total innocence." Lauren looked from the agent to Stewart and continued. "Without going into all the specifics, a member of the operation defected in our favor. You two are among the first to know. I would appreciate keeping this under wraps until we can make an official announcement tomorrow."

Stewart nodded slowly, still processing this explosive piece of information. Everything they had done, Mina, Lucas, the Senator... for nothing? More surprisingly, why was it affecting him so? A mere five or six hours ago, he would have been celebrating the operation's collapse.

"Do they know?"

"The others?" Lauren was a little perplexed at the question. "Well I don't think so. Except Lucas Roberts."

She frowned. Hopefully Rubger would be transferred soon so she could speak with him. The things he had done for her company...

"Lucas knows?"

Something about his tone threw Lauren off. There was a sadness in the voice she did not expect. Maybe she had underestimated the man's loyalty to his captors? Rubger's involvement had reminded her not to make assumptions—and not just because he happened to be an inside agent. He was the one who saved Fenix, and yet he was a part of the operation. It was a bit embarrassing to her, frankly, to have been so swept up in the pursuit of these men and women and so convinced of their intentions to ignore the depth of their humanity.

"Yes, he does. I'm sorry."

The news was clearly affecting the man in front of her, and Lauren searched desperately for a reprieve worth offering.

"You know, I'm not sure if they have told you this, but he is here right now."

Stewart looked at her with newfound energy. So they had captured him. But he was close, and there was only one question on his mind.

"Can I see him?"

Lauren glanced over to the agent that had escorted the couple.

"Yes sir, you may visit Mr. Roberts as soon as he has been transferred to the adjacent Courthouse."

There was no change visible in the agent's expression, but Lauren felt a hint of frustration in the statement. Clearly she was starting to overstep her boundaries, and she decided to reel it in from then on.

"I was actually headed that direction myself. Would you care to join me?"

Stewart looked over to his wife who nodded encouragingly. Before he acknowledged Lauren's proposal, he smiled at Jacqueline's unwavering patience. They had been on the verge of going home after hours and hours of action and stress, only to be side-tracked one more time by his own gut feeling. What an angel.

"Yes, thank you."

Now with one agent in front and the other behind, the three of them made their way to the exit towards the Courthouse.

11. Answers

"Lucas Roberts." Stewart read the sign above the gray door as the DCI agent pressed a button on a small panel to the left. It slid open and Stewart glanced at the agent once more before taking a step inside.

Although he had never been inside a detainment center, Stewart was aware of the level of accommodations. Those awaiting judgement were given a comfortable, three-room arrangement—living, bed, and bath—as well as a personal assistive robot. Innocent until proven guilty meant living as normal a life as possible until the Courts made a decision. If the judgement dropped all charges, which was extremely rare for those not placed on a free or monitored parole, the ex-suspect would be compensated a great deal. And for those more rare and violent criminals who were eventually imprisoned, the facilities would be almost the same, if not more spacious. The goal was rehabilitation, not punishment. Even if they were never rehabilitated, that was not an excuse not to try. Besides, the resources were all driven by robots, so almost no one was paying out of pocket, so to speak.

The door slid shut behind him, and Stewart stood at the front of the living room. There were two doors on the opposite wall, leading to the bedroom and bathroom, and to his right was a small kitchen area. On the left, nearest his current position, was Lucas, sitting in a chair on one side of a small dining table.

He stood to greet Stewart, and even though a smile came to his face, it was clear that things had not been going his way. There were circles under his eyes, and a fresh redness that came with recently shed tears. Stewart tried to forget he knew why and took the hug as it came to him.

"How are you? I didn't think you'd be free this early, but I guess it makes sense."

Why this man seemed like a lifelong friend to him, Stewart could not say, but he embraced the situation wholeheartedly.

"I'm fine, fine. What about you?"

As they spoke, Lucas made his way back to the chair and gestured for Stewart to take the one across from him. He sat while his host responded.

"I've been better. Would you like anything? Some water?"

Stewart put up a hand.

"No, no, thank you. Please Lucas, sit down."

How old was he? Stewart knew next to nothing about the man in front of him except that he had gone out of his way to save him, and ended up getting caught in the process.

"Listen, I heard about what happened, and I just wanted to come see how you were doing. Part of me wants you to tell me it's all a lie."

Lucas gave a hollow smile.

"Does this mean you agree with us after all? No, unfortunately it's quite true. But you know that—why else do you think you are here?"

Stewart didn't understand.

"What do you mean?"

"Well, why else do you think we could afford to let you out in public? You know this was done by one of our own?"

"Yes..."

"Well he happened to know a good deal, including your entire situation. Once he reversed our progress and ousted our operation, he told them all about you."

Stewart tried to ignore the suspicion growing in his mind, but all signs pointed in that direction.

"Lucas, has no one told you about Mina?"

He nearly jumped at the name, and the smile, false as it may have been, left his face. There was a cold emptiness to his demeanor, worse than any of the DCI agents he had seen that day.

"Stewart, don't say another word."

His friend's immediate change startled him, but it only validated his intuition.

"I don't have to, Lucas. They already have her."

A mixture of anger and denial replaced his expressionless visage, and Stewart fought the urge to recoil. He had clearly put the salt on the wound, although not in malice.

"What? No. How can you be sure?"

"We had to evacuate. The DCI infiltrated the base. There weren't enough air-bikes, and she volunteered to stay behind."

The fire in his eyes grew stronger, and Stewart began to think he had said too much. He did not expect this news to bring such a potent reaction. Lucas threw his fist onto the table, causing Stewart to push his seat away. What was going on?

Their eyes locked and almost instantaneously, the rage vanished. Lucas sank into his chair in dismay, still looking at his friend across the table.

"I'm sorry Stewart..."

His words were a whisper, and Stewart strained to hear.

"I'm so sorry. So much has happened today, I'm reaching the breaking point. My best friend, my trusted companion... a traitor, a defector. Do you know what he told me?"

Sniffles punctuated his words, and water started to collect in his eyes.

"He told me it was for the good of humanity. He told me these robots were his friends. What!?"

Tears flowed down Lucas's face and Stewart had no idea how to react. What was he supposed to say? What was he supposed to do?

"Seven years. Seven long years of work. It all came down to his decision. It all came down to nothing."

Here was the man who knew how to get things done. The one that had guided him along a convoluted path of adventure only to be detained and broken.

"Hope is lost. The robots will take power, I guarantee it."

Before today, Stewart had eagerly anticipated the next wave of robotics. He found the typical, robot-fearing mindset confusing, even primitive. Even now, despite his shifting position, there was a small corner of his mind wondering if Lucas was right. Or more precisely, in what way.

Previously, he had envisioned a world free of unnecessary labor and pain, where humans could do what they chose to do and the robots would handle the rest. But this, in itself, was a form of control. If they took care of human health, education, defense... who was really pulling the strings? They were already entrenched in most facets of life, and now they would be given a personality, a conscience.

Stewart reflected in silence as his friend wiped away tears. Was there any turning back at this point? Had there really been any turning back before?

"What do you think is going to happen?"

Lucas looked at him, regaining his composure.

"I can't know. These models may yet prove underwhelming. Can the strong AI horizon ever really be defined? We say it has to do with human-level intelligence now, including emotional intelligence, but how do you qualify that accurately? Somewhere down the line of this new phase of robotics, we will reach a threshold that truly defines human-level intelligence. And among those thousands of robots that are manufactured, there will be outliers that will not conform to our limitations. Maybe it will be one, maybe it will be all of them, but it will happen. And after that? Your guess is as good as mine."

His hopeless tone made Stewart uncomfortable. This man was supposed to have the answers. That was part of the reason he had come here—to see if there was a next step, a backup plan.

"What's going to happen to you?"

Lucas shrugged.

"Some sort of detainment, maybe for life."

"What!?"

Stewart's shock at the statement had him gripping the armrests of his chair.

"I thought they just put you under surveillance?"

"That would be nice."

A small smile spread across his face—almost imperceptible, but not at all hollow.

"But they won't do that, I'm too much of a risk."

"A risk? Of disappearing?"

He nodded.

"Yes. And they already had me under surveillance, look how that worked out."

"They what? What do you mean?"

"The DCI has had me on level two monitoring for the past six years."

The words were calm, almost banal. But Stewart had trouble comprehending.

"What?"

"I was a DCI trainee for four years before I quit. If you decide not to finish out the training process, or quit as an agent, you are automatically put under monitoring. It's standard procedure."

Stewart relaxed his grip and leaned back into the chair. An ex-trainee? It was obvious, in hindsight. But he didn't know such a thing existed. In his mind, a person signed up to be a DCI agent, spent ten years training, and then that was the rest of their life.

How could they have missed his involvement? How could one of their own slip through their fingers?

"You're probably wondering how I could have been a part of this operation, given my history, but it's far simpler than you would imagine. Obviously as I sit in this room I won't discuss any specifics with you but suffice to say it is possible. Think about it—I was privy to a lot of information, including how the DCI analyses surveillance, where they have their priorities... all of this being the reasoning behind the level two monitoring, but they don't really expect their ex-trainees to go against the law."

The gears were turning in Stewart's head. Skydiving, evading cameras, jammers—all of that seemed to fit the bill. But what about being tracked? The potential agents in the park?

"Did the rest of them know?"

"About my history? Oh yes, it was used to our advantage a great deal."

"But now you're sure they will detain you?"

"Positive. Criminal punishments are more severe for ex-trainees. Plus now they know how useless their monitoring was on me. They really don't have a choice, I don't blame them."

Stewart thought about the repercussions facing his friend. Was this all his fault?

"How is your wife?"

The question caught him off-guard, but confusion gave way to a smile. Lucas's thoughtful nature was what had won over Stewart in the first place.

"She's fine. She's actually outside waiting. It's been a hectic day, but we're both doing okay."

"See, you've got nothing to worry about."

Stewart didn't understand, and he showed as much in his expression.

"You two are happy, right?"

"Very."

"You've got each other. Why are you worried about all of this nonsense? In the end, as much as I might have argued against the hormones and the brain chemicals, it does come down to the happiness in your life. The pleasure. There's nothing to do now but wait and see. Why stress? If you've got love, there's nothing else you need."

The words were reassuring, but there was a sadness in his tone that affected Stewart more than he would have imagined it could. Was there something he had missed? Maybe him and Mina...

"So don't worry. Go, see your wife. Right now you deserve rest, and I'm not going anywhere. You can come visit anytime."

- - -

It took all of one glance for Lauren to realize exactly what had happened when Rubger had confronted Lucas. The man sitting in front of her was spent, a shell of emotion trying to hold on to something but not sure of what. Her heart sank at the sight of him and she began to think that all of this—the company, Bluestone, the future of robotics—wasn't worth it. No one had been physically hurt, but the emotional toll was sitting before her eyes.

"Hey Lauren."

The words were soft and careful, and she found herself missing the old, dynamic charm. She seated herself across from him at what looked to be his dining table and prepared for the worst.

"Alex. Are you okay?"

Despite it all, he managed to smile, and weak though it was, Lauren had never felt so warm from a smile before.

"I've been better. How was your interrogation?"

"Painless. Have they given you any indication of what might happen?"

"You mean to me? No, but I can guess. What about you? Free parole for now?"

She nodded.

"Thought so. That'll be gone soon enough. Sorry about dragging you into this."

"Alex, did you talk to Lucas?"

The smile vanished, and Lauren braced herself. He sighed before speaking.

"Yes. We actually spoke for a good while before the DCI intervened. Honestly I'm glad they came when they did, I was terrified of the direction of that conversation."

Taking his tone, Lauren's next words were soft and careful.

"He did not forgive you?"

Rubger's eyes strayed from hers, staring intently at the wall behind her. He shook his head.

"I'm so sorry..."

They sat in silence for a few moments, Lauren eyeing him with pity, and Rubger fixated on nothing in particular. It was uncomfortable for her, but she knew he needed her patience.

"Do you think I did the right thing?"

As she began to ponder the reasons he would ask her that question at that particular moment, Rubger's gaze came back to her. Thankfully, she didn't have to tread carefully—she could speak honestly.

"Yes, without a doubt. You saved the company, for which I am grateful, but that is less significant in the grand scheme of things. As far as I'm concerned, you saved robotics itself."

Rubger gave out a sad chuckle, but Lauren eyed him sternly.

"I am not patronizing you. Surely you have imagined the full scope of consequences for your actions? Tell me, your organization, wasn't it meant to stop the strong AI horizon?"

"Yes."

"Okay, in that case, what was the ultimate plan? Realistically, you could not have expected to thwart Bluestone and then be done with it forever. The horizon would come back sooner rather than later, no?"

Rubger nodded. "True. That was the entire purpose of the group—to monitor these developments and nip them in the bud."

Lauren gave Rubger a look of disbelief.

"That may well work for a few years, but that cannot be a final plan. There is no way to truly stop strong AI without stopping robotics itself."

He looked her up and down before responding.

"I see what you're saying. We had talked about these contingencies, and frankly they had to be put on the back-burner while we dealt with Bluestone, but you're right. There had been whispers of what the final solution would be, including a complete reversal of robotics, but it was an idea well beyond the scope of practicality."

"Of course, but you admit, the idea was there?"

"Just the idea, yes."

"Well that's the point. Everything, good or bad, starts as just an idea. And whether you believe in the eventual power of your organization or not, a future without robotics is not an idea worth flirting with. Think of all of the things that came with robotics. Who can say what the future will bring?"

He nodded, but Lauren wasn't sure he was convinced.

"I know you think I am reaching, but if public opinion keeps swaying the way it's swaying right now, who knows what might happen. Hopefully altruism will be enough to stop that trend."

She looked him up and down and sensed he had not been persuaded. However, she decided not to press the issue. There was another question that had been bothering her since he had hopped out of the PAV.

"Tell me Alex, what changed your mind? What made Bluestone so important?"

His eyes lit up the slightest amount at the question. Something in him wanted to explain, wanted to spell out why he did what he did.

"I wouldn't say that Bluestone became important. It was always important. But what I did with Lucas and the others... Our operation had always been one for the sake of humanity. That was a core belief I held above all of my personal relationships. Given my experience with the Bluestone prototypes, I came to the conclusion that my friends are wrong. There is no betterment of humanity in this project's destruction, quite the opposite. In my opinion, reaching the strong AI horizon, coupled with robotic altruism, is the proper path of humanity's future. I realize that I may not have the authority to make that suggestion, but in that case what gives them the authority to suggest the opposite? All I can do is consider what I know to be true."

A hint of strength came to his voice, and Lauren could see him sit up a bit straighter.

"Did you know that I had more extensive interaction with the prototypes than any other board member? And I don't mean by a negligible margin. Most of our colleagues would attend the routine inspections and I think I have heard of maybe a dozen individual examinations. You yourself have only been at the company officially for about a month, and you've exceeded some of their numbers already.

"At first, many of these visits were directly related to the operation. We had to assess just how realistic this venture was, and whether this qualified as true strong AI and robotic altruism. Part of that assessment was handed down to me. We had no intentions of making a premature strike, even if we began full-strength preparations a good two years before we gave ourselves a full green light.

"During the course of these meetings, I would run the prototypes and perform calculated interactions, trying to ascertain their level of emotional intelligence, and any hints of a conscience. From an outside perspective, it was just a board member keenly interested in the project's progress. I was backed by a much more rigorous analysis of the software by our roboticists, and their word was worth a good deal more than mine, but there was always room for a bit of human intuition. Unfortunately, as is always the fear with robots, we underestimated their intelligence.

"It was early last year, during one of these interactions, that the newest prototype caught me off guard. Our roboticists, they were already sounding alarms. No one had ever seen cerebral units like this, and there was a bit of extrapolation in their analysis, but the general consensus was that conscience was on its way. Up until that point I had noticed nothing unusual. The robots were intelligent, and they had a basic grasp of morality, but nothing we hadn't seen before.

"Then, directly after an answer about the role of robots in relation to humans, it asked me, 'Sir, why are you asking me these questions?' I stared at it for a moment. I was surprised. A robot asking a question is nothing new, but these are usually about objects, processes, or ideas. But motivation? I decided to test the waters, partially because of what our roboticists were saying, and partially because I was curious. I responded, 'Why do you think I am asking you these questions?'

"It didn't think about it, it didn't contemplate, it just answered. 'I think you are checking for a conscience.' I nodded, but it wasn't finished. It paused for a few seconds before continuing. Then it asked, 'Are you afraid of a robot with a conscience?' This second question left me speechless. I honestly wondered if I should bolt for the door right then. It was an eerie feeling, having this conversation with a robot, but I was already in there. I thought about answering honestly, saying yes, I was very afraid, but with the prototypes under constant surveillance and all of their interactions put into logs that dozens of our scientists would study, that was not an option. So I did what I could. I asked, 'Should I be?'

"The answer was immediate, just as before. 'No.' But the followup was unexpected: it told me, 'Your happiness brings me happiness.'"

Rubger smiled at the memory.

"Can you imagine that? Your happiness brings me happiness. I realized something fundamental about robotic altruism that day, something deceptively simple on the outside but no doubt frighteningly complex on a programmable level. Laugh at me if you will, but the only other being in the world that could say that to me and truly mean it is Lucas.

"Over the course of the next few months, our interactions grew more and more human-like. Bizarre things happened, things you would never expect from a robot. I remember one time it wanted to hug me because it missed me. Sure, robots can be made to say and do these things, fake emotional attachment and so on, but it did not try to do this until we had developed a comfortable rapport. A rapport? With a robot? That was enough to leave an impression, but little did I know that the real surprise was yet to come.

"One of the questions I always asked was 'What is your purpose?' Typically it would say 'I don't know' since it was never actually programmed with one. Occasionally it would ask me if I could divulge that information, and I just said I didn't know either. Until one day, back in May, as soon as I activated it, it proclaimed, 'I know my purpose.' Before I continue, realize the power of that gesture in itself. A robot excited about a discovery? There's so much I could say about that event on its own, but its second statement overshadowed the first. 'My purpose is to love humanity in the best way possible.'"

He smiled again and Lauren could see that he was starting to remember his motivation, why he put himself in this position, and that he was okay with it.

"*We* don't even know how to love humanity. Humans are more obsessed with loving themselves than each other. At this point, the seed of doubt was planted—I was starting to wonder if I was on the right side of the issue. Well, when it rains it pours: the prototype told me all about what exactly it meant by that statement. Like any of us humans, it struggled to put abstract concepts into words, and the occasional blunder or hiccup would remind me why these were still prototypes. But I came to a conclusion. Yes, these robots were human-like, only more benevolent. More sympathetic.

"All of this time I was walking a fine line between reporting my findings and hiding my enthusiasm. My peers were not as taken by the chain of events as I was. That should be pretty clear today. Most did not budge on the probability of malfunction, while some went so far as to claim the robot had become intelligent enough to trick me. Honestly only one argument was even remotely persuasive: so what? This one prototype seems to be a more compassionate version of a human. So what? It is still a threat to human superiority."

A memory came to him and he paused, frowning.

"This idea of exceptionalism is rather silly, although I'd venture to say it is encoded in our survival instinct. But that is beside the point. As far as I see it, the strong AI horizon is here. If we succeeded in canceling Bluestone, it would be here in a few years. Not to discredit your statements, but no amount of public opinion is going to stop this forward march. We have been destined to cross that line since robotic research began. People love to hypothesize about life beyond that horizon, but no one can know for certain. Will the robots revolt and take over, will they just up and leave, or will life go on rather similarly—no one can know. But Bluestone has always been about emulating humans. Humans, bless us, have always sought a purpose to life. Some claim to have found it, others claim it cannot be found. The prototypes, on the other hand, have a purpose. To love humanity in the best way possible. If that's the direction we are headed, I am all for it. Human superiority? That's nonsense. The robots are the superior race now, we just haven't accepted that yet. So why fight the inevitable, especially since the outcome could be less favorable the next time around. What's that old expression? Better the devil I know than the one I don't? Except these are more guardian angels. And that's fine by me."

Lauren could see the color returning the Rubger's complexion. The conversation was helping him immensely.

"I could talk about that much longer, trust me. And you know, even this morning I was still on the fence about what to do. I had formulated this plan, in case I decided to defect, but I still wasn't sure. You know what changed my mind?"

Lauren shook her head slowly.

"The operation itself. I knew what our plan entailed, but I didn't really think it through. When they disassembled the prototypes, they disassembled one of my friends."

He shook his head at the thought.

"The pain I felt at that realization was enough to send me over the edge."

Rubger smiled at her, a smile with more hope than she had seen from him all day.

"I'm not sure I agree with the idea that I saved robotics, but you have the opportunity to save Fenix. In the end, not all is lost."

He paused, holding onto the smile.

"Now I know you want to keep me company and I can't express how much I appreciate that gesture but you've got more important things to do. Go back there and get us back online."

As she prepared to object, he raised a hand to stop her.

"Lauren. I have to deal with losing Lucas. I don't know if I will ever get him back. That was my choice, and it will haunt me in the time to come. But there is one relationship that can be renewed. It will not fill the hole left in me, but it will remind me of my motivations. Get Bluestone running, and share this compassion with the world."

Rubger stood, and motioned for her to leave. She obliged, standing, and made for the exit. In front of the gray slab, before the agents on the other side opened it, she paused and looked back to the man in the room.

Something was wrong with this picture. Everything Rubger had just described seemed out of place, off-putting. He was using a robotic relationship to cope with the loss of his human ones. Where did that end? Millions of people were affected by this sort of thing, but she had never seen it up close. If robots were given a conscience, how would that affect human relationships?

The door slid open and she turned her attention back to the exit. These things had been discussed, of course. Fenix was convinced that human-robot relationships could remain healthy and wouldn't undermine human-human relationships. But as she stepped out into the hallway of the Courthouse, she realized that Rubger was showing the exact opposite. Now, moments from her company's salvation, she began to understand the other side.